DARKNESS FALLS

DARKNESS SERIES BOOK 3

J.L. DRAKE

DARKNESS FALLS

Copyright © 2015 by J.L. Drake.
All rights reserved.
First Print Edition: October 2015

Limitless Publishing, LLC
Kailua, HI 96734
www.limitlesspublishing.com

Formatting: Limitless Publishing

ISBN-13: 978-1-68058-313-7
ISBN-10: 1-68058-313-1

DEDICATION

To all my readers who waited patiently for the conclusion of Seth and Emily's story, I thank you.

CHAPTER ONE

OCTOBER

Seth

Boom! Boom! Rice flew in all directions as I ducked to get a better view of the shooter. My shirt was drenched in wine from when the fucker tried to remove my head. My ears still rang from how close the bullet came. My vest was sticky against my skin, but it was the least of my worries.

The sales clerk's wife had a death wish if she didn't shut the hell up.

"Hard left, Connors," Garrett hissed over the radio.

Shit! I scrambled to my feet and made the turn before he saw me. I spotted Garrett off to my left, and he pointed to our backup, who had just arrived.

"Hey," the woman screamed from behind the counter, "you have a gun! Do something!" I put my finger to my mouth, but she was too far gone to care.

"Oh, officers," the shooter yelled. I saw his reflection in the fridge door, which only meant…

Boom! Boom! His shotgun blasted inches from my head.

"Fuck!" I dove one row down and tumbled into a display of Gatorade. Two more shots were fired. That was it; he should be out. I heard his shotgun fall to the floor, then the cock of a handgun. *Shit!*

We got a call there was a robbery at a convenience store. Little did we know the shooter was hyped up on Flakka. He was fifty, with the strength of a twenty-year-old. Two shots to his shoulder, and he was moving like the fucking Hulk. I'd encountered his brother before, although his choice was a machete. I would prefer that right now.

"Stay down, Connors," Campbell rang through the radio. "I have a clear shot."

"Ten-four," I mumbled. I didn't want to draw attention to my location.

A bullet broke through the glass door, just missing the shooter.

"You," *bang,* "want," *bang,* "a piece," *bang,* "of me?" The shooter stopped right by my side. *Now or never.* I jumped up, wrapped my arms around his waist, and hauled him through the market with a driving force. We slammed into the wall and fell to the ground, our fists fighting for flesh to hit. Garrett head-locked the shooter and pulled him off me. He gave me just enough time to get to my feet and reach for my gun.

"Oh, look at the piggy now," he spat at me. I waited until he stepped a little closer, then twisted my body and swiped my leg along the floor and under his feet so he fell backward. It gave me a moment to grab my gun, but I was too late. The sound echoed around inside my skull right before the pain registered. It wasn't a deep ache, just a wicked burn. Three pops, and the shooter went down.

Garrett appeared above me. He ripped open my shirt and checked me out.

"Knee," I groaned as the pain sank in, "fucking knee."

Just as quickly as it started, it ended. That was when my brain could separate the fact I was moments away from being blown to shit, to going back to the station and having a hot shower, then heading home to my girlfriend. It was how I operated. It was how I survived.

***

Emily

"Why kill someone? Is it to get your fifteen minutes of fame? Revenge? Love? Or maybe it's a mental illness? An obsession with the opposite sex? There are so many possibilities why someone would take someone else's life, it's terrifying. For the average person, the thought can cross our minds daily, but actually following through with the act is something else. Most have a conscience—the inner sense of wrong and right. But imagine for a moment not having one, not having any form of empathy. You murder someone over a bowl of Frosted Flakes and show up dressed for Mom's Sunday dinner. Well, Tony Lace did." Professor Dean turned to the screen, clicked a button, and showed a mug shot of the man. "Tony was hunted by the police for eleven years, until at the ripe old age of forty-five, he got sloppy and killed his boss in the middle of the office in the middle of the day. Just snapped and lost it." Small gasps escaped from a few people.

"When they interviewed him later, he felt nothing for his crimes. He killed twenty-three women over eleven years, without even so much as a glossy eye. So," he sat up on his desk in his normal casual manner while we all clung to his next words, "the point of all of this is don't piss people off. You never know if the person sitting next to you might actually be plotting your murder." He winked as he clicked the screen off. The class erupted in some nervous laughter, everyone discretely eyeing one another.

"Drink?" Scott asked as he snapped his laptop shut. "Or maybe a light sedative, 'cause, wow." He laughed as he packed up his bag. We both decided to take this class again. There was something about Professor Dean that made you think outside the box, then want to run the hell back in. His class was fascinating, and every year he had new material to teach. He was excited to see we returned for a second year. We sat in the middle where the rest of the repeaters generally gravitated.

"Yes, to the first," I answered, pulling out my phone and giving Seth a quick call. It went directly to voicemail, which was unusual, considering he never turned it off. I gave a mental shrug and followed Scott to The Goose.

Erin and Alex were sitting at our table, and Ronnie the bartender was already nodding as I came through the door, knowing I'd want my normal four o'clock drink and snack. *I come here too much*, I laughed to myself.

I stole a fry from Erin before she started in on her usual banter. "How was the sexy professor's class this afternoon? Who done it today? Mr. Green in the library?"

"Nope." Scott quickly thanked Ronnie for his beer. "Today we learned what makes people kill."

"Oh." Erin's face scrunched up, looking disinterested.

Alex piped up. "So, Scott, what would make you snap? And who would you kill?"

"Mr. Wittgenstein from last semester. That man nearly killed me from boredom." He made everyone at the table laugh. He was so quick to lighten the mood.

"Are the guys joining us?" Erin asked. She saw me checking my phone. Sadly, it was still a habit, thinking I should check in a few times a day. Seth wanted me to, but since there was really no reason, I'd been trying to pull back. I needed to remember that everything was fine.

My phone rang, and it was him. I held up a finger to Erin while I answered it.

"Hey." I smiled like a fool in love. "How are you?"

"Hey, babe." He sounded tired. "It's been a long day. Are you at The Goose?"

"I am."

"Umm, okay, I'll meet you at home."

"Oh." I felt a pang of disappointment as I headed toward the door for some privacy. "Is everything all right?"

There was a pause.

"Yeah, just going to be here for a little longer. I'll get Johnnie to come to the house and—"

"No, you won't, Seth Connors," I scolded. "I do not need those men babysitting me anymore. I lived on my own in that house for many years without any of you. You know I'll be fine. Jimmy Lasko is dead, and Hank Wallace is behind bars. I'm not in danger anymore." I used his work therapist's words at him, knowing they were true.

He sighed heavily, but didn't push it. We went through this same discussion at least twice a week now. He was so damn controlling and protective that he couldn't let the past go.

"Fine, I won't be long, then I'll work from home."

I groaned a little, just wanting him to relax. "Seth, you can't be with me at all times. Life has thrown us some shit, and we fought through it. Now it's time to move on and be normal." I lowered my voice, lacing it with a husky undertone. "I'll meet you at home later, and if you think you're going to get any work done, think again."

He did his frustrated, sexy growl. "Fine," he relented. "Just text me when you get there."

"Only if you say please," I joked.

"No." The phone went dead. A moment later, a text came through.

Seth: TEXT ME!

I laughed. Seth would always be Seth. It was simply in his DNA.

***

The ocean was calm, and only a soft breeze could be heard through the long palm leaves. The moon was full and hung brightly over the water, casting its endless orange path to nothingness. I loved my home, though to be honest, I wasn't comfortable on my own yet, but I wouldn't let Seth know. It would only fuel his fire. So I tried to focus on repairing myself on my own. Therapy was not something I was interested in. It didn't help when my father died, and it wouldn't help now. I just tucked everything away neat and tidy inside my head.

I wove through the crosses and spider webs, past the coffins and Dracula, and hit my porch, thinking this would be the last year I gave Pete free rein of my house when I wasn't home. That man was obsessed with decorating, no matter what holiday. He convinced me to let him do Halloween with no limits, since last year we didn't even celebrate due to the fact we had just closed the case on Lasko. It was those damn eyes of his; they got me every time.

I stuck my key in the lock and smiled when I saw he'd set up two pumpkin men on my porch swing. Then I saw it. "Oh my God, Pete!" I gasped, removing one of their hands off the other's private parts. I did a quick scan and saw all of the decorations were involved in some kind of rude act. "I'm going to kill him!" I hurried over to the orgy of witches, removed Dracula's blow-up doll, and snatched the Grim Reaper from the moaning ghost. I quickly texted Pete, but rolled my eyes when I saw he'd once again changed his name in my phone.

Emily: You're so dead!

Sensuous Pete: What? My theme was a haunted brothel.

Emily: Travis has nephews!

Sensuous Pete: Who do you think helped?

Poor Travis. I glanced at his house, seeing he was home. Maybe I should go speak to him.

Sensuous Pete: You have to admit, Michael Myers is funny!

I quickly scanned my property, trees, balcony, and roof, then I saw him over in the shadows being bent over and smacked on the ass with a paddle by a drawn-on blow-up doll. Wow, he left nothing to the imagination with his drawings. I jammed the doll into the trash can, not letting on that I could hear her deflating. I'd laugh at the irony of it, but I was too damn embarrassed.

Emily: I hate you.

Sensuous Pete: I love you too, love.

Travis's kitchen light was on. Better address it now.

"Knock, knock," I said through the open patio door a few minutes later. Travis was cooking something that made my stomach grumble.

He didn't turn as he told me to come in. "Sorry, my hands are covered in batter. Help yourself to a drink." He nodded to the open wine bottle on the counter. I poured myself a little, knowing if I didn't, I'd have to hear about how when he was little, if your company didn't take the drink, it was a sign of disrespect. "You just get home?"

"Yes." I shook my head, almost blushing at what Pete did.

He smirked. He knew why I was there. "They love him, you know, my nephews." He started to laugh. "They had a ball."

I covered my face with my free hand. "I'm sorry, Pete is a breed all his own."

"Emily, the boys are fifteen. Sex is always on their mind. They came up with half of those ideas themselves. Besides, Pete kept them busy while I got some work done." He washed his hands after he coated the pork chops. "Now I have the weekend to relax."

I laughed through a sigh, moving to look out his grand, open window. A cool, late October breeze washed over my face. "Well, thank you for not being upset." I sipped my wine and watched the water lap at the shore.

"Seth working?" Travis asked as he came up

9

next to me, leaning on the door frame and watching the specular view.

"Yes." I nodded, wishing he weren't.

"You hungry?"

I smiled and thought how lucky I was to have him as a neighbor. I could have gotten another couple like the Stones; I'd barely even seen their faces. I was sure I ran into them at the supermarket and never knew it was them. I patted my pocket and realized I'd left my phone in my purse on the porch.

"Thanks, but I should get back."

"You know, it's all right to spend more than fifteen minutes here at a time." He flashed me a smile. Travis really was a good looking man. I wasn't entirely sure why he was single. Lord knew every woman in town had tried to make a move, but he didn't seem to bite. He reminded me of a taller, thicker Jude Law. "What are you thinking about?" He pulled me from my thoughts. I guessed I was staring.

"Sorry, I just realized who you remind me of."

"Oh? Enlighten me, please."

"You ever see Sherlock Holmes, the newest one?"

He rubbed his brow. "Jude Law, right? I get that a lot." He studied me for second. "I used the English accent once to get a girl in bed." He chuckled into his glass. "Not my finest moment, but the ladies sure love the British."

I covered my mouth in fear I might spit my wine out. I wasn't expecting him to say that. Once I regained my composure, I cleared my throat. "I guess we kind of do."

He turned to study me better; he used this look on me sometimes. "Emily, I know something big happened to you last year. I don't need to hear the details, but you should know I'm always here. I keep a spare key in the planter by the garage if you don't want to be home, and I keep the guest room ready for company. This is not me hitting on you, just me being a concerned neighbor and friend. You have a big house, and more than half of it is surrounded by woods. I can imagine as a woman living by herself most of the time; it would get a little scary."

It did. "Thanks, Travis, that really means a lot." I headed back into the kitchen. I went to the sink and washed out my wine glass and dried it, putting it back where I found it, then turned to find him watching me. "What?"

He shook his head like he was debating telling me. "You want to me walk you back?"

"No, I'm all right. Thanks for the talk."

"Anytime."

I needed to stop wearing heels when I decided to visit Travis. The woods were taking a toll on them—and my ankles. I followed the glow of my house where it peeked through the thick branches. I really should have taken the road. A snap from a twig behind me stiffened my spine. I turned to try to see around me, but it was pretty dark. I squeezed my eyes shut at the sound of another snap. "Stop," I whispered, forcing the images back.

"Emily?" His voice cut through my fear. "Speak so I can get to you."

It took me a moment to find my voice. "I'm

here…you're close." His huge body stepped in front of me. He reminded me of a panther sometimes, like he could just pounce from a treetop without even a sound. "You scared the hell out of me, Avery."

"Sorry." He looked above my head. "Just saw someone walking through the woods and thought I better see who the mystery guest was. Didn't think it was the host returning from…Travis's."

I ran my hand over my eyes, hating that all the guys disliked him. They didn't see he was only trying to be a friend. I moved around him, only to have his hand grip my upper arm, helping me through the heavy brush. Once we hit my lawn, he let go.

"You looking for the guys?" I asked, sitting down on the porch steps to remove the dirt from my shoes.

He took a seat next to me. "No, just didn't want to go home, I guess." He glanced at me. "I suppose you didn't want to either?"

"I had other reasons for not staying home tonight." I leaned back and stared at the clear sky. "Has the sergeant assigned you a new partner since the last one didn't work out?" Poor Avery lost Matthews last year, then his last partner decided to transfer back to Arizona for some unknown reason.

"Yeah," he dug his sneaker into the dirt, "actually, Riley."

"Seriously?" I was thrilled to hear this. Riley was thinking of going back to San Francisco, but I guessed he'd changed his mind. "Are you all right with that?"

Avery shrugged. "Could be worse. They could have given me Davis." He smirked at me, knowing my weak spot for the little charmer.

"As someone who spent a load of time with Riley, I'll tell you he's good people."

Headlights blinded us momentarily, and I saw spots. A slam of the door and heavy footsteps made Avery mutter that I was in trouble.

Seth dropped his bag near my feet, and I noticed the bandage above his eye. I jumped to my feet, but he stepped back when I reached out to touch him. I saw he had a small limp too.

"What happened?" I pulled up his shorts and discovered a large white bandage wrapped around his knee. "What happened?" I asked again, but directed at Avery, since Seth was not speaking.

"Flakka battle." Avery shrugged at Seth. "You know she won't stop until you tell her."

My hand flew to my stomach. "Flakka, as in the drug that makes you invincible?"

Avery nodded. "That be it."

"Why didn't you answer your phone?" Seth asked, not listening to us.

I shook my head and tried to catch up with the two of them. Flakka? Holy shit! "I had to go deal with something."

"Which was?"

"Are you hurt anywhere else? What happened to your knee?"

Avery gave a heavy sigh. "As much as I do enjoy watching the two most stubborn people butt heads, I can't do it tonight. Seth got lured into an attack." He pointed to Seth's knee. "Bullet grazed his muscle,

13

and he's off for a week, but he'll be fine." Seth hissed something, but it didn't stop him. "She was at Travis's, don't know why. I found her on her way back home and helped her through the woods."

"Avery!" I yelped, wanting to kick his ass for mentioning I was in the woods. The one place Seth couldn't handle, since that's where I was taken from him. "Really?"

He stood and shoved his hands in his pockets. "I'm just speeding things up."

"Avery, could you give us a moment?" Seth flicked his head toward the door where my keys were dangling from the lock.

"I think I'm going to go." Avery turned toward his car. "I know how your bickering ends."

Seth started up the stairs slowly. I wanted to help, but also wanted to play catch-up with what I just heard. Gunshot to the leg? Really? I sank back down and let my bottom hit the wooden step hard.

***

Seth

I tossed my bag on the couch as I headed for the kitchen, grabbed a beer and an ice pack, and headed out back to the patio. Swallowing two painkillers and chasing it with the beer, I decided if I was forced to take leave for five days, there was no harm in enjoying a little buzz. The thought made me nervous. I normally didn't like to feel numb; I liked to keep myself very aware. But today had been rough, and there was a moment when I thought my knee might be screwed, and my career would have been fucked.

I shook my head to clear it. No use worrying about what could have been. Focus on the fact that my spitfire of a girlfriend was spending time with our neighbor. Travis Murray had a little secret that he was hiding. It surfaced a while ago when Garrett was digging into a case that led him to Texas, then back to our flirty friend next door. Travis had a court date in a few months. Why? We weren't entirely sure, but I'd bet good money it wasn't going to be pretty. That man had rubbed me the wrong way since the day I met him. I couldn't mention it to Emily without getting into trouble, and it could possibly push her into his life more without meaning to.

A plate of chicken, roasted potatoes, and carrots was set in front of me, my beautiful girl looked down at me, and her big blue eyes fell on the bandage above my eyes. I could see the worry on her face, the look she got when she was trying to be brave, acting like she could handle the dangerous side that came with being an officer. Before she moved away, I grabbed her wrist and pulled her in front of me between my legs.

"Does it hurt?" she asked, running her smooth finger along the edge of the bandage. I shook my pills at her, showing her the label. "I've never known you to take anything stronger than an Advil." She read the bottle—oxycodone. "Guess it's good you have the week off."

"Physically, maybe, not mentally," I mumbled, knowing this was going to be hard. "Why didn't you text?"

She sighed and leaned against the table. "Let's just say I arrived home to a full-out Halloween orgy." My eyebrow rose. "Pete felt festive and included Travis's nephews in the planning. I headed over there," she pointed through the trees, "to apologize, and ended up staying for a drink. When I remembered to text you, I was there and my bag was here." She rubbed her head. "It wasn't anything but me getting distracted." She looked over at me running my hand over the curve of her hip. "You need to relax a little, though, Seth. *He's* gone, I'm safe, you protected me, but you don't need to anymore."

I shook my head, not sure I could describe the feeling I had. "Not going to happen, Em. It's who I am with you. If I could stick another bodyguard on you, I would."

"Why?"

I bit my tongue, not wanting to scare her, but something didn't feel right. It hadn't since a week after we celebrated at dinner, after I told her I loved her at the beach. Call it a sixth sense, but I started getting the feeling someone was watching me, maybe watching us. Something was off. I just wasn't sure what it was yet.

She stepped forward and ran her hands through my hair while she tugged at the roots the way she knew I loved. "What is going on in that head of yours, Seth Connors?" Bending down, she kissed my lips. "What I wouldn't do to see inside you." She smiled, but it didn't hit her eyes. There was worry there, and I wanted to kick myself for letting her see mine.

After dinner, I found Emily on the couch, laptop on her knees while she watched some horrible TV show. I stood behind her and pulled her silky blonde hair off to one side, then hooked my fingers around her tank straps and slid them down so they were out of my way. The moment my hands touched her warm skin, she leaned her head into my arms like she'd been waiting for my contact. I kneaded my thumbs gently into the base of her neck, creeping them up and down, squeezing into her tight muscles.

"Mmm," she moaned, which made me strain against my zipper almost painfully. "That feels nice."

I bent over and used the couch to support me, since my knee wasn't in the best shape. Brushing my lips over her ear, I gave it a nip and got the response I loved—her chest heaved and her nipples hardened. They pushed through her lace bra and gave away her desire. Sliding one hand into her cleavage, I cupped her heavy breast and felt the fullness that came when she got excited. My fingers inched further, straining against the lace to find the little bud. Once I did, I gave it a slight twist.

She purred as I rounded the couch, and I saw her eyes were dark and wild.

"You're a tease." One side of her mouth raised.

"Maybe I just like to see if I can get that look to run across your face."

"Mmm…" She went back to her work.

I fell in beside her and wrapped my arms around her waist and pulled her in close. She handed me the remote and muttered something about how she should be studying. I gently rubbed my hand along her bare thigh, tucking her in closer. I kissed her head, flicked the channels to *Cops*, and settled in. God, I loved us.

***

Avery

I opened my cabinets, seeing the labels perfectly in place staring back at me. Everything had its spot, and was in order. The eggshells broke easily, and the yolks fell one on top of the other in the pan. I set the burner just so before I returned to cutting my peppers and cheese in precise squares. The coffee was brewed, and the whole-grain toast should be ready in forty seconds, which left me enough time to feed the dog who was staring at me through the patio window. I scooped the kibble into the dish and placed it in front of the hungry yellow-eyed beast.

After washing the smell off my hands, I served up my breakfast. My knife and fork were placed on my napkin precisely as I liked them, before I removed them to eat. I liked order, unlike my brother. I sat and enjoyed my food, allowing myself a little self-contemplation.

The only things Jims and I shared were blood and the love of fucking with certain people. That was pretty much it. He was messy, loud, impulsive, a drunk, and his sex drive was twisted in the worst way possible. Jims was a sloppy killer, and most times I had to step in and clean up his mess.

I, on the other hand, was clean, quiet, and thought things through. I drank, but never lost my composure, never touched a drug, and was sexually driven in the *best* way possible. When I killed, it was quick, clean, and left zero trace of me ever being there. That was why I'd never been caught—I used my head.

My cell phone alerted me it was time to take my vitamins. They rested on top of my Bible. My vision blurred as I became lost in memory.

"Again!" she shouted, nearly spitting on my face. That look had taken over, just like father used to have. "You know this, Alexander. Recite it correctly."

I scrambled to remember. I could see it, but I was nervous to mess up again. "You shall love the Lord," I swallowed past her fearful eyes, "your God with all your heart, and with all your soul, and with all your strength, and all your mind, and your neighbor as yourself."

"And?" She inched the ruler closer to my face.

"Luke 10:27." My voice cracked at the end. I questioned if it was Luke or Matthew. My hands broke out in a sweat while she leaned back and tucked that wooden ruler back in her pocket.

"Good." She nodded and picked the Bible back up. "Now, where were we?"

I sagged into my seat, only to get a pointed look from her. My spine straightened and I sat as perfectly as I could. My hand tried to soothe my aching knuckles, but it was no use. I was sure she would beat them twice more before the end of the day.

She liked to instill pain; she said pain brought fear, and fear equaled respect. It was strange to me. I didn't choose to live with her, but after my parents died, the court ordered me to live here until my Aunt in Germany got Jims and Julia straightened away...That was three years ago.

I shook off the memory, washed up, and headed out. I had a full day ahead of me.

A half hour later I was standing in the station house prepared for the day.

"Hey." Riley held up a cup of coffee for me. I took the nasty smelling brew and thanked him, and wondered if I could drop it so I didn't have to choke it down. "So I guess we're working the eighteen-hundreds beat? Let's hope we don't have a repeat of Connors's day."

I nodded into my cup but blocked the hole with my tongue as I pretended to take a swig. He followed me to the squad car and slipped into the passenger seat. "Good boy," I whispered as he took his seat. I didn't have the patience to teach him that he worked for me. That he would take a bullet for me. That his life was insignificant compared to mine. Really, Riley was just a prop to toss in front of a possible threat. I dropped my coffee under Johnnie's car and slid behind the wheel. I checked the mirrors, the internal temp, and my seat settings. Riley watched me, but I ignored him. He had no idea what I was capable of, and if he was smart, he would keep his trap shut. I tapped the brake twice, then eased out of the parking lot.

***

Seth

I felt her wiggle out of my hold, as she broke free and left me cold. "No," I whispered and tucked her back in place, "take the day off." I nuzzled into my favorite spot on her neck.

She sighed and kissed my hand. "I can't."

"Mmm…" My hips pushed into her back. "I'll make it worth your while." She went to turn, but I held her in place. "I won't let you use your big blue eyes on me this morning." She laughed. She knew I was on to her. My hands moved to her lace panties and shifted them down enough so I could slip my hand around to cup her warmth. One finger skated around her opening, and it showed me she was ready. Her legs clenched around me. She wanted it, and so did I.

"Seth," she moaned, "I don't have time. You're going to make me—" I lifted her leg, lined up, and gently pushed inside of her with ease. She was like velvet, so soft and smooth.

"Make you what?" I murmured into her neck and pushed deeper, until I was fully in. I held my breath as her tight walls eased up around me. My hand slid up between her breasts and sprawled out against her chest, pushing her harder into me. "Late?" I rolled my hips and started to ease in and out, and her moans made my dick twitch. I fought not to pound her hard from behind. I liked it rough, and so did she. It was a thing we had. Sometimes I thought we picked fights just so we could have angry sex. I didn't care if that wasn't healthy. It was hot, and we both got off on it. It was something we needed. It was our outlet for all the shit we'd been through. I guessed you could call it our own brand of therapy. I rolled her nipple between my fingers. She flexed around me.

"Yes," she panted as her hand roamed between her legs and cupped my balls. She gave them a little squeeze. "I need to…" Her words slipped away as her beautiful, plump breasts bounced when I picked up the pace. "Please."

"Front or back?"

"Back," she nearly cried.

I hooked my arm around her waist and rolled her over. Pulling her to the kneeling position, I settled in between her legs, all the while never leaving her. I leaned forward, gripped the headboard, and tested out my knee. It was weak, but I could manage. She must have sensed this and started to move, but I gave her a crack on the ass, which made her still. I clutched the rail, pulled out almost all the way, then thrust in deep and hard, and her body shot forward. She screamed, so I did it again, and again. I increased the force, which drove her wild. I loved the sound our skin made, the way her ass looked with me behind it. The way her body quivered around me, showing me how much she liked it when I controlled her. She was so fucking sexy, I could hardly tear my eyes away. My knee grew weak quickly, so I stood and leaned over her. I drew her up a little higher and came at her from a different angle. I nearly fell when I sank back in at a speedy rate.

"Seth! I can't! It's too intense!" she cried, but she met my thrust just as hard. "Don't stop, oh my God."

"That's my girl." I was so close I could taste it. I let go with one hand, then my fingers found her spot and softy pressed inward with a flick to the left. That's all it took to make her clench around me and lose all sense, and I took off chasing her orgasm.

I dropped to the bed and brought her with me, but sadly this moment was lost when she glanced at the clock and jumped up with a curse.

"Dammit." She started to run around the room. I propped up on the pillow, one hand tucked behind my head. "Seth, you and your..." She shook her head. "My professor hates when people are late."

I stopped my eyes from rolling. Professor Dean was in love with her. Emily could do no wrong. "Then skip his class and stay home with me." I grabbed my erection. The mere sight of her red cheeks and wild eyes made me hard again. I moved the sheet and gave her a little show. She stopped dead in her tracks, and I thought she was about to agree when her face dropped into a scowl.

"Like whenever I've asked you to take time off in the past?" Her arms folded and pushed her breasts up. She made it hard to focus. "You hardly ever take days off, Seth. You work way past your hours. Why should I bend to you when you never do to me?" Shit, she was right, and she knew it. *Well played.* She sighed and reached for her clothes.

I waited until I heard the shower door open before I stepped into the shower with her. I spun her around to look at me.

"You're right, and I'm sorry." A few moments later she gave me a little nod. "Let me make it up to you." I scooped down and caught her lips with mine, my tongue pushed my way into her mouth, and three swipes later she gave in. I grabbed her ass and lifted her against the wall. I didn't mean to come in and do this. I was going to show her I had control, but I didn't, not when she was mad, wet, and so damn sexy. I zoned in on the little mark on her neck I made last night and started to suck ever so lightly. "I need you again," I whispered as I lapped my tongue around the water drops.

She wiggled out of my hold, so I placed her back down. "I don't have time." She turned and squeezed some shampoo into her hand. I sighed and watched her lather her hair and felt like an asshole. I thought with my dick, not my head.

I stopped her hands, gently pushed them aside, and took over massaging light circles into her scalp.

"Sorry," I whispered as my fingers inched toward her temples. Her frustration faded slowly, and all the while I gave myself a mental ass kicking. *Way to rub your time off in her face, jackass.* I turned her into the spray, washing her free of the suds. When her eyes opened and I saw she was still a little pissed, I kissed her cheek and let her be.

After a brief nap on the couch, I cleaned the kitchen, did laundry, fixed the patio door, and restrung some lights around the barbecue. It was only two thirty in the afternoon, and I was going mad. I needed to do something. I didn't mind having a day off, but five was going to bury me.

I texted Garrett, but he was busy and bitter about

having been stuck on desk duty today. He said he'd come by later.

Seth: You in class?

Emily: Nope, how's the knee?

Seth: Fine, where are you?

Emily: Good, get some rest.

Seth: Why are you avoiding my question?

Emily: Not, just I know you, and you'll show up and be a distraction…like this morning.

Seth: You didn't seem to object the first time.

Emily: And I didn't want to the second time, but you made me late, and I had to see Prof Dean after class to explain.

Seth: And he didn't care, right?

Emily: You know what?

Seth: What?

I waited and wondered if she was going to respond. I headed into the kitchen to make myself a late lunch. It wasn't until I was cleaning up that a text came through.

Maddy: You have the day off! Yippie! Gretchen said she's going to drop me off at your place in ten. YAY!

Oh shit. My head dropped into my hand. An afternoon spent with a fifteen year old girl…I was screwed.

Seth: You're dead.

Emily: Sorry, baby, but you made me.

Seth: What am I supposed to do with her?

Emily: Be her big brother, she loves you, and you did promise to spend more time with her.

I gave Pete a quick call; he'd know what to do.

Sure enough, fifteen minutes later my little sister bounced on my patio and rang my doorbell like it was going out of style. I opened the door, only to have her leap into my arms and give me a sloppy kiss on the cheek.

"Hey, Seth!" She beamed up at me with big, round, blue eyes. "I couldn't believe when Em told me you had the day off and nothing to do." She dropped her bag on the floor and looked around the house. "Wow, this place is nice."

"You want something to drink, Mads?" I closed the door behind her, then headed toward the kitchen. "Coke, Pepsi, water, juice?"

"Pepsi." She followed me, and I realized she'd never been here before. "Wow, that's quite the patio." She opened the door and whistled. "I can see why you never come home." I felt a pang of guilt. I really needed to work on that more.

"I work a lot." I handed her the soda. "So I don't enjoy it as much as I'd like to."

I pulled out a seat for her at the patio table and sat across from her. "So, why aren't you at school?"

She sat and downed nearly half the glass. "It was mainly Halloween festivities today and tomorrow, and when Em told me you were off, I came home early to come see you."

I nodded. "Right on. What's Mom up to?"

Her face dropped, and the excitement faded from her eyes. "She's up north, seeing Dad."

"Oh." A loud crack from my water bottle gave my tension away.

"Yeah, I heard Mom on the phone last night. They were arguing about one of Dad's clients coming by the house Friday. I wasn't home, so I didn't see him, but I guess he scared Mom a bit." I cleared my throat as a way to stop my outburst. *Fuck my father.* "Dad gave him the passcode, so he didn't even have to check in at the gate. Came right inside when Gretchen opened the door." She shrugged her little shoulders. "Anyway, Mom called Dad to talk to him about it, and I guess he was a real dick." She looked up at me to see if I was going to give her shit for swearing. I didn't. She was right— he was a dick. "Somehow he convinced her to come and visit, so she's there until tomorrow morning."

"I see." I nodded and attempted to keep my cool. "All right, well, I'll get the watchman to change the gate code, and make sure he keeps an eye on you guys. Does Nick know about what happened?"

She shook her head as she stirred what was left of her soda. "He'd have to pick up his phone in order for him to hear anything." I rolled my eyes. Nick loved to avoid any kind of drama, even at the expense of our little sister.

"Sorry, Mads, we're bad at communicating."

"It sucks." She looked up at me. "Like I miss hanging out with you. But Emily is great, and we talk all the time. She even took me out to lunch the other day."

Really? "She did?"

"Yup." She grinned a little, and I could tell she thought it was great I didn't know this. "We even went shopping. She helped me pick out a dress for the Halloween dance."

"Good." I needed to remember to kiss Em extra hard for doing this. I glanced at my watch. "You ready?"

"For what?"

"I have someone I want you to meet." She was going to love this.

***

"Oh my God, Seth, I can't believe you did that!" Maddy squealed while she scrolled through her pictures on her iPhone. "How in the world did you pull that off?"

"Pete." I couldn't help but smile at her excitement, although my ears still hurt from her screams as Zayn Malik came out of the sound booth to greet us. I wasn't sure what all the hype was with him. He reminded me of someone you'd find on one of the soaps Gretchen watched while she cooked.

Maddy scrolled through her iPhone before she removed mine from the cord and plugged in hers. "Listen, this is one of their older ones, but one of my favorites." Moments later, I heard a peppy beat strum through my speakers. Maddy started to sing along. I leaned my arm out the window and wondered if I should roll the windows up before anyone witnessed this show. "Oh, come on!" She started to dance, trying to get me to loosen up. She belted the chorus, and I laughed at her moves. "Fine." She turned down the music.

Her face said it all. *Shit.* "Give me your phone." I checked the stoplight to see it was still red, then quickly pressed play and brought that horrible tune back into my car. She looked at me, confused. I held up my finger to make her wait, then I forced myself to remember she was my baby sis, someone I'd give my life for. I gave her a look before I popped my collar, turned my hat around, and did it. I started to sing the lyrics, with a little douchebag dance. *Fuck me, no one better see this.*

Her mouth dropped open as I sang the words just as they did. Hell, I even added hand movements.

"Oh!" She squealed and clapped her hands with an infectious laugh. "This is amazing!" She joined me at the chorus.

When the song ended, I turned down the music and gave her my scariest face. "You tell anyone what just happened here, I will deny it for the rest of my life."

"Promise." She giggled and beamed at me, and

that made it all worth it. I turned my hat back around and smoothed down my collar. "Can I ask how you know the words?"

"I live with a woman, who loves *all* music." I pulled into my driveway. "A woman who sings *all* the time. You tend to pick up the words after hearing them eighty-seven times." I opened my door but noticed she didn't. "What?"

"Shouldn't you take me home?" I saw her eye Emily's car. "I mean, I don't want to overstay my welcome."

"Mads, get out of the car." I wrapped my arm around her shoulders as we climbed the stairs. "Just because I don't see you much, doesn't mean I don't want to spend time with you. I'll take you back later, but for now you're staying."

Her face lit up, then she looked past my shoulder. "Doesn't that witch look like she's spanking that ghost?"

"Pete," I hissed as I steered her away from the dirty scene.

A male voice from the kitchen prompted me to step in front of Maddy. I opened the door and found Travis nursing a beer as Emily sprinkled cheese on top of a homemade pizza.

"Oh, hey, man." Travis nodded at me as he took a swig of his beer. He didn't rise out of his seat like a man should do. "Wow," he said when he saw Maddy, "you must be his sister, because you're a mini Seth."

"I am," she replied and smiled proudly.

"Hey, Maddy," Emily said while she brushed her hands clean. She moved over and gave her a hug.

"Hey, baby," she said to me and gave me a kiss on the lips. Then she mouthed, "Be nice."

"Oh my God, Emily," Maddy said, following her over to the counter, "Seth took me to meet Zayn Malik! I got to listen to him sing, and I got a bunch of pictures."

"Seriously?" Emily grinned at me. "From One Direction?"

"Yup!" Maddy pulled out her phone. "Look!"

"One what?" Travis asked and downed the rest of his beer. Both girls turned to look at him. "Is that a person?"

"Band," they both answered together.

Garrett came into the kitchen but stopped when he saw Travis, who looked mighty comfortable at the table.

"Hey, Garrett." Travis stood to get another beer, but Emily beat him to it. She pulled out three and handed us each one. Garrett gave her a quick hug before he eyed me.

"Hey, Maddy." Garrett waved. "What are you guys looking at?"

"Don't ask," I muttered in fear they'd play the song again. "So, Travis, what are you doing here tonight?" Emily shot me a look, but I acted like I didn't see it.

"I came over to borrow some flour," he said into his beer. This guy had zero respect for me. "Guess I got caught up having a drink with Emily."

"Or two," Garrett added, and Emily glared at both of us.

He picked up the container of flour and placed his beer on the counter. "One and a half," he stated, then turned to Emily. "I'll return this later. Thanks, as always."

"Anytime." Em gave him a smile, but her cheeks were pink from blushing.

Once Travis was gone, she turned to both of us. "Really, guys? That was rude."

"He's hot," Maddy chimed in. "Does he always wear his shirt open like that?"

"Yes," Garrett muttered as he sank into a chair.

"Maddy." I scowled at her.

"What?" She watched him walk through the woods. "It's not like I stand a chance. I'm just sneaking a peek."

Oh fuck. "No peeking."

"I'm fifteen, Seth." She rolled her eyes. "A little peek is fun."

"Ah!" I shook my head. "Just stop."

She laughed over her shoulder as she headed for the restroom.

I glance over at Emily, who looked mighty pissed at both of us. "Must you guys be so rude to him? I would think you'd be happy he's a friendly neighbor. He's always home, and you aren't. If I was to get into trouble, he's here, a few yards away. Isn't that just as good as having one of your babysitters?"

"No," I said without missing a beat.

"Nope," Garrett added. "He likes you, Em."

"So?" She tossed the dishrag in the sink and shoved the pizzas into the oven. "I don't like him that way. Doesn't that count for something?"

"It should, but it doesn't." Garrett sipped his beer.

I crossed my arms. "When a guy like him likes a woman like you, he'll make a move. It's only a matter of time."

"Okay." She leaned against the counter, and I could see she wasn't going to back down on this either.

"Okay?" I felt like I wasn't going to like this answer.

"Okay, when *or* if he makes his move, I tell him no. Then if he doesn't get that I'm not interested, I stay away. But I'm not pushing away every guy you two think likes me, or I'd have no friends."

Garrett smacked me on the shoulder as he pulled Maddy into the living room area to give us some privacy.

"Seth," she held her hands up, looking tired, "please, please don't start this whole jealously thing again. First Scott, then Vince. I can't do Travis too."

I wanted to point out that both Scott and Vince had feelings for her at one time and probably still did, but I knew better right now.

I took a few steps so I was in front of her and cupped her cheeks so she would look at me. "Can't blame a guy for being crazy jealous over someone flirting with what's his, baby. Just because you don't see it yet doesn't mean I don't." I leaned forward and sealed my lips over hers, tasting the wine that lingered on her tongue. "Don't be mad."

She sighed when she heard Maddy in the other room. "Yeah." She moved away to check on the pizza.

CHAPTER TWO

Avery

My body was perfectly still behind a large tree, my senses heightened to every single sound around me. I was dressed in my normal attire for when I was watching, all black. I blended perfectly, trained to stay still for endless amounts of time, and have the patience of a saint, though I was anything but.

I could see perfectly into the kitchen window, see Emily and Seth get into one of their famous fights over her blind stupidity and his over the top jealousy issues. They were a bit like oil and water.

Travis was stopped a few feet away, watching too. Little did he know I was watching him with as much curiosity. My instincts told me he was hiding something, and I knew Garrett found something because I overheard him with Seth. I made a mental note to look into him further. I had plans for Travis, and the fact he was interested in Emily and not nervous of Seth's territorial issues made it that much more fun.

Travis suddenly looked in my direction, his eyes locked onto mine. I slipped into predator mode. I noted all the areas my knife could slice and dice into his flesh, ending his life quickly with no sound at all. I had a plastic sheet hidden a few yards away, along with some rope for times like this when it could get messy fast. My truck was a quarter of a mile due east. Travis was a big man. I would guess two hundred-some pounds, at six feet. I could carry him, but there was a chance I might have to drag him, so I would need a break. So, add all that together, if I had to kill my pawn, I'd be looking at least an hour or two of dealing with this shit.

Travis's eyes unlocked from mine and scanned the trees. His phone grabbed his attention, and he suddenly headed back toward his house. He walked right by me. If he were to lean to his right even an inch, he'd feel me. He had no idea how close he came to being carved into something spectacular tonight.

My attention was drawn back to the window when I heard Seth's little sister laugh. She brought the fight to a halt. Fuck! I hoped for some more tension. I guessed I'd have to step it up a notch.

***

Emily

My hands sought the warmth of my coffee, and I held it close to my chest as the cool morning breeze brushed my skin, leaving a thin layer of sea spray. My toes flexed in the sand, and the sun rose behind me. Ever since I was a child, I'd tried to beat the sunrise so we could wake together. It was like an old friend who no matter what would always be there.

I pushed last night's events away, feeling a little a lost with them. I focused on the fact Maddy and Seth had a great day, and she seemed to be bubbling over with happiness. Lord knew the poor girl needed someone to look up to while Martha figured out how to deal with Jack's messes. Seth's father needed to be taken out back and dealt with.

I dug at my pocket, shocked to see Maddy was up so early.

Maddy: Have you decided on your costumes?

Emily: Why aren't you sleeping?

Maddy: Excited! So…

I rubbed my head, trying to get my head in the game.

Emily: Yes, should be arriving today or tomorrow.

Maddy: Yay!! Will you give me a clue?

Emily: Your brother will be happy.

Maddy: So you're going as cops?

Emily: Ha! No, you'll just have to wait and see.

I laughed. I was lucky enough that he agreed not to go as a cop. He claimed he and Garrett already had the uniforms, and they didn't see the point in being anything else.

Maddy: I had a lot of fun yesterday, thanks a lot.

Emily: You should know you're welcome at our place anytime, Maddy. You never need an invite.

Maddy: Thanks, I needed to hear that. xo

I closed my eyes and breathed in some warmth from the rays and tuned in to the waves. I should get ready for school and hit up the library, but I didn't want to move.

His warm chest found my back, and his arms wrapped around me as his legs settled in next to mine.

"Morning." His raspy voice sent a jolt to my system. I leaned back and rested my head on his broad shoulder. I loved how I felt in his arms. "You're up early." I nodded and nuzzled deeper into his hold.

"I was saying hello to an old friend."

"Oh?" he asked, then kissed my temple. "Have I met this friend?"

I looked up at him. "Yeah," I closed my eyes and kissed his neck, "you have."

He made the connection and remembered the last time I did this, at the beach the morning after he told me he loved me.

"What's on your mind, baby?"

I watched as a seagull dived into the water and came back up empty. "Nothing really worth getting into." He didn't push; he got what I was talking about. We didn't need to beat a dead horse again. "Seth?"

"Mmm?"

"Do you see us together in ten years?"

His left hand found mine and held it tightly. "Emily, if you're not in my future in ten years, what is there to live for?"

I felt the passion he had for me, but was it enough? "You think, with how we are, with how stubborn and crazy we are together, we'll make it?"

He leaned to the side to see my face. "Do you?" My finger traced circles in the sand, truly trying to find the honest answer. "Em, you fought so hard for us last year, so let me fight for us now. If you're second guessing things, tell me now so I can make them right. I don't want to do me without you." His hand caught a tear I didn't even know was falling.

"I don't want to either," I whispered. He waited and studied my face to see how upset I was, then moved back and pulled me closer. He wrapped his arms around my waist and rested his chin against my shoulder.

***

"How's he holding up?" Erin asked through a bite into her apple. The library campus was surprisingly empty at three thirty in the afternoon.

We decided to study outside since it was so cool, and you could smell rain in the air. I loved that scent; it meant the temperature would drop. I just hoped it held out for Martha's Halloween party.

"All right. I guess these past four days have been interesting, considering the guy hasn't taken more than a day off work since he started at the station. He's visiting his mom today."

She grinned. "You set that one up too?"

"No, this one was all him. Guess there have been some problems with Jack again."

"Oh." She set her book down and gave me her full attention. "Anything you're worried about?"

"Not yet, but I guess I'll find out tonight." Erin fiddled with the corner of her book. I could see she was thinking about something. "Out with it, E."

She shrugged, then looked over my shoulder. "How are you dealing with…you know, the whole thing? It's been a year since Jimmy Lasko messed with your life."

"Honestly…" I looked around. We were pretty much alone. "I don't know."

***

Avery

I sat in my normal spot, on the edge of their bed, on his side. I turned the central air down and made it abnormally cool. I liked it that way; I could think better. I hated the heat, and I only came back here because of him. I really preferred Chicago. The winters were great, and the food was decent, but it didn't have what I needed—what I needed was here.

I removed my sneakers and leaned back on the pillows. Emily's shampoo smell was all over the place. I turned on the TV and watched a few shows, not really paying attention, just going through the motions one would if they lived here.

My eyes fell on a new picture on the dresser. It was of Seth's family. Everyone was there but his father. I closed my eyes and tried to remember the last time I ever saw my family's picture. No, I couldn't even imagine it. I didn't think we ever did one, but there wasn't really much time.

"Zooommm." I ran around the living room with a sheet tied my around my neck. I pretended to be a superhero. My arms were stuck out straight, and I imagined myself flying above the clouds at lightning speed. "I see you," I shouted to the bad guy below, stealing a motorbike. I dived to the ground, rolled under a chair, and dodged the laser beams that just missed my arm. I jumped up and grabbed the bad guy, which was actually my teddy bear Digger, and tackled him to the ground. I held him in a super death grip that no one could escape from.

"Shut up, boy!" My father chucked the TV remote at me, and it smacked me in the cheek. The impact split the skin, but I didn't say anything. I was not even allowed to cry–that only made him angrier. I quickly stood up and held Digger as a shield between us and handed the remote back to him. "You wanna see my belt again?" he screamed in my face. Spit striking my cheek felt like acid, but I

didn't dare wipe it off.

"No, Father," I whispered while I lowered my head.

"Get the fuck outside. I don't want to see your face until tomorrow."

"Okay." I hurried to the back, pulled open the patio door, stepped out onto the cold cement slab, and wished I had grabbed my shoes. I took two steps at a time as I made my way up to the treehouse tucked away out of sight of the house. It was the only place where my father couldn't hurt me. I pushed the trap door up and lifted myself onto the floor.

It was nothing like other kids' treehouses, but it was mine and Jims's. We kept what we needed up there for times like this. I covered my shivering body with a blanket, then I tucked Digger in and made sure he was warm. I opened the plastic container where we kept our emergency supply of food. Crackers and peanut butter got old, but it was better than being down there with him. I peeked through a crack in the branches where I could see the lights flicker from the TV as my father had another beer. He drank a lot, and he hit a lot too. He said our cries made him mad. He hit everyone but Julia, and I wasn't sure why. I hated Julia, but Jims made sure she was never alone with me. I guessed because she was so mean. The moonlight was bright enough so I didn't need to waste the flashlight batteries. The comics were in a sack next to me. I chose my favorite and pretended I was Clark Kent until my eyes grew heavy.

Gunshots from the TV brought me back to the present, but the feelings from my memory still weighed heavily in my chest.

I turned off the TV, smoothed the bedspread back in place, and puffed the pillow to leave no trace of an intruder. I knew I shouldn't, but I turned the picture frame around. Sometimes I just couldn't help myself. I scanned the room, when I suddenly heard footsteps on the stairs. *Shit!* They must have come in when I was lost in my memories. I hurried across the room and in behind the huge velvet curtain that concealed my body perfectly.

"I swear, Pete, if I come home to one more orgy—" I leaned to the side just enough so my left eye peeked out and saw Emily on the phone. She put him on speaker and tossed it on the bed. "I don't care if you think it's funny, people are going to think it's me doing it." She pulled her dress off over her head and kicked it to the side. I slid my phone out of my pocket and snapped a few photos. Emily was like a lingerie magazine; she always matched. Today she had a soft pink and black lace set that showed off half her perky ass. Her plump breasts jiggled as she laughed at something Pete said. She was a pretty little thing, and I knew why Seth was so damn protective. Any man with a dick wanted a piece of her. Didn't help that some of the guys talked about how they screwed in the on-call room. She was a wild one in bed, and I knew she was up for anything. I knew because I watched all the time. She loved to give up control, loved to be completely dominated by him.

I was hard, not for her, but for the idea of a

woman giving herself over completely. I'd screw Emily, but it'd be like used goods. She belonged to Jims, not me. I took a deep breath and forced my control to come back. I couldn't afford to lose it now. She moved into the bathroom and ran the shower. I stepped from behind the curtain, about to make my way out the door, when she came back into the room. She stopped three feet in front of me. I froze. Thank God her head was down, hair flung forward as she scooped it into a ponytail. I took two swift steps behind the closet door just as her head came back up. I was not seen. She grabbed her phone and disappeared into the bathroom.

The edges of my mouth rose as the high spread through me. I got this rush. It happened a lot with Emily, almost daily. I loved to play with my pawns.

A car door slammed, and I hurried to the window to see a FedEx truck driver on his way up the driveway. I hurried down the stairs and caught him at the door.

***

I didn't even notice I was at The Brick until I parked. I reached in my bag, double checked the thick envelope of money was still there, and recounted to be sure it still added up to a thousand.

The building was an old warehouse in the middle of an abandoned part of town. If you didn't have a membership and walked in, you'd think the place was a photography studio. That was the front the owner used, and no one seemed to question it.

"Hey there, sunshine," she said as she held the

door open for me. I glanced down at her outfit. I wasn't aware they made shorts that short, but whatever. "I'm doing well, thank you for asking." She rolled her eyes and handed me my key. "I had a flood at my apartment, and my dick landlord wanted a blow job for payment, even though it was the guy above me who did it." She rambled on, and I started to say something, but she was too lost in her story to notice I'd walked away and was punching in the passcode.

The door opened, and in walked one of the regulars, who eyed her long legs and slim waist.

"Hello, Edward," she grinned and gave him a playful smile, "you've been gone a while."

Edward tucked his hands into his dress pants and gave her a flick of his head. "So you've been waiting for me?" He pulled out a card and slid it over the smooth granite counter. "You could always call me."

I slapped my hand down on top of the card and balled it in my fist. "Would you please get me some water?"

"Umm…" she started to say, but when she saw my face, she nodded. "Of course." She hurried off to the back room.

"Do we have a problem here, Adam?" Edward laughed under his breath. "Never known you to claim one before." He headed toward the keypad, then slipped into the dimly lit hallway. We didn't use our own names here—everything was kept confidential.

"Here." She slammed the water bottle in front of me. "What the hell was that?"

I jammed the card in my pocket, reached for my bag, and headed inside. I didn't have the time or desire to deal with this shit right now.

***

Seth

The smell of coffee found me and pulled me out of my groggy state. I peeled myself off the couch, where apparently I spent the night, and headed into the kitchen.

Emily was arms deep in laundry, and she sang along to the music that was plugged into her ears. Her back was turned as I poured my coffee. I leaned back and watched her shake her ass in her short, silky robe. She jumped when she spotted me.

"Like what you see?" She laughed and tugged her earphones out and tossed the last of the folded sheets into the basket.

"I do," I murmured into my mug. I saw her blush, which was comical because she was such a dirty little vixen. "Come here." I took her arm and tugged her over to me, then bent down and kissed her soft lips. "You didn't wake me."

She shook her head and wrapped her arms around my neck. "You were out cold, and you needed sleep."

"I needed you more." I nuzzled her neck to warm my cold cheeks.

She gasped. "I'm here now." Her hand dipped under my shirt, and she raked her nails down my back. I grew hard instantly, grabbed her waist, and twisted around and sat her on the counter. She spread her legs as I moved in between and hauled her close again.

"Do you have any idea what you do to me?" I slid my hands up her bare legs and squeezed her tight ass while I nipped at her earlobe.

"You know," she whispered, "I really don't. Why don't you show me?"

I took her hand and slid it over my chest. "Feel that?" My heart pounded against my ribs to show her she made me wild. "And this?" I lowered her hand over my erection. Her fingers wiggled out of my hold and started to massage me, and I grew even thicker. My hands steadied me on either side of her, and she kept her eyes locked with mine as I fought the urge to take her right there on the counter. "I want to be in you when I come."

She untied the belt and let the robe fall away, to leave her in only a tiny scrap of silk. Her nipples were hard and strained against the fabric. She inched the nightgown up to expose the evidence of her arousal. She glistened around the seams.

My pants were off, and I lined up with her in a matter of seconds, pushing in slowly. I felt her tight little walls contract around me. Her legs wrapped around me, as she lifted her hips off the counter to pull me in deeper. It was perfect. I loved how she was just as needy as I was. My hands flew to her hips to hold her still as I gave a few good thrusts, which earned me a sexy little moan.

"Hello?"

Emily's eyes darted up to mine. "Travis!" she hissed. I grabbed her waist and carried her into her father's old office and locked the door behind us. "Seth, put me down." She tried to push free, but I backed her against the wall while I steadied myself. "Seth!"

I started to thrust inside her again, deep and hard. She tried to protest, but it soon was lost as her orgasm built.

"Anyone home?" Travis called as he walked into the kitchen. Fuck, this guy had some balls walking in here. If I wasn't buried deep inside her, I would flip out on this asshole.

"Seth," she begged, but at the same time was clawing at my back to pull me closer. "Stop! He's going to hear us!"

I grabbed her face. "Then you better be quiet, because I'm not going to stop until we both come."

"Seth," she whimpered.

"He is in our home uninvited, so if he hears something, that's on him, not us. Now..." I sat her down, turned her around, and raised her arms over her head. I pumped back into her from behind. My lips hovered over her ear. "Don't be thinking of him while I'm inside you," I growled.

She tried like hell to stay quiet, but I could see she was struggling. Travis moved about just outside our door, as I thrust deeper and deeper and sent myself into overdrive. My hand dipped down and cupped a handful of her breast, and I twisted the nipple between my fingertips. I was so fucking angry that he was here *again* for her.

"Seth I-I..." she cried as she came. I pumped a few more times until I joined her, filling her with everything I had. My anger fueled me. I could barely think while I carried her over to the desk, laid her down, and entered her again, semi-hard now, but I stiffened by the second. She moaned and muttered something I couldn't make out.

I didn't care about anyone but her at that moment. I pounded out my frustration, and she didn't seem to mind. Her hands massaged her bouncing breasts.

"Harder," she demanded. That made me go crazy. I increased the speed, until nothing but skin slapping skin could be heard. It was all incredibly sexy, the noise, her face, her breasts, the look in her eye—all of it was mine. Her nails clawed at me, and her quiet screams were enough to send any man buck wild. I wanted to be deeper, I was gone, lost in pure animal instinct. I knew she saw it, and she suddenly pulled me down, cupped my sack, and gave it a hard tug as I pounded her senseless.

"I'm yours, Seth," she just barely whispered as she came along with me. She was all mine, and she was perfect. Emily was the light at the end of the tunnel.

I shook off the after sex jitters and helped Emily to her feet and let her know I'd get her something to cover up with.

"Hey," Travis said as he came into the kitchen, then stopped when he saw it was me. "I was looking for Emily." He held up a FedEx package. "This came to my house yesterday, thought I'd deliver it."

"Most people would knock, wait for an invite, and leave it by the door if no one answered," I muttered, annoyed. He had become a little too comfortable. I snagged one of my t-shirts and handed it to Emily, who waited behind the door.

"You really don't like me, do you?" Travis leaned against the patio door.

I poured some coffee. I wanted a fresh cup now that mine was cold. "Just don't have a ton of respect for someone who openly flirts with someone else's girl."

"Hey, Travis." Em gave me a look of death. "Joe delivered this to you?" She read the label. "That's strange. I was home around the time he would have come by."

"Mmm, strange," I mumbled and thought it was incredibly convenient that Joe messed up the delivery.

"Well, thanks, I appreciate it. I need this tonight." She showed me the label. *Oh shit, it's our Halloween costumes.*

"Sure." Travis gave a tiny smile, then looked at me. "I guess I'll see ya later."

"Okay, thanks again." Emily moved to the door and closed it behind him. She turned to me, hands on her hips. "That was a little uncalled for, Seth." I shrugged. I didn't care about what Travis thought. "Whatever." She opened the box just enough to peek in, and when I went to look, she slammed the top shut. "Not yet."

"Why?" I peered over the rim of my mug.

"Because I like watching you squirm about your costume." She laughed and headed upstairs, leaving me to watch Travis disappear into the tree line. I wondered if he watched her like Lasko used to.

"Seth?" I looked behind me at Emily, who held up my handcuffs. "We should really use these more often." I grinned. "Maybe I'll use them on you?"

"Not on your life."

She tossed them on the couch with a shrug. "Maybe I'll find someone else to use them on then."

I lunged forward, only to have her yelp. "Yeah, you better run."

***

Avery

I jolted awake from the sound of Emily's scream. At first it was terror, but when I heard Seth's voice call after her, I knew they were playing.

I moved undetected from the guest room closet where I had fallen asleep waiting for them to return, and slipped into Emily's room. There was a spot behind her shoe rack that hid my bottom half perfectly, and her dresses hid everything but my eyes. The great part was she had these shutter-style doors so I could watch without having to move from my spot. This was good because a few times she opened the closet unexpectedly. I quickly moved her father's memory box over so I could get a full view of the room.

Emily suddenly laughed and ran into the room. She raced around, then grinned when she looked at the closet. She flung open the doors and moved inside, clicking the door closed just as Seth came in.

"You think you're safe, baby?" He laughed as he scanned the room.

Emily was so close, and if she were to look back to her left, she'd see my face. She panted, out of breath as she grinned at him. Her skin was flushed and her hair was messy.

Slowly, I moved my hand up. It ached to wrap around her vocal cords. The need to steal her life made my mind spin with consuming thoughts. I blinked and swallowed as my hand grazed her hair. She shifted but was too wrapped up in Seth to notice me. My other hand went into my pocket and pulled out a long, skinny wire. *In a flash, I saw myself wrap it around her neck and tighten it so it ripped through her flesh. Her eyes locked onto mine with such shock it made me smile with delight. Blood poured down her front and dripped at her feet. The tin smell of human blood heightened my excitement.*

Just as the urge became overpowering, just as I prepared to make my move in my crazed state, Seth opened the door and hauled her free.

Fuck! I pressed myself flat against the wall and waited. Now wasn't the time. But it was coming, and when it did, it would be my most passionate kill yet.

***

Emily

"Wow." Vanessa gawked at my costume as I fastened the red ribbon around my ankle just above the black high heel. "What an elegant, sexy looking dress." I winked as I stood in front of the mirror and fixed the leather overlay on top of the puffy tulle. I was in a black and red corset, with black lace sleeves and a rather stylish popped collar, a leather skirt with red tulle underneath, fishnet stockings, and black high heels.

"I hope I can do my master proud." I grinned and thought about Seth, who was off helping his family prep for the Halloween party they held every year. I told him not to worry, that Garrett and I would meet him there.

"Do you think your master will be all right going as Dracula?" she asked as her fingertips grasped the zipper on her dress, then slipped on a pair of glasses.

I removed the contact from the solution and replaced my bright blues with a deep yellow. I laughed at the thought of Seth's face. "Something tells me when he sees his bad-ass cane, he'll be fine with it." Vanessa's costume looked perfect. "And Campbell?"

She shifted her wig in place. "Well, he owes me one, so..." I looked over to find her chuckling. "This should be fun."

"You know what the difference is between you and me?" Garrett stood in the doorway and pulled on a pair of sunglasses. "I make this look good."

"You make a hot MIB agent, Garrett."

"Thanks." He sat on the bed playing with his little memory eraser. "You two look very good—" He paused at Vanessa, and I could see him putting the dots together. "Oh shit, does that mean...?" He rolled his hand over his mouth. "Wait-wait, I need to make sure my phone is fully charged so I can take pictures."

We arrived at the Connors family home, and it

looked completely different. "Wow," I gasped, impressed at the decorations, "this place puts Disneyland to shame."

The entire house had been decorated to look like a haunted mansion. Purple lights helped intensify the fog that made the house look like it was almost floating. Flashes of light flickered throughout the windows where silhouettes were placed to look eerie.

Vanessa tucked herself closer to my side. "Seth says she even hired people to walk around the property to reenact scenes from movies." Garrett chuckled and moved us forward, and we headed toward a door where a man took our name and nodded us through.

"Ready?" Garrett asked over my shoulder. I smacked his arm and tried to hide my nerves. Vanessa's hand slipped into mine as we walked into the entryway. It was dark, but a bright black light enabled spider webs to lead the way. Music was being pumped above us, the slow beat of a drum making my stomach twist, and I couldn't help but smile. I knew this was all fake, but it seemed very real. Someone ran in front of us, and we both screamed. Garrett was still in hysterics behind us, but we ignored him and continued until we made it into the living room, where someone was sitting in a chair by the fireplace. Wow, Martha really had thought of everything. I wondered who this actor was supposed to be. Before I had a chance to guess, I heard Garrett's laugh belt out over the crowd.

"Not one word, O'Brian," Campbell shouted, pulling at his tights.

"Ohmygod!" I cupped my mouth. The sight was almost too much to take. Campbell, one of the biggest, grizzly-bear type guys, had managed to stuff his massive body into a full spandex Superman costume.

"I hate you all." His face remained deadpan, which only made it funnier.

Vanessa whispered something in his ear. He rolled his eyes but did pull her in for a long kiss, a kiss that made me want to find Seth immediately.

We made our way out to the patio, where again I hardly recognized the place. The theme was famous couples, and everyone had put a ton of effort into their costumes. There must have been at least two hundred people there. The lighting was spectacular, following the same look as the front, a haunted house.

I was handed a tall glass of champagne, the base of it shaped like a bird claw. Campbell pulled Vanessa away to visit someone, and Garrett was at the bar. I scanned the faces to see if I could spot Seth, but mostly everyone was wearing some kind of mask or face paint.

"Mmm," a voice called out from behind me. "Well, well, well, it's been a while."

I smiled as I took a drink. "It has."

"How do I look?" he asked as some of his friends came and joined him. They eyed me like a slice of meat, and I scanned behind them and wondered where Garrett was.

"Very dashing." I smiled politely. I had no issues with Nicholas; I just didn't like how his friends were watching me.

"Three guesses who we are." One guy snickered. I wasn't entirely sure what his problem was.

I pointed to Nicholas. "Porthos." I pointed to the quiet guy. "Aramis." Then I pointed to the cocky one, bloody well knowing he was Athos, but said, "Lady Winter?" Nicholas grinned at my answer.

"Very good." He nodded in approval. "And you are?"

"My wife." Seth appeared out of nowhere and wrapped his arm around my waist and granted me a kiss to the side of my neck. "Hello, my missus," he whispered.

"Master." I smiled at the excellent job he did on his Dracula costume. He was even wearing the contacts I got him.

"Master?" He pulled away. His eyes raked down my front, and his tongue darted out to lick his lips. "Mmm..." A low growl came from deep in his throat. "Now, I like the sound of that."

"Dracula and his wife." Nicholas sounded a little impressed. "Nicely done, guys." He looked at his friends before he stepped closer. "Seth, have you spoken to Dad?"

"No," Seth hissed. "Don't, Nicholas, not tonight." He pulled me away from the group, but Nicholas came after us.

"Seth, you need to talk to him. He won't listen to me."

"Why?" Seth nearly shouted, and a few guests stopped and stared. "I have no interest in speaking to that sorry excuse of a father. I will not do him any favors." He moved closer to Nicholas, which made me nervous. I wasn't sure what was about to happen, but it's wasn't going to be good. "You can be his lapdog, do his dirty work, but I won't. Never have, never will."

"Seth," I whispered and placed my hand on his arm, "can you help me with something?" His attention snapped back to me, and I could see how upset he was. "Please."

"Yeah, sure, baby." He turned back to his brother and shook his head. "No more."

Nicholas nodded but glanced me, and he mouthed, "Later."

I steered Seth to the side of the house and tucked him away in the shadows. "Are you all right?" I wanted him to take a moment to catch his breath. "Can I do anything?"

He cupped my face as he lowered his yellow eyes to meet my gaze. For a moment my stomach dropped, remembering Lasko's dog and the basement, but I pushed it aside. "I love you, Emily." Before I could respond, he sealed his lips over mine. He pushed me flat to the wall. I could tell he was bothered, but I let him be. Seth was not someone you pushed. He'd come to me when he needed my help. My fingers played in his hair as his tongue danced with mine, and his hand reached under my thigh and hooked my leg over his hip. He ground his erection into me, making me squeak.

"Have you seen Emily?" Maddy's voice came from no more than ten feet away. Seth growled as he pulled away, nearly panting with need.

"This family." He squeezed his eyes shut, then looked down at me. He ran his finger from my lips, down my throat, to the center of my breasts. "This is sexy." His eyes were hooded. I could see he was weighing his options, but there was no way I was having sex with this man ten feet from a pile of family and guests.

"We should go," I muttered, only to have him push me gently back. His free hand ran up the back of my leg, under my skirt, and over the curve of my ass. "Seth, we can't," I whimpered as my body betrayed me with a tingly sensation.

"Just let me do one thing." His hot breath blew over my neck. "I just need to feel." His fingers ran along my opening ever so slowly, and my eyes rolled back as the sensations shot through me. "You're ready for me." He grinned darkly, but I could see he was hiding something. "I like knowing that." He pulled away and tugged me into his side as we walked back around the corner. "While you're mingling, think of my fingers there." I didn't think I had a choice.

"Emily!" Maddy shouted as she bounced toward me. "Garrett told me you were here, but I couldn't find you. Wow, look at you two! How perfect. Look at your eyes, so creepy." I blocked out her rambles when I saw Seth's eyes full of promise for a night of pleasure. "Come on, Emily, let me show you around." She pulled my arm, but I was still lost in Seth's world. "You don't mind, do you, Seth?" Her face always softened when she looked at her older brother. There was so much love and respect there, it nearly broke my heart, but in a good way.

"Not long," he growled playfully as he leaned in and kissed me on the neck. "That's an order from your Master." He gave my ass a little pat before he left, flipping his cape dramatically. Garrett popped out of nowhere, blocking his path.

"Aww," he pointed to Seth's cane, "all I got was a stupid lighty-up prop. Why didn't I think about a cane?"

Seth waved it around. "Pretty bad-ass, right?"

"Yeah." Garrett reached out and touched the handle. "Can...can I try?"

Maddy and I burst out laughing, and both guys turned and glared at us. They huffed as they walked away like they didn't just share a moment. *Men.*

"Okay, so here is the bobbing for apples area." She waved her hand around. "The photo booth, in there is the makeup artist in case you need a touch-up, the 'guess what you're touching tank,' and..." she rubbed her hands together, "six haunted houses." She beamed when she showed me one door, explaining that once inside, it led to six different doors you could pick, depending on how much of a wimp you were.

I listened but heard no screams. "How scary is the sixth door?"

Her face changed as the ass from earlier, Nicholas's friend, took over our conversation. "Did you ever see the first *Saw* movie?"

"Yes." I swallowed hard and remembered how scary it was.

"You ever see the show *Twisted Sisters* or *The Birds* by Alfred Hitchcock?"

"Unfortunately, both." I glanced at Maddy, who shrugged at her brother's friend taking over her fun.

"Well, combine those two fears, modern and classic, and you have door number six." He stepped closer to me and put his face close to mine. "Is the pretty little blonde bimbo scared?" I wasn't sure what I'd done to offend this guy, and I decided to ignore him.

"Well, thanks. Maddy, you want to move on?" I threaded my arm through hers.

"Wow, she *is* scared," he said and grinned a little. "Nicholas said you had balls, but I've yet to see them." He crossed his arms. "Looks to me like you're a bit of a pussy. Who's got fifty she can't do door six?"

The quiet friend piped up, "I have sixty she can."

Shit! I felt my braver side come out, the side that had gotten me in my fair share of trouble in the past.

"No, Emily, ignore them." Maddy gave me a pleading look. "Sorry, but Nicky's friends are assholes."

"No, it's fine. You know I love a good challenge." I swallowed down a lump.

He waved a hand down the stairs toward the door. I waited for Maddy, but the ass stood in front of her.

"No, alone. She knows all the tricks, so what's the fun in that?" He moved to open the door. "House six is waiting."

I smiled back at Maddy, who looked as if she might be sick. Frankly, I felt the same way. I looked over her shoulder at the house before I stepped into the darkness.

The hallway was pitch black, nothing but cool air was with me, and I reached out to run my fingertips along the wall. I moved a slow step forward, knowing the only way I was going to get through this was if I moved. My movement triggered music, and "Custer" by Slipknot flooded my ears. I recognize it from Seth's workouts. My knees were weak as I shimmied forward and reminded myself it was just pretend. It was all pretend. A strobe light started to blink to the beat of the song. Once my eyes adjusted, my heart came to a halt mid-beat.

A dark figure stepped out from the wall as ice water shot through me. He was covered head to toe in black, his face concealed with a hoodie. Ever so slowly his head rose, and I nearly fainted at the clear plastic mask that hid his face. His head tilted to the side like he was very interested in me. *It's all pretend, it's all pretend.* My heartbeat matched the strobe light's rhythm, and my mind screamed at me to turn around, but I couldn't. He stepped to the side as if to tell me to pass, but if I did, we would be so close. I knew I had no choice but to pass by him, so I swallowed hard and placed a nervous step forward, then another, and another. All the while my brain battled with me to turn around and get the fuck out of there. I swore the temperature dropped so low my breath could be seen.

I was a step away from the actor—I was sure he was an actor. All I needed to do was take one more step, then I could pass. I was nearly in tears, but I managed to hold it back. I was strong, and this was ridiculous. I moved in front of him, but I didn't turn my back. Instead, I stared into his dark eyes.

A series of emotions ran through me. Holy shit, the mask looked just like Jimmy Lasko! *Run Emily!* I was screaming inside, but I wouldn't run. *There was no reason to*, I tried to reason with myself. Lasko was dead. This was just my mind and its screwed up, dark thoughts. The man squinted slightly, then stepped back into the dark, and just as he did, I heard him whisper, "Emilyyyy."

I turned and hurried around the corner, shaking uncontrollably. I used the wall to help me race through the maze. The fog got thicker as I moved on, and it made it hard to see. Lights flashed, music screamed at me, and my head swarmed with images from my own nightmares. I swore I was not alone. I could feel someone there, and it didn't feel like an actor.

Finally, I hit a dead end, which led to another door. *Fuck!* I yanked on the handle and tossed myself forward and slammed it behind me. I reached around the wall for a light switch, but nothing. *Think, think, think!* Okay, everything seemed to be on motion detectors. I stepped forward and triggered a bright red light. My stomach dropped, tucked, and rolled as it hit the foot of a man who dripped in blood standing four feet away, staring directly at me. Blood seeped over his eyeballs as he stood motionless between me and the other door.

But what made me really want to scream was the hooded man in black was back. He was in the corner, and something told me he wasn't supposed to be there.

***

Seth

I got a few feet from the bottom of the stairs before I heard my father's voice. He was in his office. The door was almost closed, but I could hear him. Normally, I blocked out anything that had to do with him, but his tone was so desperate. I moved a little closer to peek inside, and saw he paced in front of his fire place with his cell phone to his ear.

"No, I said take care of it," he shouted, then downed the rest of his drink. "Do I pay you to question me? No, I pay you to make things disappear. I don't know who leaked this, but you better fix it or you'll join the last guy you let slip through your fingers. Last chance, Cale." He chucked his phone on the chair and sent his glass into the fireplace. "Fucking bitch!"

"Seth," Mom whispered from the kitchen as she gave me a look begging me to leave.

My father suddenly appeared at the door. His face looked like I just caught him doing something wrong.

"What do you want?" he snapped at me.

I smirked and thought how sad it was that this man was my father. "Nothing from you," I muttered.

"Watch your mouth, son," he barked.

"Jack," Mom came forward to calm the situation, "please, let's just enjoy the party."

"Or what, Father, you'll punch me again? Toss me up against the wall?" I moved closer. I towered over him by a few inches. "In case you forgot, I'm all grown up, smarter and wiser."

His eyes flickered, and I knew he'd love to haul off and punch me. Jack never liked to be threatened, which was why so many feared him. But he didn't scare me, not now that I saw what a sad man he had become.

"Seth!" Maddy flew into the hallway. "Seth!" she shouted again, not at all reading the situation. "I need your help."

"Not now, Mads."

"Please," she begged, and something in her tone made me follow her outside while she filled me in. "He basically pushed her into going. But she should have been out by now. I don't know, I...I have a bad feeling because, well...you know."

I beat my way through the sea of people to the front and headed through a side door. Once inside, I glanced around at the holding room for the actors. It was small, but it gave them a moment to rest before they went back into the rooms to play their part. My mother sank a hefty amount of money into Halloween, and she went all out for her haunted houses, but to someone who scares easily, no matter how much she denied it...house six was the worst.

"Anyone see the blonde in house six?" I called out. "Any idea where she is in the maze?"

"Third room," a guy dressed all in back, head down, holding a cloth to his face growled.

I hurried down a tiny hallway and slipped into the room that was a riddle. It was empty, and I quickly turned a handle, which made a door pop open. That was when I saw Emily, back pressed to the wall, fingers madly scratching along the fake window to find her way out.

"Em." I made my way down the hall, but she couldn't hear me over the loud music. The moment I touched her hand, she screamed. I covered her mouth and whispered in her ear, "Open your eyes." She did, and when she saw it was me, she lunged into my arms. She was shaking, but she seemed all right. "You okay?" She nodded, but I could see she was beyond terrified.

"Get me out of here." Her eyes were wide. "I don't like this."

I moved her through the last room, where I shook my head at the actor who was about to do his performance. Emily's grip on my hand almost made me sad that she got so scared.

Once outside, she sagged against the wall and took a moment to regroup, then she started to laugh.

"Should I be worried?" I asked, worried she might be losing it.

"No." She leaned forward, hands on her thighs. "But I think I may have hurt one of your actors. I elbowed him in the face." She cupped her mouth as she laughed harder. "Oh my God, Seth, that was so fucking scary." She stopped, and her face fell a little. I started to hold her, but she held up her hand to stop me. "I just need a moment."

"Okay." I leaned beside her and made sure she was all right. I wanted to kill the ass who tempted her to go in there. "Why did you go in?" I had to know.

She took a deep, trembling breath and let it out. "If I tell you, Seth, you can't judge or be worried, because really, I'm fine." I waited for her to go on. I could see she was wondering how I was going to react. "I'm not sure how to explain this."

"Try." I pushed her because I needed the answer.

She looked up at me and pressed her lips together. "Have you ever watched a horror movie, and the suspense has you so wound up, you just need that release of the person jumping out of the bushes so you can let go?" I nodded. "Since Lasko died, I've had that feeling. I'm wound up so tight, I just needed a good jolt to the system to feel better, to feel release. I thought going in there would give it to me, but instead I ended up seeing Lasko's face, hearing the way he said my name. That poor guy," she pointed at the house, "he just reminded me so much of him. Christ, even his eyes, and the way he looked at me, even the way he tilted his head. It's like he was reading my thoughts." Her hands started to rake through her hair. "He was in every room, and at one point he came up behind me to block my path, and I freaked out and ended up elbowing him in the face." She squatted down and covered her eyes. "It was stupid to have done that. I should go apologize."

I bent down in front of her. "First, this is not the only time one of those guys has been hit." I chuckled. "They kind of know it comes with scaring the hell out of people. Second, he wasn't supposed to follow you room to room, so that's just taking advantage of the situation. And third," I removed her hands so I could see her beautiful face, "I know how you feel about being wound up so tight inside because I feel it too."

"Really?" she whispered.

I moved a piece of her golden hair off her face.

"Really." I stood and held out my hand. "You ready to go back to the party?" She nodded but stopped me when she spotted the ass who taunted her. "Is that the guy?" He was next to go in.

"Yes."

"Stay here." I rushed inside through a side door, gave instructions to one of the directors, and returned a moment later.

"What did you do?" She reached for my hand.

I grinned down at her. "Nothing." I kissed her head and wished I could witness what that asshole was about to walk into.

***

After the dinner was cleared, everyone seemed to be in good spirits. Emily was back to her old self. Although she bounced back quickly from things, I was not completely blind to the fact that she was struggling. We were, after all, right around the date I killed Jimmy, ending that whole ordeal. There were many questions that came to mind about that case, but the one that haunted me the most was how and why Jimmy picked Emily. I wondered if I'd ever know the answer to that question.

My arm was wrapped around the back of her chair, my thumb brushing the back of her neck. There wasn't a time when she was near me that I didn't want to touch her. She still had the pull that gravitated me to her. She grounded me, awakened things in me I didn't know I had. I loved this woman with all my heart, but sometimes I wondered if it was enough. We had a huge history, one that she didn't have with someone like Travis or Scott. Christ, those two were like sharks circling, waiting for a chance to swoop in and snatch her away. There was no doubt she loved me, but I knew history could sometimes destroy the future if you weren't careful.

Her hand fell onto my leg, and I looked down as she drew circles over my pants. Such a simple act to let me know she was thinking of me.

Nicholas's curse stole my attention. He stared at his cell phone, then looked back at the house. He slammed his glass down and headed inside.

Garrett had seen it as well, and he nodded to let me know he would keep an eye on Emily for me. I leaned over and kissed her on the neck. "I'll be right back."

"Everything all right?" she asked as she looked around the property. I hated that it was a reflex for her.

"Save me a dance."

I headed inside and checked the kitchen, the living room, my father's office, then I heard something coming from upstairs. I took the stairs two at a time and followed the noise to the library, where the doors were not completely shut.

"I need this, Nicholas!" my fathered shouted in my brother's face.

"I can't, I just can't anymore. You're out of control, Dad." Nicholas was nervous. "I won't lose my job digging in places I don't belong."

"Lose your job?" My father laughed. "Nicholas, I can have you thrown behind bars for the shit you've done."

67

"That's nice!" Nicholas tossed his hands in the air. "Trying to win father of the year, here? 'Cause you're doing a fine job."

My father turned and pointed a finger in his direction. "You want to get smart with me, son?" He shoved Nicholas in the chest, which sent him back a few feet. "You think you can talk to me that way, boy?" He shoved him again, but this time Nicholas was ready and stood firm. "You're a dirty cop, *son*."

"Yeah, well, you're a dirty lawyer, *Dad*."

My father hauled back to punch Nicholas, but he ducked and sent my father tumbling forward. I'd seen enough and hurried into the room and stood in front of my younger brother.

"What the hell, Dad!" I shouted and felt my fists harden as they curled. "You think it's all right for you to hit us?" Father stepped forward and hissed with anger. "We're your children, your fucking blood. If you're going to treat one of us like a punching bag, at least punch the one you despise the most." He went to swing like the coward he was, but I ducked.

"You're a disgrace," Nicholas spat at his feet.

Father turned his attention on him and sent a sucker punch into Nicholas's ribs. I took my father by the shoulders, turned him around, and punched him straight in the jaw. He fell back but quickly recovered and charged me with his arms locked around my waist. He plowed me into the wall. The impact hurt but soon dissipated with the adrenaline pumping through me.

Nicholas pulled him off me and chucked him to

the floor. We both stood, out of breath, and stared down at him while we waited for his next move.

He stumbled to his feet, and anger poured off of him. I knew he saw he wouldn't win, so he headed over to the fireplace, where he pulled out an envelope and tossed it into the flames. I glanced at Nicholas to see if he knew what that was all about, but he shook head, confused.

The punch to my father's face had split my knuckles open, and I felt them starting to swell.

I moved so he saw my face. "You ever lay a hand on anyone else in the family, I promise you, you won't leave this room again."

"That's quite a threat, son," he grunted with his back turned to me.

"Nah, Dad, just a promise."

***

Avery

I pulled off the hoodie once I was far enough away from the house and jogged down to where my car was parked outside of the gate. Once inside, I turned on the light and took a look at the damage. *"Shit!"* My whole left eye was swollen, and the cheek was puffy and red as well. *Stupid bitch!* I needed some painkillers and some ice. Voices behind me had me on edge, so I started the car and headed home.

After I swallowed three of Jimmy's white pills marked painkillers, I held a bag of frozen peas to my eye. I let myself sink into the recliner. I wondered how I was going to get out of this one. I had work in six hours. I soon gave in to the effects of the drugs. My eyes grew heavy, and I drifted off.

There were so many lights, they lit up our entire street. If I wasn't so scared, I would think it looked like a Christmas parade like I'd seen on TV. People were in tears, my sister's eyes were turned toward the ground, Jims' arms were around me to make sure no one touched me. What I couldn't understand was where Mommy was. She always made things better, she always came and visited in the treehouse after Daddy hit me. But she didn't this time. Instead, I came down when Jims called for me.

"What's going on?" I asked Jims, who was covered in blood, his pants were undone, and he smelled like bubblegum. Julia always smelled like bubblegum. I hated her. She was mean to me. "Where's Mommy, Jims? I want Mommy."

Jims hugged me a little tighter. "Sorry, Alexander, Mommy got in the way. She won't be coming back."

I didn't understand, and I started to cry, I tucked my face into his side. Maybe if I closed my eyes real tight Mommy would come back to me.

"Are you Jimmy?" an officer asked as he bent down to look at us. "Are you Alexander?" I nodded, but Jims stayed quiet. "Can you tell me what happened here?"

"I..." I hiccupped and rubbed my runny nose across my sleeve. "I don't know, I was up there." I pointed to the treehouse where just moments ago I flew across the city about to save a bank from

70

getting robbed.

"What about you?" The officer looked at Jims. "Can you tell me where this blood came from?" Jims didn't move, but I did notice he glanced at Julia, who watched us carefully. She seemed fine. Maybe she didn't know Mommy wasn't coming home. But she wouldn't care. She spent a lot of time with Daddy. Daddy always said she was his special little girl, and that he'd take her pain away. They even had sleepovers together. I hated Daddy. He didn't care about me. Just Jims and Mommy did.

The officer nodded at a woman, who came over to us. She said her name was Lindsay and that she'd find us a place to stay tonight. And in a few days we would be moved to another home. This scared me. I looked at Jims and hoped he'd help, but he was too busy watching people snap pictures around our house.

Three days later, after a lot of questions, I was handed a small book bag of clothes and one stuffed animal and was told I had to stay with my grandmother. This was not okay. Grandmother was just like Daddy.

Jims gave me a quick hug. "I'll be back, Alexander."

I grabbed his arm as I started to panic. I didn't want him to leave me. He was all I had left. "Jims, please," I sobbed to anyone who might listen, "I don't want to go with Grandmother, please, I'll be a good boy. Please take me with you!" My heart raced, and sweat broke above my hairline. "I just wanna go back to the treehouse! Please please please," I screamed as someone grabbed me from behind and pulled me away from him. "Nooo!"

I kicked into the air, but before I could break free, I was carried outside and placed in a car where I was taken to Grandmother's.

A knock to the door found my head in a swarm of thoughts. I dried my face. I hadn't realized I had been crying. I forgot how much I looked up to Jims. Funny how things changed. I awkwardly got out of the chair and dragged my drugged body to the entryway. The fucking dog barked sharply from the patio. I threw Grandmother's Bible at the glass, but it only made him bark louder. Stupid dog! I flipped on the light and opened the door without thinking.

"Wow, dude, what the hell happened to your eye?"

Fuck me! I grabbed him by the collar of his shirt and pulled him inside. Without hesitation, I stuck my gun to his neck and pulled the trigger twice.

CHAPTER THREE

Emily

This was the best, when I woke up before Seth. It gave me a moment to study his features without him aware of it. Just Seth without his guard up so he couldn't hold back or be closed off, only my love sleeping peacefully next to me.

I loved his dirty blond eyebrows, his long lashes, the way his nose aligned with his cheekbones. His hair that was long enough to run my fingers through. The morning scruff that made him look like an ad for Calvin Klein. I tugged the sheet away gently to admire his strong muscles that dipped, curved, and sculpted into perfection. My fingers tingled with the idea of tracing his six pack down to his pelvis.

"My body's your playground." He grinned with his eyes still closed. "Let loose, McPhee."

"Just looking." I shrugged and rolled onto my back. He grabbed the sheet as he quickly rolled on top of me. He hid us both from the morning light.

"Well, I'm not." He laughed as he dipped down and kissed me. His hand roamed down my leg but stopped when his alarm went off. "To be continued."

I grabbed his arms and held him in place. "You wanna tell me what happened last night?"

He smiled, but I could see something bothered him. "Not yet." He kissed the tip of my nose before he rolled off the bed and headed for the shower. He gave me a grin over his shoulder; he knew I would admire the view. I chewed my lip and thought how much I wanted to bite that fine ass of his. "Such a dirty girl," he teased.

"You have no idea."

After I got ready, I met Seth downstairs, where he poured me a cup of coffee, then eyed my dress. I looked down and thought maybe I skipped a button.

"Damn, baby, you look mighty fine in lace." His voice was still hoarse. "I'd hate to be your professor. No doubt I'd end up in jail."

I cut up an apple and bit into a piece. "Professor Dean is four years older than me, and I'm over sixteen. No jail time is needed."

"Is that so?" He crossed his arms, which made him look larger than he already was.

I leaned over and patted his arm. "I meant if you were the professor." I rolled my eyes. "How could you ever think I'd love anyone more than I love you?" I glanced at him. "Besides, you'd scare anyone who dared talk to me. I'd be single for life."

He came up behind me and trapped me with both hands against the counter. His lips hovered at my ear. "Damn straight, baby, no one will have you but me." I turned my head up toward his lips just in time to see that possessive look that made me weak in the heart. It was a look I'd loved since the day we met at the party. "I love you." He kissed me and ground his hips into my back, leaving me breathless as he swiped an apple and headed for the door.

"Hey," I called out, and he turned around.

"We still on for our date tonight at Franco's at seven?"

"Wouldn't miss it." He looked me over once before he shook his head. "Have a good day, baby."

Saturdays were my favorite lately. I met up with Erin to go over some notes, study a little, then have lunch at the beach and go to our yoga class. I headed back home to get ready for dinner, then showered and changed into a new dress Seth hadn't seen yet. It was red, tight, and hugged my hips perfectly. I paired it with black heels and a long black sweater. I left my hair in long, big curls, just a little makeup, and a tiny spray of his favorite scent—Vanilla by Victoria's Secret. We hadn't had a date since, well…I guessed since he told me he loved me. That was a year ago. Wow, where did the time go?

I was pleased with my appearance, then turned to inspect the bedroom. I had a bottle of champagne chilled, roses on the desk, candles waiting to be lit. I didn't care if it was cheesy. I wanted cheesy romance tonight. We deserved it. I closed the curtains and made everything just so. I pulled out the gift I got him and set it on the night stand. I knew he'd love it. He'd mentioned several times before that he wanted to know what happened to his grandfather's watch. After a huge hunt and Martha's help, it turned out it was passed down to his uncle who had no use for it and said it'd been in his safety deposit box for the past few years. He was more than willing to pass it along to Seth. So I had it cleaned and polished, and now it sat in a navy blue box. I sneaked a peek at the Hublot Big Bang. I couldn't wait to see how excited he'd be. I had no idea watches could be so expensive. I nearly had to pay the man a fee just to touch the damn thing before he'd even consider cleaning it. I carefully closed the lid. One last look at the room, and I decided it was perfect.

***

I checked the time again—seven forty-five. I smiled at the waiter who brought me another glass of wine. Thankfully, I took a cab. We were supposed to drive home together. I sipped my second glass and started to worry. I called again, and for the fifth time it rang and rang, then clicked to voicemail. I cleared my throat and decided to leave a message this time.

"Hey, umm, I'm here in a booth wondering where you are." I swallowed down my worry. "I'm just checking in, making sure you're all right." I fiddled with the napkin and watched the candle burn around a puddle of wax, evidence of the length of time I'd been there. "All right, well, I'll be here waiting. Call me when you can. I love you." I hung up and saw the waiter glance over at me. The restaurant was busy and I was embarrassed that it looked like I got stood up. I could only imagine what the wait staff would say. I shouldn't care, but I did.

When eight fifteen rolled around, I asked for the check and flagged down a cab. I nearly made it home before the tears started. I finally gave in and texted Garrett.

Emily: Hey, is Seth with you?

Garrett: Yup, he's helping Ronnie out with some paperwork. You good?

I stared out the window as the cabbie parked. I dried my tears and handed him a twenty.

Emily: Yeah, all good.

I sat on the porch stairs, stared up at the moon, and watched the clouds hurry by. My head fell to my hands, and I let the tears fall. I allowed myself an ugly cry. I was so hurt he forgot our big date. I spent a long time and a lot of prep work to make it just so. For what? For him to forget? I stopped my pity party and told myself I was sure there was a reasonable excuse.

Seth: I'm so sorry, baby, I totally forgot! I'll come home ASAP.

He forgot. Just forgot. Okay.

Emily: Don't bother.

I shook my head, but stopped when I saw Travis walk across my lawn. I set my unfinished, unsent message on the step and quickly dried my face.

"Hey," he waved as he came to the stairs, "I'm sorry, but I saw you over here, and you sounded upset."

I tilted my head back to stop the tears. "I'm all right."

"Well, where I'm from, when people are dressed like that," he pointed to my outfit, "and are crying on their doorstep, it normally means they either got into a fight, or got stood up." He sat next to me but kept his eyes on the ocean.

"Yeah," is all I said as he handed me a tissue from his pocket. "Thanks."

He smiled over at me. "Of course." He held up his hand to show me his intent. I didn't really register what he was doing until his thumb swiped under my eye to clear a tear. It was an incredibly intimate act, and it left me feeling like I'd done something wrong. "Anyone who can stand up such a beautiful woman is a fool."

I turned my head away. I didn't like his words. Seth might have been an ass for forgetting, but... "I love him," I said to make sure he knew where I stood.

"I know." He gave me a reassuring nod. "But the question is, is he worthy of it?"

I felt confused, and a little lost in my emotions. Sure, this wasn't the first time Seth had stood me up on something, but it had always been for a legitimate reason. It wasn't like he worked a desk job from nine to five. Things happened. I stood, needing a moment to think.

Travis stood as I did, then came up behind me. "Em, sometimes we can be overshadowed by what we *think* we have rather than by what we *really* have. If you're second guessing yourself, maybe you should be second guessing your relationship." He gave me a little pat on the shoulder. "You know where I am." He walked away.

"Thanks," I suddenly called out. I thought I owed him that much.

"That's what friends are for." He waved right before he disappeared into the woods. Was that a friendly conversation? I wrapped my sweater around my shoulders and convinced myself it was. Travis had always made it clear he was my neighbor and nothing more.

I went inside and lit the fireplace; I was cold. I curled up on the couch and rested my head on the pillow. I watched as the flames crackled and popped across the log. It wasn't long until I closed my eyes and fell into a stressful sleep.

***

Seth

Asshole was all that came to mind when I thought about myself. I couldn't believe I got caught up at work. It was a curse to be good at IT. Shit, I was always the first person they called when something happened. I parked and saw all the lights were off. I raced up the stairs and cautiously opened the front door.

The fire was on and Emily was asleep on the couch. She looked beautiful in a new red dress. I set the alarm and ran upstairs to change. My stomach dropped when I saw the room was decorated with flowers and candles, and champagne was in a pool of water. I sank down onto the bed and covered my face.

How on earth would I be able to make this up to her? My hands dropped when I saw a box on my nightstand. I opened the lid and my insides twisted in a knot. She got me my grandfather's watch! My hands shook as I pulled it free and slipped it over my wrist. Emily must have done a ton of searching to get her hands on this. I loved it; it was just how I remembered. After a small amount of gawking, I returned it to its box, changed, and headed downstairs to an empty living room.

Emily's back was to me as she washed the last of the dishes. She was barefoot and looked tired.

"Hey." I came up next to her and leaned against the counter to face her. Her hair was all around her face, so I couldn't see her very well. "I'm sorry about tonight." She nodded. "I got caught up with Ronnie and some paperwork. The computer wasn't working, so I had to fix that first. Anyway, the night got away from me, and when Garrett said you texted him, I couldn't believe the time."

"Was your phone broken too?" she asked quietly. I could tell she was crying.

I closed my eyes. I knew this was about to sound bad. "Ronnie's was, and I loaned mine to make some calls. I didn't know you called."

"Yeah." She turned to walk into the laundry

room, reappearing moments later. "I'm going to head to bed." She went to leave, but I blocked her path.

"Hey, I really am sorry. You know I'd never purposely hurt you."

She took the corner of her sweater and dried her eyes. "I know that. I was more worried than anything." Her eyes dropped away. "I was just looking forward to it."

I pulled her close and rested her head on my shoulder. "I know. I was too." I kissed the top of her head and took a moment to breathe in her scent. "You smell good." She pulled out of my arms. I thought she was going to walk away, but she didn't. Instead, she took my hand and led me upstairs.

***

The ring of my phone pulled me out of a deep sleep. I untangled myself from Emily and snatched it off the side table.

"Yeah," I choked into the phone. I wished I had checked to see who it was first.

"Connors, you should come down to the station."

I squinted at the time. "Ronnie, it's three thirty in the morning, and I don't work tomorrow. I don't appreciate being called this—"

"Trust me, you'll want to be here for this." The line went dead. I flopped back down and wondered why Ronnie called and not Garrett. Ronnie was new to the force and was pretty ballsy to have called me this early when I wasn't working. I sent Garrett a quick text saying I was on my way in ten.

Emily tucked herself into me, and her hot skin warmed mine. My fingers ran along her side and the curve of her soft breast. I allowed myself a few more moments with her. I started to move, but Emily slid her body over of mine. She straddled herself over top of me, then bent down and started to kiss my chest. Her silky hair fell all around her.

"Where are you going?" she asked between kisses.

My hands gripped her hips as I dug the tip of my erection into her wet folds. "Work," I grunted as I teased myself at her opening. Her lips moved up to my neck with a playful bite on my shoulder.

"You have the day off. You're mine to do what I want."

I groaned. She was so right. I wanted to lie there, spend the whole damn day naked with her. Show her countless times how sorry I was for last night.

"I'm sorry, baby, but I have to go in, hopefully for just an hour." I gently slid in. I didn't stop until I was nice and deep. Emily leaned back and let out a delicious moan that had me grinding her hips in circles. Fuck, the things this woman made me feel. She started to rock her body, moving like a wave. It was such a sexy sight. Her breasts, full and heavy, bounced forward and begged the palms of my hands to cup and squeeze them. She leaned back and held her ankles to change the direction I was hitting her. I tried to tame the animal inside that was clawing to get out. I tried like hell to give her some level of control in bed. She must have seen my look, because her sexy mouth turned up as she slowed her pace. She knew damn well what she was doing. I held her hips a little harder to calm myself, but the slow flicks were maddening. Sweat broke out around my brow as she let out another moan, and it was my undoing.

In a moment I tossed her back, stood next to the bed, took her legs, and plowed back inside. It was heaven, like her little body was meant for mine. She fit me perfectly in so many ways I sometimes lost myself in her. The sight of her legs spread wide as she took me deep, and that look that she was almost there, were bliss.

"Seth, I'm so close," she cried, and her hands clawed at the sheets. "Harder!"

I picked up the pace. I had to hold on while she shot forward. I felt the moment she came. Everything tightened, her nipples hardened, and her screams drove me wild. I plowed on. I was so close but held off until she finished.

"Shit," I grunted as I let go and flopped over her sweaty body.

* * *

After a hot shower, I changed into plain clothes. I sat next to Emily, who was on her side, her bright blue eyes peeking out through her hair. The TV flickered over her face. I could tell she was disappointed, but she wouldn't say anything. She knew I had to leave. I brushed her hair away and kissed her lips, lingering a little longer than I meant to. I knew I'd never get out of there if I didn't pull away, so I did.

"I love you, baby."

"I know. I love you too."

I pointed to the watch. "I don't know how you did it, but thank you for getting my grandfather's watch."

She sat up and pulled the sheet along with her. "I had help." She gave me a quick peck. "Leave so you can come home to me."

**

Garrett texted me an address to meet him, and when I got closer, I saw sirens and a ton of officers at the corner. I parked, flashed my badge, and hurried to find the sergeant.

"Isn't it your day off?" he asked and rubbed his head the way he did when he had a bad vibe about something.

"Yeah, what's going on?"

"Thanks for coming. We're going to need everyone on this." He pointed to a dumpster. "Body, burned, teeth removed, finger prints, hair, everything gone."

"DOA?"

"No," Detective Michaels answered as he came up behind me, "two shots to the neck, then moved here to be burned. No witnesses, no camera, so whoever did this knew what they were doing."

I stared down at the charred body which still smelled fresh. "Who found him?"

"Homeless man." Sarge pointed to a man next to a shopping cart, watching it like someone might take it. He was dirty, his clothes torn, and he looked hungry. He kept his eye on Campbell's bagel. "I need you to keep the newbies in check, make sure no one passes through, and listen for talk among the crowd."

"Yes, of course." I hurried back to the other officers. Campbell handed me an OPD jacket so I had some kind of identification on.

I scanned the crowd, watching people's mannerisms to see if they showed any signs of enjoyment, fear, or lust. We had no idea what we were dealing with here.

"You think he's here?" Ronnie appeared out of nowhere.

I shrugged and zipped the jacket up. "A lot of times the killer will come back and watch." I spotted Garrett, who held up a coffee. "Excuse me."

"Hey." I gladly took the hot brew, needing some kind of jolt. I looked to see where Ronnie was. "Why did I get a call from Ronnie this morning and not from Sarge or you?"

"Really?" He looked confused. "Sarge called me and told me he's got someone on the call list, so not to worry, just to meet here."

"Strange." I sipped my coffee while I scanned the crowd.

"Hey, guys." Johnnie stared at his cell phone. "Umm, have any of you heard from Davis? I've been trying to get hold of him since the Halloween party. He said he had to make a stop at Avery's, but Avery said he never showed."

"No." I looked at Garrett, who shook his head.

"Okay, I'm going to go talk to Sarge." I gave Johnnie a friendly slap on the shoulder as he walked away.

Garrett checked the time. "Not like Davis not to check in."

"No, it's not."

***

Campbell bent his head down and smelled his shirt. "I don't think I'll be able to get that smell out of my head for a while."

"Fucking sick," Riggs chimed in right before he bit into his burger. "Gotta say, glad the guy was shot first, because that's a hell of a way to go."

"One of my biggest fears," Riley added and reached for the mustard from another table. "I won't even burn a candle at home."

"Pussy," Riggs said and grinned with a greasy mouth.

"You're scared of mascots, Riggs," Riley pointed out. "We all saw it at the hockey game a few months back."

Riggs dropped his burger, then stuck a finger in his direction. "It's not right having an abnormally large head." The table broke into a loud roar. "It's unnecessary to be that disproportioned." He made an exaggerated quiver sound and went back to his burger.

"Okay, so you wouldn't have a mascot hanging around your house?" Riggs gave Riley a look. "Right, so no candle, no fire, no barbecue death for me."

"Oh, speaking of barbecues..." I caught the table's attention. "My place, Friday, seven."

Riley shook his head. "That was so wrong,

dude."

"Holy shit," Campbell hissed toward the front door just as Avery headed to our table. "What happened to you?"

Avery sat in an open chair and signaled at the waitress to bring him a beer. Both of his eyes were black, and his nose appeared to be fractured. "Wrong place, wrong time."

"Well, that explains why you weren't there this morning." Riley pushed his plate away. I could see he and Avery had some issues with working together. It wasn't easy filling the shoes of a dead partner.

"What happened?" Campbell asked quietly.

Avery thanked the waitress, who looked a little startled. "Took a shortcut home, walked up on a drug deal, they weren't too pleased. Anyway, a few punches later, they backed off."

"You get a good look at them?" I asked and wondered where this went down. Avery didn't live that far from us.

"Not really." He downed half his beer. "But if I see them again, I'll deal with them."

I looked at the rest of the guys. "Yeah, we all will."

***

Avery

The bottle sat in front of me, half empty. I squinted through the colored glass, and the TV flickered behind it. My face pounded with my heartbeat. I let myself go back over how I dealt with my face. I sought out a few dealers, pretended I wanted to buy some coke, and then ran off with it. I turned left, though I knew it was a dead end. I waited for them to approach, then let them beat my face in. When I had enough, I took out my pent-up anger on them. One probably wouldn't be able to walk again, but whatever.

I looked at my phone to check the time, then stared for a while at the picture I kept for show on the lock screen of my computer. It was of me and Matthews at the Triangle. There was a small part of me that missed him; he always had my back. I should have known he wouldn't have been able to handle Jims and his crazy ways. When Jims caught sight of Emily and moved his attention there, Matthews really flipped out. He couldn't do that to Seth, blah, blah, blah. Yeah, after he met Emily, things went south. I thought he was going to be able to work it out, but that night he followed me to Jims's cabin and saw the basement where Jims was going to keep her, I knew it was over. Matthews just didn't have it in him, and his constant moral battles with himself had to end.

My eyes started to close.

"Hey." Matthews opened the door and moved aside to let me in. "You want a drink?"

"Sure." I locked the door behind me and slowly closed the blinds. "You here by yourself?"

"Yeah, Mom came for dinner, but she left about an hour ago." He handed me a beer and poured himself a rye and Coke, his favorite. "Cheers." He

nodded at the couch. "You hungry?" I waited for him to set his glass down on the table.

"Yeah, I kind of am. You have any leftovers?"

Matthews headed for the kitchen, and when he rounded the corner, I pulled out a baggie of crushed painkillers. I poured the seven pills' worth of white dust into his glass and stirred it with my finger. It quickly swirled and disappeared in the glass.

"Meatloaf all right?" He handed me the plate and fork.

"Great, thanks, man."

I saw a little dust settle on the bottom of the glass. Shit, it was taking a long time to dissolve. He began to reach for it, so I started to cough and asked for a napkin. He rolled his eyes and jumped up to go grab one. I stirred the drink one last time.

"Here." He handed me a piece of paper towel. "Anything else?" he joked. I gave him the finger.

I ate the disgusting meal and watched him slowly sip his drink. It didn't take too long before he started to yawn. His body relaxed and his eyes grew heavy. He set the glass down, and I saw there was still some left. He needed to drink it all for his heart to stop.

"You all right, buddy?" I moved over closer and saw him slowly nod. "Here." I held the glass up to his lips, and encouraged the rest of the drug down his throat. "You don't want to waste this." He looked at me funny, then he made the connection.

"Why?" he slurred as he sank deeper in the couch.

I took the empty glass and tucked it into a Ziploc bag and shoved it in my coat. I headed over to the bar, slipped on my black gloves, and poured a glass of rye and Coke, just a little, for show.

"You never would have gone through with it," I said as I took a seat next to him and pressed his fingers to the glass and dabbed his lips to the edges. "I know it doesn't seem fair, but you know too much. I've worked too hard to get close to Connors for you to fuck this up." Matthews squinted and tried to follow along. I stood and pulled him like a rag doll toward the bedroom. He tried to push me away, but he was too weak. I flopped him down on the bed and placed the pill bottle next to him.

Matthews started to cry. This part always fascinated me. The part where you knew you were about to die, and there was nothing you could do to stop it. I often wondered how that felt. I let out a sigh and sat on the bed next to him. I dug deep and remembered Grandmother's words. "Even though I walk through the valley of the shadow of death, I will fear no evil, for you are with me; your rod and your staff, they comfort me." I shook my head. That didn't feel right. "That doesn't bring me comfort either." I spotted a baseball Matthews had signed as a kid and remembered my mother used to sign them for me during the baseball season. I placed my hand on his arm, and started to sing "Take Me Out to the Ballgame." *Only a few moments later, I felt his heartbeat stop, saw his chest fall one last time, and everything that was Matthews was gone. He was now just a shell of the man, a man who knew too much.*

***

"Travis, right?" I stopped in front of his cart, noting it was full of baking ingredients. Fuck, this guy was a male Martha Stewart. "You're McPhee's neighbor?" I loved to play dumb with dumb people.

"Yeah." He pointed his finger at me. "Avery, right? You work with Seth at OPD?"

I smiled and showed off my teeth. People seemed to like that smile. "I do." I motioned for him to grab the peanut butter he was about to reach for before I came up. "So, I have to ask." I turned to him and lowered my voice like I was about to share something private. "How can you stand living next to someone like McPhee? Frig, that girl is something." I winked playfully. I saw his face change, I knew he wanted to say something, but he stopped himself. I changed paths. "Look, Travis, I've seen how those two operate. There's a ton of tension between them after what happened. I give them a month before you see the moving van outside her door."

Travis looked around to see if the coast was clear. Shit, what I wouldn't give to ram his stupid face into the grocery cart handle, maybe break his nose, fuck up his jaw. "I don't know what happened, but I can tell you she's been hurting lately. Crying, looking for comfort from other people. I think you might be right about him moving out."

Perfect. My hand flexed on the handle of the basket. I was just itching to break something of his. I promised myself I'd hit up The Brick tonight before I headed over to McPhee's. I made a face to show I was on his side. "If you're interested in

McPhee, I can give you some pointers." I waited and dangled the bait. I knew the cocky fucker would bite. He smiled and moved in closer. "Flowers, candy, she loves wine and martinis, with three olives."

"Three olives?" he interrupted me. I was really fighting hard to hold back the urge to punch him in the throat. *Fuck, are manners dead nowadays?*

"I know, strange, but yes, three." I waited to see if he had anything else to add. "Just be there a lot, she loves company, and despite what she says, she hates to be alone. Why do you think I'm always there?"

"Speaking of which..." he interrupted again. "You seem interested in her, no?"

I shrugged and pulled out all my fantastic talent. "Nah, after everything that happened, we're way too close to go down that road. Kinda like a sister, you know."

"What did happen?" he asked.

I felt a tiny bead of sweat break out along my neck, but I played off my anger as compassion for Emily. "Let's just say she became someone's obsession and it didn't end very well."

"Oh, and there's still tension from it, with Seth?"

I chucked a jar of jam in my basket and moved on to make a show of reading a label on something else. "Some people deal with stress in different ways. Connors doesn't deal well with people touching his things. After what happened with McPhee, he's convinced she was forced into sex, and now he's not that interested." I gave him a sad face. "Who knows what happened, but bottom line is that girl deserved better than to be questioned by the man who supposedly loves her, right?" I squeezed his shoulder. Contact in a sad moment tends to deepen the impact of the words. I tried to be friendly while I fought to chase my evil thoughts away. "She's invested a lot of time into Seth, and it won't be easy for her, but if she knew someone else was there, she might see the light." I started to walk away, but I stopped. "Oh, Travis, 2011 St. Michelle Merlot." I glanced toward the roof and thought Jims would love that one. "It was nice to see you again, Travis, take care."

"Yeah." Travis sounded a million miles away. "Yeah, you too, Avery."

I smirked as I dropped the basket by a sales clerk and headed out to my car. Oh, how I loved to meddle when I got front row seats to the show.

***

Emily

I pushed the shopping cart through the aisles and thought about all that I'd need for the barbecue tonight. Steaks, chicken, potatoes, Caesar salad stuff. I bent over and saw a pair of sneakers come up next to me.

"Do you come here often?" Travis asked as he gazed down at me with a killer smile. He offered a hand to help me up and took the sack of potatoes out of my arms and placed it in my cart.

"Thanks." I brushed off the dirt from the bag. "Quite the line."

He pushed his cart behind mine and let an older gentleman go by. "It's one of my best, but I have several others if that didn't work. I have, 'Baby, your eyes are like the stars, and I am the tide. Do you feel that pull we have?'" I laughed and thought how funny he could be. "So," he looked in my cart, "you having company?"

"Yes, the guys are having a barbecue. It's been a while—" I stopped. I didn't want to get into that right now. "It's long overdue."

"How nice for them. Do you do all the cooking too?" I stared at him for a moment and wondered why he asked that. "I just mean it's very kind that you shop and cook. Seth's a lucky man."

I shrugged while I reached for the flour. "I don't mind, I enjoy the cooking. Besides, Garrett will be there, so I won't be handling the meat. He's a tad OCD with barbecuing." I chuckled, thinking of his secret sauce. "Besides, the guys are great with the cleanup, and that's the part I hate the most."

"Well, that's good." He turned the corner with me into the wine section.

"St. Francis." I turned the bottle to show him the label. "This is one of my favorites." I placed two in my cart, and I noticed he did the same. "Alamos," I grinned and added the bottle to the cart, "and…" I scanned the shelves, "Francis Coppola. These are my go to wines. They aren't too pricey and are delicious."

Travis took the Francis Coppola out of my hand and read the bottle. "If you like this one, you should try this." He handed me another bottle. "William Hill, it's one of my favorites."

"Then I shall try it, thank you." I snagged the bottle and added it to my collection. "If you're not busy, you should come by. They're a great group of guys. You know most of them in passing, so why don't you stop by and get to know them better?"

He was quiet for a moment, and I thought he was going to decline when he answered, "What can I bring?"

"Nothing, just yourself."

"That I can do," he laughed. "All right, Emily, see you later. I need to pick up my dry cleaning before they close. You, my friend, enjoy the rest of your shopping experience."

"Oh, that I will." I waved goodbye.

I finished shopping and headed home, unlocking the door awkwardly with all the groceries stacked on top of one another so they wouldn't fall. Once inside, I carefully set them down and started to punch in the security code. I stopped dead in my tracks.

Oh my hell! Jimmy Lasko was on my couch in his usual posture, crossed legged, hands entwined, eyes burning into mine.

"Hello, darlin'!" His voice was as clear as day, every word pronounced just so. "Miss me?"

The security alarm screamed at me. My brain questioned what the hell was going on, but my body was frozen, rooted in place. Every ounce of fear I had carefully tucked away smacked me in the face.

"How?" barely fell from my lips.

"It's not about you." He fixed his jacket, like he needed something to do.

"What?"

"It's not about you."

The door burst open and Riggs and Campbell, weapons drawn, moved about the room, scanning everywhere.

"Emily!" Riggs shouted as he turned around to face me. "What happened?" He had to shout over the alarm. "Are you alone?" I shook my head and saw Lasko press a finger to his lips to keep quiet. "What are you staring at?" Riggs followed my line of sight but didn't react.

Campbell stepped in front of me and ducked down to look at me straight in the face. "What happened, Emily?"

I shook my head and finally snapped out of Lasko's hold. "I-I..." I moved to see the chair was empty, no sign that anyone sat there. My hand flew to my mouth. *What the hell?*

"Em?" Riggs made me look over at him.

"I-I just..." I stopped. They'd think I was insane. "Nothing." I begged my legs to move and turn off the alarm. I did, and suddenly the place was too quiet. "I'm sorry, guys." I wrapped my arms around my mid-section. I felt cold and eyed the chair. It still felt like he was here.

"Did you hear something? Or see something?" Campbell asked, but watched Riggs answer a call.

I shrugged, not sure how to answer that one. "Yeah, I guess."

"Yes to both? Or yes to just one of them?"

"I don't know, both?" I couldn't seem to get my head in the game.

Campbell studied my face, then nodded. "You want me to get Vanessa to stay with you until

Connors comes home?"

"No." I managed to smile. "Erin will be here soon. Thanks, though."

Campbell signaled to Riggs to leave. "All right, well, call us if you need us."

"Will do."

Riggs hung up the phone. "Call Connors when you get a chance, all right?"

"I will. Thanks, guys."

I locked the door and turned around. I half expected to see him again, but the place was empty. I took a deep breath and tried to get past the haunting feeling Lasko gave me. I didn't want to admit to myself that I just saw him. He was dead, and my mind was just playing tricks on me. Mean, evil tricks.

***

I called Seth, but it went straight to voicemail. I called Garrett next, and his did the same. Strange, they must be out of service. After I tried one more time, I called Avery.

"Hey, McPhee, you all right?"

"Yeah, I'm fine. I was wondering if you know where Seth is."

"Ummm," there was a pause, "he's helping Ronnie."

"Oh." I sighed but wondered why both of their phones were off if they were in the station. "Who's Ronnie?"

"The newbie, Ronnie. Ronnie wants Connors's help."

"Okay, well, please let him know I tried to get hold of him, but seeing that their phones are off, I tried you."

"Their phones are off? Are you sure? Because Connors texted me as we speak." I sank down onto the chair. *What the hell is going on?* "He may have to ignore your call, you know, being that Ronnie is right there. Who knows? All right, I'll let him know."

"Thanks, Avery," I whispered. Moments later, Erin pulled up.

***

Seth

I slammed the locker closed and shoved my arms through my sweatshirt. To say I was pissed was an understatement. Emily didn't call. I didn't know what was going on with her. If it wasn't for Ronnie needing my help *again* and the call that came in for a possible robbery across town, I would have gone home and checked in on her.

I stewed the whole way home, but when I arrived, I saw Erin's car in the driveway, and I reined in my anger. I dropped my bag at the door and headed to the kitchen, where I found Erin mixing a salad.

"Hey," she said over her shoulder.

"How is she?" I asked and tried like hell to remove the bite from my voice.

Erin shrugged. "She won't talk about it, but I think she just got spooked. She's a little spacy, and something is clearly on her mind. But you know Em, she needs to process everything, store it away before she'll even think of sharing it."

The cap off my beer landed on the counter as I listened to Erin prattle away, and all the while I watched Emily set up the table on the patio.

"Seth," she said a little louder so I would look over at her, "don't pry too much. I just finally got my friend back."

"Yeah," I muttered and opened the door.

Emily gave me a tiny smile, but I could tell she was pissed off about something.

"Is your phone broken?" I asked.

She turned to glare at me. "Is yours?"

"Come again?"

She set a handful of forks down on the table and placed her hands on her hips. "I did call you, and Garrett too, but both phones went straight to voicemails. So I called Avery to let him know I'm all right and to pass the message on to you." She rubbed her head. "You were too busy with Ronnie to get back to me."

I shook off her last comment. "What happened today?" I asked, but I was curious why Avery failed to mentioned she had called.

She went back to fixing the table. "Just heard a noise and thought someone was in the house. False alarm."

I moved to stand by her. "That would have been convincing if your voice didn't crack at the end."

"Lovers, I'm home!" Pete shouted from the kitchen. He hung outward holding the door frame when he spotted us. "Why don't you have a drink in your hand, love?"

"I was just finishing up, then I was going to grab one." She glanced up at me. "Please let it go, it was nothing."

"Right." I knew I wouldn't get much further with her on the topic.

I showered, changed, and headed downstairs. I heard some people arrive, so I pasted on what I hoped was my best welcome smile. I met Garrett at the stairs and allowed myself a brief expression change to rest my face, which made him look at me with a question. I took the bag of meat he brought and had him follow me into the kitchen. Emily must have changed. She was now in super tight jeans that made her ass look amazing. I fought the urge to grab it as she walked by. She gave me a sideways glance. I knew she was still upset. I'd bring it up later, but I wouldn't tonight. I knew how she operated.

"Hey, you," Garrett leaned down and gave her a huge hug, "you look nice."

"Thanks." She looked down at her black halter top. "You thirsty?"

"Yes, ma'am!" He headed for the fridge.

Music pumped from the speakers. Pete must have had the controls again. I greeted Riley, Riggs, and Campbell as they headed out to the patio. Emily came in just as Avery did.

"Oh, shit," Avery hissed and closed his eyes. "Connors, I'm really sorry. I meant to mention McPhee called, but you were dealing with Ronnie again, then you got called out. Man, I'm sorry."

"It's all right, Avery." Emily shook her head.

"There really was no reason for me to call anyway. It was stupid, what happened."

"Thanks." He gave her a side hug as she glanced down at his pocket. "That's my phone." He laughed and pulled it free, then he rolled his eyes as he glanced over at me. "Your girlfriend is looking for you."

"Who?" I asked, confused.

"Ronnie, who else?"

"Nope, I'm off the clock, not interested in helping out." Emily came up next to me and poured herself a glass of wine. "New jeans?"

"Yes." She peered at me over the edge of her wine glass. "You like?"

"Very much." My eyes flickered from hers to her deliciously moist lips. "So much indeed, I wish you'd change."

She rolled her eyes. "Everyone here is like a brother, except you," she winked, "and you can have all the dirty thoughts you want as long as you describe them to me later."

"Shit, Connors, will you just call Ronnie?" Avery jammed his phone back in his pocket. I was so lost with Em I forgot he was still there.

"Knock-knock." Travis appeared into the kitchen. "Hey, guys."

I gave Garrett, who came in behind him, a quick glance, then let Em play hostess. I was not interested.

"Hey, you came." She gave him a hug. "You hungry?"

"Actually, I won't stay long. I just wanted to ask what you thought of the William Hill." He pointed to her open bottle on the counter.

"I love it, thanks. It will now be one of my new favorites." I looked at Emily, then Travis, and wondered when they spoke about wine. Garrett was doing the same thing.

"Em, the steaks ready?" Garrett cut in without caring.

Emily opened the fridge and removed the platter of sea-salt marinated steaks. "Just as you instructed me to do via *several* text messages, Garrett." She handed him the dish. Garrett inspected the meat, then gave an approving nod.

"Yum," Riggs called out as he carried a case of beer, with Campbell and Vanessa behind him. "I'm starving! Here, Garrett, let me help you with those."

I swore the entire place went silent as Garrett stared at him, then around at all of us as he saw we were anxiously waiting for his reaction.

"What?" Garrett smiled. "I'm not *that* bad." He went to leave, but looked at Riggs. "Stay!"

"Wow, you weren't kidding." Travis laughed at Emily, and I fought the urge to roll my eyes. I didn't like how comfortable he was.

Pete poked his head in the door. "Love, my liver called, said it would like another drink. Would you mind passing me another beer?" I watched Travis as she got the beer. He watched her the way *I did*, with a mix of lust and protection. My fingers gripped the edge of the counter. I didn't need him to see how much he bothered me.

"Well." Travis pushed off the wall. "I should get going."

Smart plan.

***

Avery

I casually stepped back into the shadows as Travis and Emily emerged from the house. I loved how the darkness enclosed me like a shield. My grandmother hated how I could move about undetected. She said I was like a cat in the night. I enjoyed that analogy. I caught her many times in situations she didn't want me to know about. I watched, but never told her what I saw. Let's just say I had the upper hand over Father Thomas and would use it if I had to, but it never came to that. I left before I could destroy him.

My thumb slid my phone to silent, and I leaned back against the wall of the little tool shed. Travis's eyes were glued to Emily's ass while she walked a few feet ahead, completely oblivious to what was going on. She stopped at the tree line, just a few yards from me.

"Thanks for coming," she said with her hands tucked in her pockets.

"Thanks for the invite." Travis looked over her shoulder to the house. He saw Seth and Garrett at the barbecue. Pathetic in my eyes. Emily had always been loyal to the guy, but Seth had issues. "You have a little," Travis reached over and pulled something out of her hair, "lettuce?" he laughed as he tossed it to the ground. "There." He grinned. "Well, if looks could kill, I'd be dead a long time ago." He nodded toward Seth.

Emily waved at Seth. "A lot happened last year."

103

She shrugged at Travis. "I don't blame him for being protective. I just bounced back a little faster than he did."

"Mmm," Travis muttered, "well, there's being protective and being smothering."

Fuck, Travis! I shook my head. *You're coming off way too strong there.* I'd have to play damage control later.

"Seth has been like this since day one. It's nothing new, and it's everything I love about him." Emily took a step back.

Fuck!

Travis ran his hand over the back of his neck. "Sorry, that was uncalled for, Emily. I guess sometimes as an outsider he can seem a little controlling, that's all." He placed a hand on her shoulder. "Thanks again for the invite. I'll talk to you later."

"Of course." She waved goodbye as she turned to walk away. Travis walked a few feet into the woods, then stopped and watched her.

I waited a beat, and then pinched my zipper on my jeans and walked onto the lit patio like I just took a piss in the woods. Vanessa shot me a gross look, and I shot her a playful wink. I didn't like Vanessa. She was a nosy bitch who had inserted her life into Campbell's way too quickly. She was one of those girls who saw security and grabbed it by the balls, squeezing until it surrendered. She didn't get in my way, so I left her alone...for now.

I opened a beer and listened to Emily speak to Seth as she approached him.

"You know, you are one of the biggest men at

this party, and you really don't have to use your stare to scare people." She placed her hands on her hips. Seth took a step toward her and towered over her petite frame.

"And you need to open your pretty little eyes and see." He pointed his beer at Travis's house. "That man is interested in you."

She sighed heavily. "And you need to see that I'm not interested in anyone but you."

"Oh, I know that." He almost grinned, but held it together. "But it doesn't mean I need to be friendly. He knows you are mine."

"It's true, Em." Riggs closed the grill after he stole a peek. "Travis is sniffing out someone else's property. There's a man code, and he's pissin' all over it."

I fought the urge to rub my hands together in excitement...*wait for it...wait for it...*

I almost felt Emily's pulse speed up. "Property?" She cringed at the word. "You speak as though I am something you bought and set out in the yard for dogs to piss on!"

"That's not what I meant—I'm bad with words, Emily." Riggs closed his eyes, clearly regretting what he just said.

"Hey." Seth hooked an arm around her waist and tugged her toward him. "I don't trust him, I don't like him, and while he's hitting on you, I will be making damn sure he doesn't touch what is mine." His hand slid into her hair and tilted her head back to look at him. Seth was a natural Dom without even knowing it. "You don't have to like it, but it's going to happen." He hovered above her lips and watched her closely. "You are mine, Emily, remember that."

She suddenly snapped out of the spell he had over her and wiggled out of his hold. "Shall I remind you?" She turned her head to study him. She seethed with anger, but she pulled it in and let her emotions take over. "Who fought for us?" she whispered as she headed into the kitchen, only to leave Seth to curse under his breath.

I stepped down the stairs and slapped Seth on the shoulder. "Give her a minute." I clinked my bottle to his, while really I imagined breaking the bottle over the table then jabbing it into his stomach so I could watch the blood drain from his body. "Any man can see he's into her. He certainly doesn't have a problem stepping over into your territory, does he?"

Seth sighed heavily. "No, he doesn't."

"Well." I pressed my lips together and thought about how to play this just right. "Maybe you need to go have a talk with him. Let your friendly neighbor know where he belongs." I moved my head in Emily's direction. "And where you do."

"That's a thought." He nodded.

Ha! This was too easy.

I sank into a chair at the table and helped myself to a rather large hunk of steak. I grinned to myself. How I loved to fuck with their lives. There was so much they didn't know, and it was so easy to mess with them, like child's play. I saw Emily glance at Seth, letting him see she was hurt by his assumptions. *That's right, my puppets, dance.*

***

Emily

I avoided Seth most of the night. I just needed some space, and I hated that he thought I would ever cheat on him. In fact, I was a bit insulted. It wasn't like I hadn't put my time in to prove how much I loved the friggin' guy! I chucked the trash in the bin and jumped when I heard footsteps behind me.

"Sorry." Garrett looked guilty. "Just wanted to check in. Make sure you're all right."

"I'm fine." I slammed the lid down. "Will he ever trust me, Garrett? 'Cause, honestly, it's getting a little old."

Garrett leaned against the rail. "He trusts you, Em; it's Travis he doesn't trust."

"Such a *you* answer." I went to move inside, but Garrett stopped me.

"Right, because it's the truth." He stared down. "I spend more time with the guy than you do. I know what he's thinking almost before he does. I've never lied to you, so hear me when I tell you he does trust you, but neither of us trusts Travis."

"What is it that you guys don't like about Travis besides his supposed hitting on me? Is it something I don't know? Something else?" I stepped closer to see if there was something there, but he turned to look away. "Right, so it's just a jealousy thing. Perfect."

Pete appeared in the doorway. "Hey, all, we're heading to the beach pit. Thought the fire might be nice."

The three of us headed down to the beach, where the guys had already started the fire and were settling into beach chairs. Vanessa joined me and handed me a Bailey's hot chocolate. The evenings sure cooled down in October.

"Thanks." I caught sight of Seth, who was reading something on his phone. He looked annoyed as he sent a quick text. I made my way over and sat on the arm of his chair. I couldn't help it. I loved to be near him, no matter how angry I got. My body was naturally drawn to his.

Moments later I felt him wrap a blanket over my shoulders as he tugged me onto his lap. I tucked my legs up and curled into his chest. He kissed the top of my head. "Don't be mad, baby."

"Too late for that."

I heard him growl deep down in his throat. His mouth pushed my head away from his chest so he could whisper, "Can you blame me?" His stare held me in place. "Any man wants you, any woman wants to look like you, you have a personality men only dream of, you're incredibly smart, and you're not married. You, Emily, are the perfect catch." I couldn't help myself. I reached up grabbed his head and pulled his lips to mine. He didn't hesitate, and he swiped his tongue inside my mouth. He took over the kiss and reminded me of his intense love for me. I gave in until I heard Riggs crack a joke about us.

"You're not off the hook, but thank you for saying those things," I whispered.

"So, tell me something." Vanessa pulled our

attention to her. "I never heard the story of how you two met."

I sat up and wrapped my arm around Seth's shoulders. I'd be the storyteller, since Seth didn't talk too much about anything personal.

"Three years ago, Erin and I went to a party of a friend of a friend's." I glanced at Erin, who loved that she was involved in this story. "It was mid-summer hot, I was itching to hit the pool when we ran into a bunch of friends who were in our Soc class. We started chatting. More and more people started to arrive, the place was filling up fast, but at one point I had this feeling someone was watching me. I was in mid-sentence when I looked up and saw this guy watching me from the doorway. His eyes were shaded by his baseball hat, but I knew he was staring at me." I looked down at Seth. "You didn't smile, you just watched." He nodded and remembered with me.

"Then what?" Riggs asked and made us all laugh a little. Riggs didn't seem like he cared.

"Well, I couldn't really think straight with him staring at me, so I had to turn a little and focus on the group."

"I didn't like that," Seth muttered.

"Yeah, I know. After an hour, I checked to see if he was still there, but he was gone. I won't lie, I was disappointed, but what did I expect? For him to hang around while I chatted in the heat? So I finally decided to take a dip in the pool. I ended up in a volleyball match where we were one player short. Someone, who I now know was Garrett, called over to his partner, and soon enough we had a full team of me, Garrett, Seth, and some guy named Tony."

"I played against them," Erin chimed with a wink.

"Yes, you did." I grinned. "You may not want to brag about that, E." I took a moment to sip my hot drink. The Baileys was just right. "We started to play, and by the time it ended, it was well into the night. Garrett and Tony vanished and left me and Seth all alone in the pool, and, well, the rest is history." I took a quick drink.

"Oh no!" Everyone started to shout. "You can't leave it there."

"Come on." Avery raised an eyebrow. "Share the good stuff."

"Nope." Seth grinned up at me. "That's our moment." I gave him a quick peck on the lips and laid my head down on his shoulder and listened to people protest. Finally, Vanessa started to tell about how she and Campbell met, and the attention shifted to them. I stared at the fire and remembered the rest of our story.

"Great game." Seth's smile made my stomach jump in excitement. He was incredibly hot. His shorts were dipped low, showing his tan line and part of his V. I had to look away before my body betrayed me. "Seth." He extended his hand. I slipped mine into his and noticed how much larger he was than me.

"Emily." I tried to play it cool. He waited a beat before he released it. "So, Seth." I leaned against the edge of the pool. "What is it that you do?"

"I just got hired on with the Orange Police

Department," he said proudly, making my bloody brain picture him in the uniform. I could see my chest rise and fall as he stepped closer. "And you, Emily?"

"I'm taking some time off, but I want to eventually enroll in Orange University. I would like to be a teacher."

His stomach flexed as he reached next to me for his drink. He was close. I could feel his body heat. "Looks like I'll be seeing more of you, then. My partner and I patrol that area."

"I think you'll have to make a better effort than that, Seth. I'm not one for getting into trouble." I smirked in a playful manner. "But you can find me at the campus pub, The Goose."

"Is that so?"

"It is." I looked over his shoulder at Erin, who was coming toward us.

"Sorry for interrupting, Em, but Alex wants to head back. You want to leave or…" She gave me a shake of the head as if to say, 'stay!'

Seth faced me. "I can take you home." He looked at Erin. "I'll get her home safe. You've met my partner, and you know who I am."

"That's true." Erin beamed at me. "That cool with you, Em?"

"Umm, sure."

"All right, call me when you get home." She waved goodbye.

Once alone again, he turned back to me, still only a foot between us, just an arm's length away from his perfect steel body. "I have to know something, Emily. Are you seeing anyone?" I was thankful for the darkness because I felt my face heat.

"Why do you have to know?" I played.

"Well." He leaned against the edge of the pool next to me. "I spent more than half the day watching you, the other half with you, and I want to know if I am stepping on any man's territory here."

"Why were you watching me?"

"Because you're beautiful. I have to know." He smiled playfully. "Are you seeing anyone right now?"

"If I am, then what?"

"Then I'd be horribly disappointed, but I'd think of a million ways to show you we're a better match."

"You're pretty sure of yourself." I smirked; his confidence was sexy.

He shrugged. "I am, so?"

"Single." I saw his blue eyes brighten up in the little light there was. "So now what?"

"Now I make sure you get home safely." He hopped up and headed to the table where our towels were. I followed and took the towel he offered me.

"It's all right. I can call a cab."

He looked at me strangely. "No, I said I'd take you home, so I am."

"Are you warm enough?" he asked as he pulled out of the driveway and onto the road.

"I'm fine." I let my hair out of the elastic, and it fell all around me. It was nearly dry. Soft music played in the background, and I felt comfortable with Seth, even though he was quieter than earlier. My phone rang, and I dug it out of my purse.

"Hello?"

"Emily, is it a good time?"

Dammit!

"Hey, Christopher, umm...not really. What's up?" I snuck a glance over at Seth, whose jaw appeared to be locked in place.

I could tell Christopher wasn't pleased I wouldn't give him much of my time. "Are we still on for Friday, six thirty at The Rhubarb?"

"Umm, yeah, Friday, Rhubarb, six thirty. I'll see you then." I hung up before I could hear about anything he had planned. I tucked my phone in my purse and stared out the windshield.

"You have a date?" he asked quietly.

"Sort of." I shrugged. "If you take the next turn, that's my driveway there on the right." He turned down the long, dark driveway and into my spot.

"You live here by yourself?" He opened his door as I gathered my things. He came around and offered to take my bag as I stood.

"My father passed away a few years ago, and my mother..." I closed my eyes. I didn't even know where I should begin. "She's in Africa saving anyone who's not me." I pushed away the painful thoughts. "I love the quiet, so it's perfect." It was a bit of a lie, but I didn't care. I was sure I wouldn't see this guy after tonight anyway. Men like Seth weren't interested in women. I could see he was a workaholic.

I unlocked my front door but stopped myself from going inside. "Thank you for the ride home."

"Of course, it was my pleasure." He scanned my property, and I wondered what he was thinking.

"What?" I looked around to see what he saw. "You're kind of scaring me, here."

His face changed into a sexy smile. "Sorry, habit, I guess. It's just you live in such a remote area. Are you all right with being here all on your own?"

"I don't want to give up my house. I fought hard enough to keep it. Sometimes it gets a little big, a little lonely, but that's the price I paid to keep what's mine." I was curious as to why in the hell I was telling him so much. "Wow, that got heavy quick." I stared down at my shoes and mentally kicked myself. "Sorry."

His finger lifted my chin so I'd look at him. "Why are you sorry? You're very refreshing, Emily, in so many ways." I nodded and resisted the urge to step forward and kiss him. "Now." He handed me my bag. "Please go inside, lock your door, and call Erin so I can say I dropped you off safe and sound."

A tiny ping of disappointment hit me that I wouldn't get a goodnight kiss, but at the same point, Seth seemed like the perfect gentleman, so it was nice.

"See you around, Seth." I opened my door.

"Yeah, you will, Emily." He gave a nod and watched me close my door on quite possibly the sexiest man who ever lived.

***

"She'll have a margarita," Christopher said to the waiter, "and I'll have a whiskey." He scanned the menu without even so much as a look at me or a *request for my input. "She'll have the duck with baby potatoes, and a salad with light ranch, and I'll have the duck with mashed potatoes and coleslaw."*

Wow, really? I leaned over the table. "Actually, I'll have a dirty martini with three olives, and a steak, medium, with fries." The waiter grinned a little as he took my menu. I noticed he made a quick retreat.

Christopher closed his eyes in frustration. "That was rude and demeaning for me."

"What was rude, Chris, was you not asking me what I'd like. You just assumed."

He pulled at his tie and glanced around the busy restaurant. "You really should eat healthier. Too much red meat is fattening, and the fries are full of salt."

I wanted to toss my water at him for even referring to my weight at dinner. I ate healthy and exercised every day. If I wasn't fit enough for him, then find someone else!

After a mind-numbing dinner, a painful dessert, and three martinis, I found myself looking out the window. I wanted to be anywhere else. Christopher talked about his father's company he was taking over, blah, blah, blah. If he thought it impressed me, he was so wrong. He was cocky in all the wrong ways.

"So," he muttered as we walked along the sidewalk, "that was a nice time." Really? I barely said two words while he chatted the entire time. "You want to come back to my place?"

"I don't think that's a good idea, Christopher." I stopped at his car and wished I had driven. "I had a

nice time, but I think we'd be better off as friends."

I didn't see him coming in for a kiss until his sloppy lips smacked into mine. I squeaked and tried to push him off. He took it as an invitation and stuck his tongue into my mouth like a dead slug. He pushed his body into mine against the car and pinned me with his weight. I pounded on his chest, but he didn't stop. He was the worst kisser. He barely moved his tongue, and he created too much saliva. Get off me! I want to vomit!

One moment he was on me, the next he was slammed to the ground and rolled across the pavement.

"You all right?" Seth held onto my hands while he madly looked me over.

"Yea-yes, I-I'm okay." I was a little shaken, but no harm done. Christopher moved to his feet and held his elbow.

"What the fuck, man!" He cursed at Seth, who turned and tucked me behind him. "She's with me."

"No, she's not," Seth said calmly. "You forced yourself on her. I should be arresting your ass, but I won't if you leave right now and never talk to Emily again."

Christopher looked at me, then Seth. I thought he was weighing his options. "Whatever." He dug his keys out and shimmied into the car, then spun the tires as he drove off.

I wiped my mouth. "Just in the neighborhood?"

"No." He looked at me after Christopher was out of sight. "I wanted to make sure you got home from your date."

116

Then I remembered Chris called when I was in the car with him the other night. "Well, thanks for following me." I laughed. "You're handy to have around."

"Someone told me you get yourself into situations without meaning to. Thought it was my duty to make sure this one went all right."

"Someone?"

"Erin." He shrugged.

"Oh, you spoke to my friend?" He nodded as he led me toward his car. "Why?"

"I wanted to know more about you." He helped me inside. "I ran into her and asked."

"Ran into her?" I asked, knowing that was a flat out lie. He winked and shut my door.

We chatted a little on the way home, but mostly he stayed quiet. I moved to face him better, right before we turned into my driveway, and studied his face. He had a strong jaw, dirty blond hair just a little bit long, and the bluest eyes I'd ever seen.

"What?" A little grin appeared.

"Nothing, just looking."

"Thanks for the ride home, again," I said as we climbed the porch steps. I stopped at the door. I made a face and remembered the taste of Christopher. Suddenly I wanted to gag.

"What?"

I felt stupid. "I can still taste him."

Seth suddenly cupped my face, dipped down, and pressed his strong lips to mine. It was a closed-lip kiss, but then he pulled back slightly to see if it was all right to continue. I moved toward him; I wanted more. My hands slid up his chest, over his

117

shoulders, and around his neck to get closer. He whirled me around so I was flat against the wall, then he grabbed one of my bare legs and hooked it over his hip. He ran his fingers down my thigh and squeezed my ass, while his other hand ran into my hair. He took over the kiss in a dominating way. My body jumped awake, my breasts strained against my bra, my hips rolled into his giant erection that made me moan as his tongue swept mine. Yes! This was the way you were supposed to feel when a man touched you. I finally let go and allowed him to steer the way, and it was amazing. I felt the moment he realized I gave myself over to him, and I swore he was even more turned on by it.

His hip started to vibrate, and he pulled away and took out his phone. His face dropped, and he looked down at me as if he were torn.

"I'm sorry, I have to go." He seemed a million miles away. I lowered my leg off his hip and felt the mood shift between us. "Umm, I'll call you later." He kissed my lips one more time, but it was different.

"Right, yeah...sure." I just wanted to be alone now. Something seemed off. Oh my God, what if it was a girl? "Well, thanks again for being there. Drive safe, Seth."

He sighed as I closed and locked the door behind me. I listened until I heard the engine fade away. What the hell was that?

Little did I know Seth would spend the next two years fighting off any man who spoke to me, but would keep me an arm's length away.

CHAPTER FOUR

Seth

I glanced down to find Emily was still awake. "You're quiet." I rubbed her leg under the blanket.

"Just remembering the night you rescued me from *nasty* Chris," she whispered with a smile, but she still had an uneasy edge to her. The party slowed down. Only Vanessa and Campbell were left, and they were on their last drink.

"Well, guys," Campbell huffed just as his cab pulled up in the driveway, "thanks again for a great night. It's always a pleasure."

"Yeah, thanks, guys." Vanessa sagged into his side and waved goodbye as they veered toward the cab. I turned off the fire pit and walked Emily back up to the house.

Emily fell asleep right away, draped over my body, and my hand rubbed along her arm while my other was tucked under my head. I stared at the ceiling, remembering that night with Emily and Chris. It was the night I got the text.

Maddy: Please come home, Seth! Dad's here and drunk.

I looked down at this amazing, sexy woman. We were both so pent-up we could hardly catch our breath. And now I had to go. This was fucked up!

"I'm sorry, but I have to go." She pulled away from me, and I ached all over. I said the first thing that came to mind. "I'll call you later."

She nearly smiled. "Right, yeah…sure." She paused. "Well, thanks again for being there. Drive safe, Seth." She closed the door, and I waited for the click of the lock.

I wanted to scream at my father. He had perfect timing for when to fuck with my life again! I hurried down the steps and made my way back to my parents' house.

Seth: Be there in ten.

Maddy was on the front steps in tears, and she jumped to her feet when I headed toward her, "Seth, he's really scaring me and Mom. I don't know what to do."

"Where is he?"

"His office, the last I saw. Mom is in the kitchen with Gretchen."

"Go to your room, lock your door, and stay there until I come get you." She ran inside and upstairs.

First I headed to the kitchen where Mom, with bloodshot eyes, sat quietly at the table. Gretchen gave me a sad look as she poured my mother a cup of tea.

"What's happening, Mom?" I asked from in the doorway.

She took a moment to gather herself before she addressed me. "He lost a case, dear. He just needs some space right now."

"Did he hurt you?"

"No." She pulled her sweater around her more. "You know your father. He's just verbally lashing out. Your sister got caught in the crossfire, though. Poor baby didn't need to hear she was a mistake."

My blood boiled to the point of pain when I heard that bastard hurt Maddy.

"He didn't come alone. One of the Marrone family members is here." Her face twisted. "He's a delight."

Is that so? *I sent a quick text to Garrett to let him know the situation in case I needed him. I made my way over to my father's office. I didn't knock before I walked in.*

My father was in front of the fireplace with a large glass of scotch, and his friend was sitting at my father's desk with his feet propped up.

"What the hell do you want?" my father hissed at me from the corner of his office. "Larry, meet my oldest, Seth, the cop who will do no wrong." Larry looked me up and down, and I mirrored his action with a hard expression. He was one greasy son of a bitch, and looked as if he just walked off the set of The Sopranos.

"Ah, yes." Larry grinned. "Nice to meet you, boy."

"Wish I could say the same," I grunted. "Dad,

121

why are you here? Drunk?"

Larry snorted. "It was wise for your father to get out of town. He lost an important case, one that might get him into some trouble."

"Hold on." I held up a hand. "You lost a major case, and people are looking for you, and you came here?" I nearly shouted, appalled. "You're putting your family in danger now, Dad! What the hell?"

"You yelling at me, boy?"

"I'm trying to understand why you'd do that." I couldn't even look at him. I started to leave, but stopped.

"If I ever hear you speak to Maddy like that again, I'll give up your location."

I heard his footsteps and turned just as his fist met my left eye, hard. I ducked when he swung again. I slammed my fist into his stomach and sent him backward. He came at me again and clipped my jaw. I elbowed him in the nose, heard a small crack, and hoped I broke it.

"Enough!" I shouted and raised my fist again to show I would keep going if he didn't stop. Blood drained from his nose as he scrambled to his feet. "Enough, Dad!" Larry clapped and announced how entertaining that was. I turned to leave, but Dad spoke up before I got out the door.

"You nail that little blonde yet, Seth?" I froze, but blood shot to my head as my heart pumped like mad to catch up. "Yeah, that's right, son, I know all about your fascination with the McPhee girl." I could barely see now; my anger took over. "You should invite your little girlfriend over for dinner tomorrow night. We'd love to meet her."

"You see," Larry came around the desk and continued the conversation, "we know all about her, where she lives, that she lives alone, that her only neighbors are elderly and hard of hearing. I followed you." He smirked darkly. "Her mother is a million miles away, and she attends Orange University. Other than her bra size, I think we have it covered, and really that wouldn't be too hard to find out, right, Jack?"

I swallowed past the massive lump in my throat and faced Larry. "What's your point?"

"My point, son, if you hurt someone I like," he pointed at my father, "I hurt someone you like. Think about that when you want to make that call to the men who are after him."

I swung open the door and headed upstairs, and once alone in my old room, I vowed I wouldn't bring Emily into this mess.

Little did I know I couldn't stay away from her. I wouldn't touch her for another two years, but I sure as hell couldn't let anyone else either.

As time went on, I couldn't keep it up, and I gave in. I loved that woman with all my heart. She started to get bolder, and my body couldn't take it. The time we kissed in the kitchen, I was done for, but then Lasko got in the way, and I thought maybe Larry had something to do with it. I found out Larry was killed in a shooting six months before Lasko even came into the picture, so the odds they had a connection were pretty slim.

My father and I had never been the same since. When he was in town, I avoided him. It broke my heart that my mother loved him so much that no

*matter what he did, she tried to see the good in him.
There was no good in Jack Connors, just pure evil. I
hated I was his son.*

"What's wrong?" Emily asked in a husky voice.
"Why are you awake?"

"Nothing." I rolled her over and spooned her
from behind, and I kissed her shoulder before I fell
into a restless sleep.

***

Avery

They never knew I was there, never knew I
watched their most private moments, never knew I
heard some of their darkest secrets. I stood in their
bedroom door and pointed a gun at Seth's head. The
silencer would muffle the noise and allow me to
clean up the mess and escape with plenty of time to
get home before I received the call that Connors
didn't make it in to work. I shifted the gun to Emily.
I didn't feel the same rush with the idea of her death
as I did with his. Maybe because Jims never wanted
her dead. He just wanted her to be his.

I loved this part, the part where I toyed with
Seth's sixth sense. I stepped outside the doorframe
and cocked the gun. Immediately, Seth woke and
ripped his gun from the Velcro strap on the bed
frame. Once his feet hit the floor, I slowly stepped
across the hall into his old bedroom behind the
door. I was dressed all in black, and it helped me
move throughout the house undetected. I also wore

Jims's mask on the off chance someone spotted me. It was fucked I wore this mask. I really hoped one day Emily would see it again.

His footsteps got louder, and I saw him enter the room through the crack. Once he opened the closet, I stepped out around the door, back into the hallway, and to their bedroom. I didn't have much time, but I moved his family picture so it faced the window and turned my attention to Emily, who was still sound asleep. I slipped into her closet just as Seth came back into the room.

Instead of going back to bed, he pulled on some pants and sat in the corner of the room with his gun ready to fire. Most men, if they felt a threat, would leave. Not Seth. I swore the man had a set of cast iron balls.

I checked the time—one fifteen. I propped myself up and settled in for a long night. I would have preferred to have slept in the attic like normal, but this would have to do.

"Will I ever see her again, Grandmother?"

"Who, your mother?" she snarled. "No, never. Her body is six feet under, and her soul is even further south." I stared at Grandmother and wondered why she hated my mother so much. "Alexander!" She snapped her ruler. "Eyes on the book." They dropped back down to the words that talked about good and evil.

I wondered if I'd see Jims again. I missed him a lot.

At four thirty, Seth headed to the bathroom to get

ready for his shift. I slipped out and made my way downstairs, where I disarmed the alarm and hurried into the woods down my usual path and into my car.

***

"Hey, Ronnie." I dropped a folder on the desk. "You overlooked the cousin's address. You'll need to grab that before you submit this to Sarge. It has to be finished tonight. If you need any help, Connors will be off at five. I suggest you use his help before you get in shit."

"Thanks." Ronnie gathered the file and hurried out.

"Ready?" Riley asked with his crap coffee in hand. Thankfully, he got the hint I hated that shit. I despised this man; he annoyed me in so many ways. I supposed it could be worse. I could have gotten stuck with Ronnie, and that idea made my stomach knot.

"Yeah, let's go."

After my shift, I stopped off at The Brick. I needed a fix. With my bag hooked over my shoulder, I headed inside. Once again she was at the counter, wearing barely a scrap of material. I stared at her boots that stopped at the top of her knees.

"Got something you wanna say?" Her hands were on her cocked hips. I shook my head as I moved across the small reception area and entered the code to get in the back. "I'm having a good day, thanks for asking," she hissed as the door closed behind me.

My room was four doors down on the right. I

undressed, before hanging my clothes neatly in the closet where I made sure everything was placed the way I liked it. Crossed laces in an 'x' form, my socks hung over the top, and my watch and wallet were squared away in a personal safe that I set with my own combination to ensure privacy.

The green light blinked above the side door to indicate she was ready. I slipped on a pair of silk pants and stepped into the dark room.

My finger swiped through the songs on the iPad attached to the wall. I selected "Make it Rain" by Ed Sheeran and turned up the volume to five, the perfect level.

My attention was pulled to the woman chained to the wall, securely bound by metal handcuffs. She was blindfolded; I never let them see my face. Sherry liked it rough with a lot of pain. She was the right match for my mood right now.

"Safe word," I commanded sharply.

A slow, lazy smile spread across her sweet little mouth. I knew she knew it was me, Number Six. We're all called by numbers to keep things private. "More." She grinned and licked her lips. It was a standard question we must all ask, but we both knew she'd never use it.

I reached for the studded paddle and made my way over to her. I could smell her arousal as I uncuffed her hands and bent her over a bench so her ass was stuck up in the air. I palmed her pale skin before I smacked her hard with the paddle. She cried out, which made her scent even stronger. I closed my eyes and relished her pain before I continued to pleasure her, being careful not to reach the point of damage.

The song switched to "Creep" by Radiohead, and I changed my method. I choose the cane and stood over her and waited for the chorus. My fingers twitched as my grip tightened. This was the best part.

***

Emily

"All right, I wanted to change it up a little this year." Professor Dean turned off his projector. "I want you to come up with the perfect murder. You will present a photo of the fake crime scene, give us a detailed summary on the victim and their family. You will present the assignment, and the class will try to solve it together." He waited until the excitement died down. "You may pair up with a friend, or you can do it solo. It's completely up to you. You have two weeks to complete this assignment. You will be marked on creativity, detail, depth, presentation, and overall outcome." He checked the time. "This is supposed to be a fun project. My only rule is don't murder anyone for extra credit—you won't get it—and the whole 'my professor told me to do it' defense won't stand up in court." The class broke out in laughter just as the bell rang. "Have a great day."

"So," Scott caught up with me as I opened the front door to head to the library. "You wanna be my partner?"

"That depends." I smirked. "How invested are

you in this project? Because I plan on pulling out all the stops."

"I'm all in, girl!" He winked, which earned him an eye roll at the obvious sexual innuendo. It had been a year, but I swore Scott still thought he had a chance.

"Emily!" I heard my name called, and every nerve in my body went on high alert. I didn't need to turn around to know that voice, and it sent my stomach into a knot *every time.* "Join me for dinner, please."

"Who's that?" Scott whispered, most likely as he noted the icy tone she brought to her voice whenever she spoke to me.

"That would be my mother." I swallowed back a frustrated sob. "I'll call you later. If we're going to be partners, start thinking."

"Yes, ma'am." He stood at attention.

I took a few shaky steps toward her. I could see she wasn't in her false friendly mode she used in public. My mind flipped through a million and one reasons why she was here or what I'd done now.

"Mother," I greeted her right before she entered the Town Car. "I once again wasn't aware you were back in town."

"I have some business to attend to," she said in a clipped tone, as she typed away on her phone.

The entire drive home was silent. I stared out the window while she ignored me.

"Are we ordering or cooking tonight, Mother?" I pulled open the fridge.

"Neither, I just wanted to get you home without a fuss." Gary came out of my father's office with a

129

file in his hand. *What the hell!*

"Oh, hey there, kiddo, I didn't know you'd be back so soon." I ground my teeth together. What the hell was that man doing in my father's office, let alone my home?

"What are you doing?" I pointed to the paperwork.

My mother pulled out a chair at the table. "Sit, Emily, we need to chat." I took the chair because my thoughts were negative enough already that I feared I might just cry. Gary joined Mother on the other side of the table. He looked a tad smug, and I wanted to smack him.

"Okay, what do you want, Mother?" I just wanted her to get on with it.

"Emily, I have a buyer for the house." All the air got sucked from my lungs. "They are prepared to offer more than the asking price, but they want to move in by Christmas."

"What?"

My mother raised her hands as if fending off my anger. Little did she know I was way past that point; I was beyond anger—I was livid! "I have been trying to get you to put it on the market for a long time now, and you've obviously been too lazy or too obstinate to get it done, so I had to do it. Now, six months later, I've had three inquires, and this latest one is very promising."

"You had no right to do that," I hissed as the words 'buyer' and 'move in by Christmas' burned themselves into my brain. "You can't legally sell this house at all. It's under *my* name."

Gary put his hand on mine but quickly moved it

when he felt me flinch as though seared by his touch. "You're right, kiddo, we can't sell it. That's why we need you to sign the house over to your mother and let us handle all the work."

Mom reached out for Gary's hand and gave it a little squeeze as she looked at me. "Honey," she had the gall to beam at me, "Gary and I got married last week." *Wow.* "Now, I really want to close this chapter of my life so I can move forward and let the past go."

Heavy, hot tears filled my eyes. I wasn't sure what I was angrier about—my mother for practically selling my house out from under me, or that she wanted to move on and forget about the life she once had as my mother. Forget about me, my father, and our whole past like we were never a family at all.

I snatched the paperwork from Gary, opened it up, and saw it was the information on my trust fund my father had set up for me. That was it...I was finished.

"Get out!" I growled at both of them, the heat of my anger making me boil. They stared at me. "How *dare* you? Get the fuck out of my house, *now!*" I slowly stood and placed my hands flat on the table to still the impulse to take a swing at one of them. "Leave now before I call the cops and get them to throw you the hell off my property. I'll have you charged for trying to sell the house illegally."

"Emily Grace!" My mother scowled. "Don't you dare talk to me like that. I am your mother—"

"My mother!" I shouted as I started to shake with the adrenaline that pumped through me.

"When have you *ever* been my mother?" I blinked back the tears. I didn't want to give her the satisfaction knowing her words tore me apart. I took a step toward her, and she stepped back, almost tripping over the chair. "Dad signed this house over to me for this very goddamn reason, *Mother*, because you wanted nothing to do with us, even then. I always felt that, but now I have proof. This is *my* home, *my* memories, this is the only piece of Dad I have left. I would fight you to the grave for this property." I looked at Gary, whose face had lost his sappy expression and now showed his true emotion—anger. "You think you're fooling anyone, Gary? I see you for what you are. My mother is a cash cow, and your ticket to the rich life."

"Emily!" my mother snapped.

Gary shook his head to stop her. "Actually, Emily, you are wrong there. Your mother needs the sale of this house. She's sunk a lot of money into Doctors Without Borders, and we need this money to start a hospital for those unfortunate…"

"Now your tactic is guilt?" I spat back, interrupting him. "Those 'unfortunate' people over there have had more of my mother than I ever have, so as far as I'm concerned, we're even."

"Jenny, honey." He suddenly took another tack. "Could you grab my phone from the car? I want to show Emily the apartment we found her."

"Of course, what a great idea." She smiled as she moved out to the living room.

I turned to Gary and saw his face had changed again. It was ugly. "Don't even, Gary. I'll ship mother's shit to wherever, but you both get out of my fucking house!"

"Watch your mouth, my dear." Gary suddenly stood to tower over me. "This isn't over."

"Wow, really? Are you threatening me, Gary?"

He gave me an icy look, then changed it to a sickly sweet smile as Mother returned to the room. "No, kiddo, I'm just making sure we're on the same page, that's all." She gave Gary a quick glance. I swore she knew what he just said to me.

"It's time for you both to leave." I grabbed my phone as if to make a call and swallowed back a little fear. I really didn't know anything about this man.

Gary wrapped an arm around my mother. "Perhaps you're right." They turned to leave, but Gary twisted back to face me before he stepped out the door. "I'll be seeing you soon, Emily."

I glanced at my mother to see if she was scared of Gary. Perhaps that was why she wasn't speaking up. I couldn't tell if she or he was mastermind on this little game they were playing. "Mom?" I nearly cried as I barely held it together.

She looked at me with a resigned expression. "All you need to do, dear, is sign the papers. I simply don't understand why you are so attached to this damn place. It's just a house. We have a lovely apartment chosen for you."

"Maybe to you, but it's not to me. Why can't you just leave it alone? For once in your life, give me something I care about without hurting me."

She shook her head and checked the time. "Always so dramatic, Emily." She sighed at Gary. "This was pointless. Let's go."

The moment they left, I locked the door and set the alarm. I hurried upstairs and into the guest bedroom, where Seth's boxes were stored from when he moved in. I yanked them free and headed into my mother's bedroom. I usually never went in there; it made me uncomfortable.

I started to shove all her belongings into the boxes, not that there was much. I didn't care. I removed anything she could say was hers. I started to cry as the conversation replayed in my head. Why did she have to do this? Why wasn't it she who died instead of Dad? The good always died first!

By the time I was done, I'd filled four large boxes. I taped them shut and tossed them down the stairs, then sat on the step and pulled out my phone.

Emily: Are you at the station?

Nothing.

Emily: Is Seth with you?

Garrett: I just wrapped things up. Seth is helping Ronnie.

I wanted to scream!

Garrett: You okay?

Emily: Any idea how long he'll be?

Garrett: At least another hour. Can I help?

I grabbed my keys and filled the car with her boxes. I just wanted to get rid of them.

"Hey, you moving?" Travis joked behind me. His face dropped when he saw I was in tears. "Oh my God, are you all right?"

"No," I kicked the last box hard and jammed it in the trunk, "I'm not!"

"Emily, what's wrong? Did he hurt you?"

I barely listened to him. All I wanted was to toss all this crap in the trash. "Hurt doesn't begin to describe how I'm feeling!"

"Here." Travis twisted the box so it fit then closed the trunk. "I knew he wasn't good for you."

"He's perfect for her! Match made in hell!" I hissed and opened the driver door.

"Where are you going?"

"I can't look at this stuff anymore. I'm over it."

He bent down into my window. "You want me to go with you?"

"No." I couldn't even smile to be friendly. "Thanks; I just need this to be over."

"Okay, why don't you come over for a drink tonight? Just so you're not alone."

I closed my eyes and fought a new round of tears. "Yeah—maybe, thanks."

I barely remembered the drive over to Gary's stupid club. I parked at a red curb, only to have the bouncer comment. *Thanks, asshole!* I opened the back door and started to chuck boxes on the sidewalk. Then I emptied the trunk as well. The bouncer merely watched. He didn't react, and he didn't offer to help. Although I imagined I looked terrible at that point, I didn't care.

"Tell Gary this is all of his wife's crap. She's no longer my problem."

The bouncer muttered something into a radio, then nodded at me. "Anything else?"

"Yeah," I pulled open my door. "Tell him to fuck off, and I'll see him in court if I have to!"

I jumped in my car, pulled a U-turn without even looking to see if anything was coming, and got the hell out of there.

***

"Hey there, Emily," Lou greeted me as I walked straight past him into the back offices. I was way beyond the point where I need to check in anyway. I nodded once, and he nodded back. "Emily." He stopped me and pointed down a hallway. "He's down there, second witness room on your left. Been a busy day, and they needed some quiet."

"Thanks." I hurried in that direction. I just needed to be in his arms before I broke down again.

I reached for the handle but stopped when I looked in the window. A long-legged brunette stepped into Seth and locked lips with him.

I stepped back immediately and into someone's chest. "Hey, McPhee, what's up?" Avery's hands flew to my shoulders as I bumped into him. He looked inside the office and closed his eyes. "Oh, Em, sorry you saw that." He rubbed his face. "She's been after him since she arrived at the station." He took my arm and hurried me down the hallway and back toward the front door.

"Who is she?" I barely got out.

"Ronnie...Ronnie."

"Ronnie? Is a...girl?" I bit my lip. This was all too much. "So all these late nights, our date he forgot, he was with her?" I held my stomach as it moved violently. The walls closed in on me. I needed to get out of there. "I need to go."

"Wait, Emily." He hooked my arm. "Where are you going? Tell me, at least." My chin quivered, evidence that I was about to lose it. "Oh, come here." He pulled me into his arms and gave me a stiff hug. Avery wasn't normally a touchy-feely person. "Life sucks sometimes, and you were dealt a shitty hand." I sobbed and held onto his arms, needing something to ground me. "Look." He pulled away and bent down so we were eye level. "Ronnie is new. Once people get word what's going on, they'll eat her alive. You know we all love you."

"Funny, I thought Seth did too," I said bitterly. I shook my head and attempted to clear the fog. "I gotta go." I couldn't think about that. "Thank you, though."

The clouds hung low, the wind picked up, and the sea turned violent. Large raindrops bounced off my windshield and sent trails down to the wipers, much like the tears that were running down my cheeks. My chest was wet with them and heavy with pain.

Only one other car besides mine was in the beach parking lot. I didn't know where to go. I felt lost in a sea of anger, hurt, betrayal, and deep, deep sadness.

***

Avery

Adler sat perfectly still, his stare fixed on me through the patio door, the rain beating off his head. I admitted he looked pathetic, but Jims trained him well. The only time the dog barked was if he was hungry. For the most part, he was a good companion if you needed one. I'd never been an animal person. They were dirty creatures with their smelly fur and saliva, and I hated their wet noses when they touched you. I cringed at the thought, and nearly gagged. I flicked off the porch light and made him disappear into the darkness. His eyes seemed to glow with my kitchen light, so I turned that off too. I headed into the living room with my drink in hand.

I just got settled into my chair when my doorbell rang. I waited for a moment. No one was supposed to come by tonight. My last unexpected company ended up in the incinerator. I removed my gun from the table and carefully pulled the blinds aside to see who it was. A hood covered their face. *Fuck!* I slowly opened the door and nearly dropped the gun.

"Can I come in?"

"Umm..." I thought about my place, and if anything was out that shouldn't be. "Sure, Emily, come on in."

"Thanks." She removed her jacket and hung it on my coat rack, then slipped off her rain boots and placed them by mine. None of this felt right. Her face was puffy from crying, and her eyes were bloodshot. "I'm sorry to come unannounced. I honestly just drove and ended up here."

"It's fine," I lied while she came further into my space. I never had anyone over, let alone one of my puppets. "Can I get you a drink? I have whiskey and—"

"Whiskey sounds perfect." She dried her watery eyes.

I slowly walked into the kitchen with her behind me. My skin crawled like it wanted to get off my bones. Every part of me screamed to kill her, but that was not my plan. She still had some damage to do first. "Straight up or mixed?"

"Straight, please." She sat on the bar stool at the counter and watched me move about. It was unnerving. I didn't like this. I needed to be in control, and right now, I didn't have it. I opened the cabinet and removed a glass. I spotted the crushed up pills that I used on Matthews last year. *No! Not yet.* Adler started to bark, and it made Emily jump. "Is that your dog?" She looked out the patio door from her seat. *Shit!*

"Neighbors," I said calmly and set the glass down to get her attention. I poured the whiskey into her glass. "He comes on my patio sometimes when they're not home. Looking for something to eat, I guess. I'm not much of a pet person."

"I can see that." She looked around.

"Meaning?"

"Meaning your place is spotless, everything is in order. It's nice."

I took a long sip of my drink and eased my breathing. She was an observant little one. My eyes moved to the steak knife, then over to the meat thermometer, then to the Saran Wrap. So many ways I could end her life right now.

She downed her drink in one swallow and I quickly filled it, trying my best to act like a good host. "Come, let's sit in the living room." Away from fucking Adler, who still barked at the glass. Maybe he sensed her? That was the last thing I needed, her seeing that damn dog.

"Are you all right?" I asked as she sat next to me on the couch. She was so close.

"No." She stared into her glass. "Not at all. Can I ask you something?"

"Sure." I handed her a tissue as her emotions surfaced again.

"Thanks." She dabbed her eyes. "You didn't seem surprised when you saw them kissing. That's not the first time it's happened, is it?"

I didn't want to underestimate Emily's ability to read a person. I'd need to play this off just right.

"Honestly, what you were reading on my face was more like 'I wasn't that surprised it came to that.' Ronnie is a sexy woman, and a few of the men have been interested in her, Garrett included. She's had her eye on Connors since she started. She has a bunch of other guys she could ask for help, but she won't. She wants him. Ronnie is one of those women who uses her body to get men to do what she wants. Before you write Connors off, remember he's a man, and we think with our dicks, not our brains."

I could almost feel her soul bleed; it was marvelous to witness. If I knew Emily like I thought

I did…

"I'm not a woman who can overlook that kind of thing, Avery."

Just as I thought. I had to take a drink to stop the smirk that was threatening my face. "I know." I lowered my voice to show I understood. "Truthfully, I wouldn't want a woman who just rolls over and takes it. I would want one who would care if I cheated. It would keep me in line, make me a better man."

Her phone alerted her she had a text. She pulled her phone from her back pocket, and I could tell it was him just by the way her chin quivered and her eyes refilled. She tossed her phone on the table, leaned forward, and rested her elbows on her thighs.

"You know, I truly thought I couldn't hurt worse than what I went through last year." She suddenly stopped. "God, I'm sorry, Avery. I mean, all *we* went through. I'll never forget about Matthews."

"It's all right." I frowned at the right moment.

She stood and moved to the window. "Do you have any family, Avery?"

I paused and wondered why she changed to this topic.

"My parents passed many years ago, only child. Only have a cousin I see once in a while."

"Yeah," she said through a swallow, "family is really overrated."

"It is," I agreed, then moved to my feet, wanting to get her away from the window. "You know what, McPhee? I have a better idea than sitting here in my quiet apartment. I'm taking you out."

"What?"

"I'm not working tomorrow, so let's go have some fun." I needed her out of my house before I shed a layer of skin.

"The Triangle?" She looked a little uncomfortable.

"Come on, we'll take a cab."

When we arrived, I opened the door and waved her through and motioned her to the bar top. I helped her out of her wet jacket and hung it on the back of the chair, then signaled for the bartender to bring us two whiskeys. Once we were settled, I showed her some of my many talents. This one was being a friend. "Here's the thing, McPhee. Though I'm very touched you came to me for comfort, you're still technically dating one of my best friends. I feel more comfortable being in public with you than at my place. You know, so people don't make assumptions. So I brought you to our bar so everyone can see I'm here with my buddy's girl as friends. Make sense?"

"Yeah." She managed a smile. I knew she'd respect that. Emily was a good person, despite, well… "Thanks."

"No thanking me, McPhee, drink." I pointed to her glass and waited for her to get a little tipsy so I could find out what else was bothering her.

Four drinks in, and I had her laughing. I hated to admit it, but she was actually a little fun to be around. Jims would have loved her. Just the thought of him made the hate seep back into my veins, and I started to remember how much I despised everyone.

"At the risk of saying something touchy, can I ask how you've been dealing with what happened last year?"

Her face fell. All signs of fun were gone, and she signaled for another drink. "Fine, I guess." She started to stack the glasses one on top of another. "If you asked me two days ago, I'd say pretty good."

"And now?"

"Now, I feel like this." She pointed to the glass stack. "Fragile, feeling like the pressure will get too much and it'll all come crashing down."

"Those are some heavy words." I leaned on the bar top as the liquor swarmed around inside my head. "So besides Connors, is something else adding weight to your glass house?"

She chuckled a little in her liquor-induced haze. "My mother," she glanced at me, "paid me her annual visit."

"Oh no."

"Yeah, with news. I have a new stepfather, and she wanted to sell my house. Already found me a buyer, in fact."

I nodded for more drinks, though I really should stop. "I wasn't aware you were moving."

"I'm not."

"Oh."

"So, after some words, I kicked them out, packed up my mother's crap, and dumped it at her new hubby's workplace, then left a message with the bouncer that I'll see them in court."

I snatched a glass from behind the bar and placed it on top of her glass tower.

"Exactly." She nodded at my point. She had a lot on her shoulders right now.

***

I shouldn't have had that last drink. I started to lose control over my own thoughts. My mind wandered in shared silence, and recklessly, I started to share. "I grew up next to this family." She looked over at me with heavy eyes. "Two boys and a sister. The father was a real asshole, beat them all the time, beat their mother too, sometimes until she couldn't see. Their mother, despite all she went through, still loved her kids. She tried to protect them from her husband. She even found a way to leave once, but at the last minute it fell through. Six months later, she was killed." I felt my own tears threaten.

"How?"

I sat up in my seat. I needed to think straight. "Her husband lost it, beat her to death."

"Jesus, what happened to the kids?"

I slipped back into a memory of Jims and Julia, so clear it was as if they were here in front of me. "They all went to different family members. I always wondered what if they had got out, moved away, and had a chance at a better life, where they would be today? I like to think they'd be a close family, you know, Sunday dinners at the mom's." I saw she tried to follow my story, and I shook my head and forced a smile. "Guess sometimes I wonder what it's like to have that, quote, big happy family."

"If you ever find one, let me know," she muttered sarcastically into her glass.

After another hour, she was nearly passed out in the booth we had moved to at some point in the evening. I pulled out my cell phone and checked the time—three thirty a.m. I removed Emily's cell from her jacket, used the passcode to get in, and looked up his number. It took me a moment to actually locate it, as it was changed to a different name. I bypassed all the texts from Connors and O'Brian.

Em: You awake?

Fantastic Pete: Yes, love, where are you?

Emily: It's Avery, we're at the Triangle. Can you come get her?

Fantastic Pete: Be there in ten.

Sure enough, Pete walked in ten minutes later, concerned as always when it came to Emily. Then I saw Connors with a look that could kill.

***

Seth

My stomach was in a knot that tightened as I laid eyes on Emily. She was pretty much passed out in a booth next to Avery, who attempted to stand when I approached.

"Hey, guys," he started to say, but I interrupted him.

"Why did you text Pete and not me?"

Avery made a face as he looked back at Emily. "That's not for me to answer."

145

"Why the hell not?"

"Look, Connors, she showed up on my doorstep. I wasn't aware she even knew where I lived. I brought her here because I didn't feel comfortable having her at my place. She wanted to talk, I brought her here to avoid any...problems. She was upset, so we talked, and once she got everything out, I called Pete. Her best friend, someone she doesn't want to punch right now."

"Punch?" I nearly shouted, leaning over Emily, who stunk like booze. "Christ, how much has she had to drink?" My nose practically burned. "Is that whiskey? She hates the stuff."

"Not tonight, she doesn't." He shrugged over at Pete. "I think it's best you take her home."

"No." I grabbed her jacket and slipped her arm over my shoulder. "Come on, baby, time to go home."

Her eyes slowly opened and something flashed over them. Pain? Hurt, maybe?

"No." She pushed me away and stumbled to her feet. "Don't," she muttered as I came near her again.

"I'm going to go," Avery chimed in. "Drink some water, Em."

"Thanks." Pete smiled a little, but kept his watch on Emily and me, looking from one of us to the other.

I noticed the bartender, who pointed to the time. He was about to close. I didn't have a clue what was going on, but the last thing I wanted was the locals I see every week to witness me having it out with my drunken girlfriend.

"Emily, time to go home." I tried to hand over her jacket, but she flinched away from me.

She ignored me. "Pete, can I come home with you?"

"No," I snapped, more scared than anything.

Pete looked at me funny. "Of course you can, love. I'm parked out back."

"What's going on, Emily?" I lowered my voice.

She cupped her mouth as her shoulders shook, then she started to cry. I reached out to comfort her, but she raised her hand. "No," she sobbed, "don't touch," her breath caught, "me."

I looked to Pete, questioning, wondering if he knew what was going on, but he mouthed, "I have no idea."

"Please, let me take you home," I nearly begged. I felt so lost.

"Home?" She almost laughed. "That's funny." She zig-zagged toward Pete. "Get me away from him."

Oh hell no. I quickly stepped in front of her, bent down, grabbed her legs, and hiked her over my shoulder. She kicked in protest, but I needed her out of the bar and out of the public eye. She'd thank me later…maybe.

I set her feet down on the ground when were outside under the eave, free of the downpour.

"Stop." She tumbled back into Pete. "Just don't come near me—I can't be near you!"

"Why, Emily? What did I do?" I couldn't take the look she gave me, almost like she was disgusted with me.

She shoved a finger in my face. "I saw you," she

fought her sob, "with her…Ronnie!"

Everything went quiet as the memory from earlier in the day flashed in front of me. She was there? How could that be? I watched her fall apart as she stepped into the rain, heading for Pete's car.

I hurried out after her. "Emily—"

"*No!*" she shouted, and whirled around. "I'm done! I'm done fighting for us! It's always been one-sided! It's always me defending myself with Scott and Travis. You never trusted me! But I've always trusted you, always, until now." She gave up and let the sobs consume her.

I wanted to cry at the thought of her seeing what she did. "Can I at least explain?"

We were completely soaked, but we didn't care. "Later," she whispered on an exhale. "I need space, I can't…" Her hand flew to her chest like it was in pain. "I can't even look at you right now."

"I didn't kiss her, Em." She squeezed her eyes shut. "I would never touch a woman like that, the way I touch you. She kissed me!"

Her eyes slowly moved up to mine. I thought she was going to say something, but instead she turned and walked to Pete, who was in his car giving us some space.

***

SATURDAY

I stayed in bed all day. No word from Emily.

SUNDAY

I worked my shift like a zombie. The whole day I managed to avoid Ronnie. No word from Emily.

MONDAY

Same as Sunday.

TUESDAY

Seth: Please talk to me, baby.

Nothing.

Seth: How is she?

Pete: Not very good.

Seth: Should I come by?

Pete: I'm thinking not.

WEDNESDAY

I felt like a robot at work. I barely spoke to Garrett, but he finally got out of me what happened and assured me she would come back. But this time…this time, it felt different.

THURSDAY

9:00 a.m.—I sent her flowers. I never send flowers.

10:15 p.m.—The flowers appeared on our

doorstep, with a note that explained she rejected them.

I worked out for three hours. I needed some kind of release. It didn't work, nothing helped. My phone pinged, and I nearly dropped the weight bar on my chest when I went to grab it.

Jenny McPhee: Since Emily has dropped off the face of the earth after last week, please let her know the buyer will be by tomorrow at 6:30 p.m. I expect the house to be spotless.

Seth: Buyer?

I was lost.

Jenny McPhee: 6:30 p.m.!

I checked the time and wondered if I should text Emily or not.

Seth: Is Em with you?

Pete: No.

Seth: School?

Pete: No.

Seth: Pete, please.

Pete: At dinner with a friend, leave her be. It's the first time she's been out since the bar.

Seth: Yeah.

I threw my phone on the floor and worked out until I couldn't feel my arms.

FRIDAY

I'd had enough of this shit, and I could tell Garrett was finished with my moodiness too.

"Dude, just call her!" he hissed from the driver's seat.

"You don't think I've thought of that? I've tried. She doesn't pick up." We pulled into the station and parked in our spot. "I sent flowers, but she sent them back."

Garrett looked at me funny. "You sent flowers?"

"I know!" I shook my head in frustration. "What am I supposed to do?"

We both stopped when we saw Ronnie with Riggs. She smiled when she saw me. I wanted to punch her. She'd destroyed my life and didn't seem to care. She barely blinked an eye when I tossed her off me that day in the witness room…wait! I looked at Garrett. "I'll be right back."

Seth: Where is she?

Pete: Not sure.

Seth: PETE, WHERE IS SHE?

Pete: I honestly don't know. I came back from the store, and she was gone. Note said she'll be

back later.

Fuck!

I started to call her, but instead it started to ring in my hand. It was my mom. I sighed and answered it.

"Hey, Mom." I sounded upbeat, but my frustration showed through.

"Mmm," she muttered into the phone. "Wanna tell me why Emily is here in my living room crying her heart out?"

My heart jolted. "She's there?" A small part of me was excited that she went to Mom for comfort.

"Yes, honey, and she's really upset."

I grabbed my keys. "Keep her there." I hung up and raced to my car. I didn't bother to change out of my uniform.

"Where's the fire?" Avery called out to me as he opened his car door. He dropped his bag on the passenger seat.

"I gotta go see Emily."

"Everything all right?"

"Yeah," I muttered, "it will be."

"Glad to hear it, man." He rolled his window down. "Oh, hey, Triangle tomorrow night. It's Johnnie's birthday, remember."

Fuck! "Right, okay." I really didn't want to go. "Okay, I'll be there."

The house was quiet. I listened for voices, but nothing. Then I heard a chair scrape outside and headed to the back patio. That's when I saw her with a mug of coffee, huddled under a blanket in front of the fire pit. My mother stroked her back while tears fell from her cheeks. There was no other way to describe the scene but heartbreaking.

I took a deep breath and opened the door. Mom gave me a look, and I instantly knew Emily had told her. I shook my head. I didn't want to get into it right now.

I sat across from Emily, and it took her a moment to realize I was there. Her eyes finally rose enough to see me. I leaned my elbows on my thighs and watched her take me in. At least she wasn't yelling at me...yet.

"Can I at least show you something?" I whispered and hoped for a miracle. To my surprise she nodded. I offered her my hand to help her stand, and she actually took it. "Thank you."

I led her to the family room, where I inserted a disk and pressed play. She stood with the blanket around her tiny frame. The video of me walking into the witness room with Ronnie behind me made my stomach burn. I breathed a sigh of relief that I was finally was able to show her proof, when suddenly the video switched to static. I pointed the remote to back it up and tried to play it again, but it still went to static.

"What the hell?" I removed the disk and checked for a scratch, but it was clear. This had never happened before; the witness rooms had great cameras. Someone had to monitor these daily, so this didn't make sense! I chucked the disk at the wall in time to see Emily leave the room. "Wait." I chased after as she threaded her arm through her purse. "Where are you going?"

"Pete's," she muttered. I approached her

carefully and took her arm, led her to a chair, and I sat on the edge of the fire pit. I didn't want to risk her running again.

"Please, baby, look at me." My voice was thick with desperation. I was so damn terrified at that moment. "I've never kissed another woman since I met you that day at the party. You have to know she kissed me, not the other way around. She was above me and used her momentum to hold me down, but only *momentarily*. I pushed her off me as soon as I got some leverage." I sank onto my knees and held her cold hands. "You have to know, no one, no one tastes right, no one kisses me like you do, and no one makes the noise you do that has me desperate for more." She started to silently cry. I knew she had to feel my truth—she just had to. "I would never risk losing the one person I want to spend the rest of my life with over some stupid kiss. Emily, you know me better than anyone else, you know we are meant to be together."

She burst into a sob and leaned forward to bury her face into my neck. I wrapped my arms around her and stood so I could lift her on my lap.

I kissed her hair and took the moment to touch her in case she pulled away. God, she smelled like home. I couldn't imagine a moment more without her. "I love you, Emily, more than anything. I'm sorry you're hurting."

She pulled away to look at me. She seemed so worn out. My heart felt like it was about burst, she looked so weathered and saddened by all of this.

"Will you come home with me?" Her chin started to quiver with a whole new wave of emotion. *Oh, my poor everything.* "What is it, Em?"

"She's trying to take him from me again." She hiccupped. "I hate her, Seth, I hate her so much!"

"Who?" I tucked her hair behind her shoulder.

She closed her eyes to calm herself. "I'm so tired," she spoke quietly, "of everything."

I wanted to press the topic, but mostly I wanted her to let me take her home.

"Please come home with me."

She moved to her feet and gave me a slight nod.

I held her hand the entire way home, scared this moment might escape from me. She stayed quiet and wiped her cheeks every so often. I wished I could crawl inside her head and hear what she was thinking.

"I should text Pete." She pulled her hand away, but grabbed mine again when she finished. This little moment made such a difference for me. At least I knew she wanted to touch me as much as I did her.

It was late by the time we pulled up to the house. We were both drained, and the idea of bed was a welcoming thought.

She crawled into bed first, and I joined her soon after. I didn't think and wrapped myself around her like always. She stiffened for a moment, and it made me angry.

"I'm not changing the way we sleep together, Emily." She went to push me off, but I held her down. "No." I hissed at the flash of hurt that stung me. She started to turn, and I let her so I could snag both wrists and lift them above her head while I hooked my leg over hers. "I said no." Her eyes filled, but I wouldn't let her push me away. "Stop!"

"Just because you explained what happened, Seth, doesn't mean it doesn't hurt like hell!" she shouted. I moved up to straddle her waist.

"I know it hurts. I feel it too!" She pushed her weight upward and used her arms to push me away, but I held them down harder. I bent down and covered her mouth with mine. She bit my lip and drew blood, but I kept kissing her until she finally gave in. Her heavy breasts and erect nipples told me she wanted it. My hand traveled down between her legs to find her soaking wet. I didn't waste any time as I slipped two fingers inside of her. I swallowed her gasp with my mouth as I commanded her with my body. I was in control here, whether she realized it or not. She was mine.

My fingers hooked, slid, and rubbed until she was almost there, than I pulled out and made her kick in frustration.

"Seth, please!" she cried.

I took her chin in my hand gently, but forced her to look at me. "That feeling," I rested just the tip of my finger at her opening, "right there." She moved her hips, desperately seeking some kind of friction. My head shook as I removed my hand. "Like every part of your body is screaming for release, your skin is so hot it burns from the inside out. That right there is how I feel when you're not with me."

"I didn't want to stay away," she choked out as tears ran down her flushed cheeks. I understood she was mad, but this was what I wanted. We needed to hash this out. "You think I wanted this? You kissed someone, either way you say it, Seth, your lips were on hers. Give me some time to process that!"

"I gave you a week," I snarled, not willing to budge. "You're not getting any more time, Emily. I need you here with me." I peeled off of her and headed for the bathroom. Until she could forgive me, I wasn't going to give her what she needed. Love could be a real bitch. I slammed the door behind me and went to sleep on the couch, where I spent a restless night.

Sunlight burned my tired eyes, and my back ached from the odd position I was in. A sound from the kitchen told me she was up. I pulled myself off the couch with a yawn and rubbed my morning scruff. I should shave, but I knew Emily liked it this way. I opened the door and stopped as a set of eyes ran down my bare chest to my morning woody.

"I looove my life." Pete grinned then went back to the stove. "Morning, pumpkin."

I muttered a curse under my breath and moved to the fridge. "When did you arrive?"

"Right around the time you started talking about flowers." Pete laughed. "Are you aware you talk in your sleep?"

"What I should be more aware about is you watching me sleep."

Pete batted me aside just as Emily always did and removed a carton of eggs. "Don't flatter yourself, Officer Connors. My man crush for you ended long ago."

I grinned before I chugged the orange juice from the carton. "I think I may be a little disappointed."

"That's what they all say." He winked and cracked an egg into the pan. "Every man wants a piece of this." He dragged his hand down his front and flicked his wrist at his hip. "Now, how is our love this morning? Judging from that," he pointed to my erection, "I'd say you didn't get any?"

I leaned back into the fridge with a sigh. "She doesn't believe it was nothing."

Pete set the spatula down and looked at me. His normal playfulness was gone. "It *was* nothing, right?"

"Yes," I gritted out. "She came on to me."

His lips twisted as he thought. "I believe you, but I can see why she's pissed. You don't trust her with anyone."

"I do trust her." I ran a hand through my hair. I felt annoyed that I needed to defend myself again. "I do, I just don't like how naive she is when it comes to men falling all over her."

"Scott showed interested in her—hell, he still does—but has she ever slept with him? Ever kissed him? Ever once made a pass at him? No." He rested his hand on his hip. "I get she's a fucking catch. Hell, I'm gay, and there's still a part of me that's attracted to her. But don't embarrass her in front of them when she's done nothing wrong."

"I'm not trying to embarrass her, Pete, but if you're trying to tell me to change the way I love her, that will never happen."

Pete flipped the eggs. "Trust me, Seth, no one in their right mind would want you to change your alpha ways. I wish all men were like you." He gave me a dramatic sigh. "I'm just warning you that she needs to see you trust her."

I poured myself a cup of coffee and stood next to

Pete as I stared out the window. Travis arrived home from somewhere.

"She likes him, you know," Pete said quietly. "She thinks he's harmless."

His tone made me look over at him. "And you?"

He shrugged. "If there was anyone in Emily's life who makes me uncomfortable, it would be that man. I can't decide if he's homophobic or he doesn't like how affectionate I am with Em."

"Have you talked to her about this?"

He gave me a look. "Not yet. She's quick to defend him since everyone else is always complaining about him. Maybe it's nothing."

"Maybe it's everything."

***

Avery

I hated it here. Grandmother had more evil running through her veins than Father did. She drank and smoked a lot of pot. To say she was violent was putting it politely. I now understood why I was home schooled. No one could ask questions about my bruises and cuts if they didn't see them. I was sixteen years old and still beaten by my seventy-some-year-old grandmother. It was pathetic, but she was all I had. What could I do?

She claimed it was the Lord commanding her to punish me for my mother's sins. I was not allowed to watch the television and only read supervised books. Little did she know after she passed out at night, I'd sneak outside and head to town to meet up with friends I'd made at church.

There was a club where my buddy's sister worked as a stripper. Needless to say, she was no longer welcome at the church, but she'd sneak us in and give us drinks just so she could spend time with him. Most of the strippers were cool. They let me touch their boobs, and one even gave me a handy. One had her eye on me. I thought she was about three years older, and her name was Misty. She had great tits, and the perkiest ass I'd ever seen. She was sexy in all the right ways, and she was working that night.

I checked one last time that Grandmother was asleep, then slipped out my bedroom window and shimmied down the drain pipe. I hit the ground and ran to the gate and slipped into the darkness.

As I ducked behind a bush, someone put a hand on my shoulder and my entire body went stiff.

"So this is what Grandmother has been teaching you?" I whirled around to find my eyes looking back at me. "What, no love for your big brother?"

"Holy shit," I hissed and nearly jumped into his arms. "Jims!"

He patted my back. "Shit, does the bitch even feed you?"

"Barely." I pulled back to take him in. "How did you find me? How are you here?"

He scanned the property. "All that can be answered on the way to my place. Go get your things."

I could hardly comprehend it. "We're leaving?"

He smirked. "You wanna stay with the Lord's bitch?"

I laughed. "Hell, no. Give me ten."

"Do you know where she hides her cash?"

I nodded and headed back into the house.

Jims was quiet on the way to his place. I asked some questions about Julia, but he had little to say. I assumed they'd parted ways once they were old enough. She was an awful person, so I didn't blame him.

I could see Jims was different than I remembered him. His mannerisms were odd, he seemed a little weird, but I didn't care. I was out of that hellhole.

"You smart?" he asked.

"Yeah, straight A's. I'm set to graduate in two weeks. Well, I was."

Jims let out a little noise in approval. "When we get you settled, I'll arrange for you to take the test you're going to need to graduate."

"Yeah, sure, okay."

He checked the time. "I got plans for you, Alexander. We have some things to set right. But first I need you to start filling out these." He reached to the back seat and handed me a large white envelope. I peek inside, confused.

"College?"

"Not just any college." He looked over at me as I dumped the paperwork on my lap. "The police academy."

"Hey," Riley called out as he knocked on the squad car window. "You wanna get back to work or sleep?"

My gun pressed into my hip and begged me to stick it in his mouth and pull the trigger. I could hide the body. We were in a back alleyway. The dumpster was full, so I could bury him well.

I unlocked the doors and let him in.

"Thanks for locking me out, dude," he muttered. I blinked a few times at him, then started the engine. It took a moment to wake up. "I'm starting to think I should ask for a transfer. You and I really aren't working out well, are we?"

I must not kill him, I must not kill him. The chant didn't help. I knew my eyes were dilated at the thought, and my heart started to rapidly pump blood through my veins. I got excited and I watched as his heartbeat drummed in the side of his neck. I could make that stop. I could hear the snap that made my body tingle. It was the control I needed. Control was everything.

He set his coffee down, and some splattered on the gearshift. He wiped it off, but there was still some residue left. Did he really think that was clean? *Disgusting.* I leaned over and opened the glove box to remove some Lysol wipes and cleaned the spill *properly.*

"OCD much?" he mumbled, and I flexed my hands. That was it, I needed him dead. I was about to reach for his neck when a call came through and stopped my thirst.

"Shit," Riley hissed as he responded to the station. "10-4, en route." He glanced at me and waved a hand. "Are we going, or do you need me to drive?"

"So close, dude, so close," fell from my mouth as I jammed the car in gear.

After work, I decided I needed a quick upper, so

I headed to The Brick. I needed to feel grounded before I hung out with them all for Johnnie's birthday.

"You look awful," she said with her tiny hands on her waist. I stopped when I got to the front desk and noticed her chest.

"Nice necklace," I muttered.

Her hand flew to the chain and lifted it briefly to her lips for a quick kiss. I pretended not to notice. I probably shouldn't have mentioned it.

She batted a tear away and plastered on her normal smile. "She's been waiting since you called fifteen minutes ago."

I started to walk away, but I stopped myself and remembered my manners. "It's really pretty." I pointed to the chain. "Looks good on you."

She half smiled, and I could see the loss in her face. "Yeah, well, you know," as her posture changed. "I can make anything look good."

I chuckled and waved over my shoulder, happy she was back to our normal sarcastic behavior.

CHAPTER FIVE

Emily

Three hours at the library proved to be a bad idea. Nothing sank in. I went over Professor Dean's assignment information three times and got zero done. Scott was oblivious to my mood. He wore his headphones in an attempt to reenact the scene he wrote, but he didn't have much success either.

So I opted out and decided a walk along my beach was a better idea. I just wanted to be alone so I could feel any way I wanted and not have to explain myself.

The sand was cold, and the nip in the air kept my mind in the loop. I knew Seth didn't have a cheating bone in his body, but the images from that day kept flickering in front of me. What was bothering me the most was he didn't pull away fast enough. Avery did get me out of there pretty quickly. Was that what was gnawing at me? Or was it that I didn't know Ronnie was a woman?

Something moved in the trees, and it caught my

attention. I squinted but couldn't see anything.

"Hey, neighbor," Travis called out with a wave. He was sweaty from his run, his chest glazed over with it. "I was wondering when I was going to see you next."

"Hey." I scanned the tree line. Okay, now I was just being paranoid. No matter how hard I tried, Jimmy Lasko still haunted me.

"You all right?"

My head snapped back to him. "Yes." I managed a smile. "Just been a day, that's all."

He nodded toward his house. "Come, I have the perfect remedy for that."

I didn't want to visit, but I didn't want to be rude either. I could probably use a little distraction.

"Sure." I followed him to the kitchen.

"Give me ten minutes to shower. Meanwhile, here you go." He handed me a glass of wine, then shot off down the hallway.

His house was quiet, with only the crash of the surf to break the silence. I scanned the photos on his wall, but stopped at one of him and a woman. They looked happy. Funny, I hadn't seen this woman around yet. I noticed she was in a few more, and she didn't look like a sister. I spotted an old family photo. His parents were spitting images of him, and again this woman showed up with him and his mother. I leaned in to get a closer look, and when I did, I saw a flash of red in the reflection. I jumped when I felt him behind me. His chest was slightly pressed into my back.

"Didn't mean to scare you." His voice was quiet. "I see you found my childhood friend."

I couldn't help but notice they looked more than friends, but I wasn't going to point that out. "She's very pretty."

"Yes, she was."

I felt uncomfortable with how close we were. "Was?" I turned to look at him as I moved back, only to hit the wall.

He nodded and leaned against the back of the chair. "Yes. Sadly, Sandy passed away a few years ago, cancer of the liver."

"I'm sorry, I had no idea. I didn't mean to intrude."

He pushed off the chair so he was directly in front of me. "You're not, Emily, I like having you here."

My phone vibrated in my pocket. I pulled it out quickly, happy for the distraction.

Seth: Are you at home?

Oh, great. I rubbed my head and wished I weren't here.

Seth: Please just answer me, baby.

"You don't have to answer him, you know." Travis eyed my phone. "You can just ignore him."

"I should go." I went to turn, but he reached for my arm. "Please don't leave."

"Travis—"

His face flashed with sympathy. "I hate seeing you hurt, Emily." He released his hold with his hands up. "Sorry, I'm just worried about you.

166

You're young and are heavily involved with a controlling man. Does he even love you?"

"Yes." I suddenly felt defensive.

"Why would he kiss another girl if he loved you?"

My eyes snapped to his. "How...?"

He sighed and looked a little guilty. "I went to check on you a while ago and heard Garrett and Seth talking about what happened. I left before they saw me."

Christ, who else knew? I wanted to crawl in a hole and die. I returned to the kitchen, grabbed my bag, and headed for the door.

"Em, wait," Travis called after me. He gently gripped my arm and tugged me back around to look at him. "Please don't leave." His face dropped. "It's lonely over here sometimes. Please just stay and have dinner with me."

I knew how he felt. It could get lonely here, so against my better judgement, I agreed. "I'll stay for thirty, but I really can't stay longer." I headed outside to the patio.

I called Seth's cell, but he didn't answer. I tried one more time, but it clicked to voicemail. I decided to send a text to Seth and Garrett.

Emily: *Going to be a little late, but I am coming.*

"Barbecue chicken all right?" Travis asked behind me with a huge grin.

***

Seth

The Triangle was packed, and Johnnie was more than buzzed, which was great because he'd been worried about his partner. We all were. Something wasn't right with him. Davis never just left and headed home before. He emailed and said he needed time off, but hadn't returned any of our calls, and that was very unusual for him. Sarge left a message for him, saying he had till the end of the week to contact the station before he started the process of sending someone to his parents' house to see what was up.

"Heads up," Garrett whispered over my shoulder and nodded at Ronnie, who stood inside the door. She spotted us and headed over.

"Hey, guys." She smiled. "Happy birthday, Johnnie." She gave him an awkward hug. Word had already spread about what happened between us, and the guys were pissed and on high alert as to what she was like. Most of us had someone, or families, so people like Ronnie were dangerous. No one wanted to be alone with her. Who knew what she'd pull? However, I could see Johnnie was interested in her. She was a pretty woman, but a little rough around the edges.

"Thanks, Ronnie." Johnnie beamed. "Have a seat and join us."

She glanced over at me and took the open seat—which was intended for Emily—and bumped my arm. "Hey, you."

I gave a curt nod and leaned back with a long sigh. This was not going to end well. I checked my phone and saw Em had called twice, and there was a text from thirty minutes ago. I wondered what was keeping her.

Seth: What are you doing?

Holding up my phone to Garrett, he checked his phone and showed me he got the same message. He texted her back to see if she would answer him.

Nothing.

"So," Campbell stood at the head of the table. "I have a timeshare in Palm Springs. Who wants to join me and Vanessa two weekends from now?"

Loud chatter and cheers erupted from around the table. It seemed some people were on board. A man with a Gibson started to sing Ed Sheeran's "Don't." I was lost in thought when a hand slipped around my arm. My head snapped over to Ronnie, who leaned over.

"Wanna get out of here?"

"Like I've said a hundred times, Ronnie, I'm not interested, and will never be interested."

Garrett suddenly straightened in his seat, and out of the corner of my eye, he gave me a look and cleared his throat. I looked up to find Emily by the door, wearing a shocked expression. I yanked my body free and cursed.

"Happy birthday, Johnnie." Emily forced a grin and kissed him on the cheek. "I'm sorry I'm late."

"You're here, and that's all that matters, McPhee. Here, take a seat." He looked over at Ronnie, then plastered a smile on before he looked back at her. "I'll grab you a chair."

"Let me get a drink, and I'll be right back." She patted his shoulder as she headed to the bar.

Ronnie started to laugh. "So, who's the blonde bimbo in the red bottom heels?"

The entire table went silent. "That woman is our family, Ronnie," Riggs explained with an icy chip to his tone. "She also happens to be Connors's girlfriend." Ronnie looked over at me, then the corners of her mouth turned up ever so slightly. Shit, she was gonna cause trouble.

I pushed my chair away from the table and went over to the bar where Emily waited for her drink. I leaned in behind her and trapped her with my arms the way I always did.

"Hi," I whispered and resisted the urge to kiss her shoulder. "Did class run long?"

"No." She thanked the bartender, then turned to face me. "I came home early, went for a walk along the beach, and ran into Travis. He invited me over for a drink."

I closed my eyes and tried to remember to be fair and not judge. "I see."

"I was going to leave earlier, but he asked me to stay because he gets lonely over there by himself. So I stayed thirty extra minutes then went home, changed, and came right here."

I could tell she was proving to me that she has nothing to hide. "Well, that was nice of you."

"Yeah." She sipped her drink. I hated how we were right now. I missed her and hated to feel so on edge with her. "So, that's Ronnie?" I nodded and kept my eyes locked with hers. I had nothing to hide either. "She's pretty."

"She's crazy," I shot back. "I don't trust her."

"That makes two of us," she muttered into her glass.

I reached for her waist and pulled her closer to me. I needed to touch her or I was going to burst. She rested her free hand on my chest. "Look at me, baby." I put my finger under her chin and slowly raised her face, but it was impossible to read. "I miss you." Her eyes closed as if my words hurt. "I hate this."

"It hurts when the person you love doesn't trust you, doesn't it?"

"Are you trying to punish me?"

"No," she shook her head. "I would never do that to you, Seth. It's just interesting that you're in my shoes for once."

I grabbed her hand and led her to the back of the bar. I pointed at my buddy, and he nodded at his office knowingly. Once inside, I pushed her up against the door, then my hands flew to either side of her head and locked her in.

"What is happening to us?" I whispered and kept my eyes on hers. "Whatever this is, it needs to stop." She suddenly stepped forward, grabbed my shirt, and pulled me down to her lips. I wanted to get lost in her, toss her over the desk, and remind her of all she'd missed out on since she'd left me. Instead, I pushed her gently off me, which was one of the hardest things I'd ever done, as emotions battled inside me. "Please, Em, we need to talk about this."

"Why?" She untied the rope that held her dress together and let it fall to her sides. I blinked at the new red and black lingerie that pushed her plump breasts upward. It was a beautiful sight...Oh hell, she had garters on. My tongue darted out and licked my dry lips. I felt hungry for her. She lowered my hand and placed it between her legs, and I nearly crumbled with the heat that poured off of her. She was wet, turned on, and ready to go. I couldn't help when my fingers twitched at her opening. Her lips quivered with anticipation as one finger slipped past her lace panties and between her soaked folds. Her eyes closed as her head flopped back against the door. I stepped closer and hooked her leg over my hip and ground my erection into her. Her hands were everywhere, but mostly at my belt, and she undid it in record time.

I let her have her moment but my head was in a fog. I needed to clear it. I didn't want to have sex until I knew we were okay. The only progress we'd made was that we were two horny adults who needed release *now!*

"Two," she demanded. She wanted more. I slipped three fingers in, only to hear her to moan louder. "Yes!" I couldn't take it anymore. I removed my fingers and held myself at her opening. "Seth!" she begged, nearly in tears.

"Do you believe me that nothing happened with Ronnie? That I never kissed her back?" She nearly bucked with frustration. "Answer me," I demanded.

"Yes!" She pushed on my shoulder, which made me let go and step back. "Yes, dammit, I believe you!" She ran her hands through her hair, then she pointed at me. "Do you trust me with Travis? And don't say you don't trust him, because if you truly did trust me, you'd know that nothing would happen, and if he did try anything, you have to trust that I'd tell you."

"I do, baby. I have an odd way of showing it, but I do."

"All right," she said quickly as she paced the room. "Now what?"

I grabbed her waist, picked her up, and sat her on the desk. I pushed between her legs and fisted her hair. "Now I take back what's mine." I snapped the fabric on her panties and thrust inward until I was fully in the woman I loved.

***

Avery

They'd been gone a while. I could see the door to the office from where I was. Ronnie eyed the door too. Little did she know that Seth was more than likely banging Emily on the owner's desk. Fuck! I'd need to step up my game. Obviously, they were stronger together than I thought.

The moment Emily stepped out of the office, she fixed the strap on her dress. That was a dead giveaway. Fuck me...I glanced at Ronnie, who saw it too. I leaned over so only she could hear.

"Welcome to how they work." I rolled my eyes. "They'll be at each other's throats by tomorrow. Besides, Emily is interested in someone else, and it's only a matter of time before he finds out."

She shook her head. "Wait, she's interested in someone else? Why don't you tell him?"

"Have you met Connors? He'll have to figure it out on his own. He suspects her neighbor, Travis." Her eyes lit up, and I could see the excitement spread through her. "Between you and me, that's why she was late tonight."

"How do you know this?"

I went for a look of secrecy and leaned back in my seat. "I'm over there a lot, and I see it. Travis is like a dog in heat just waiting for her to see the light and be with him."

Ronnie grinned just as the two returned. "I like a challenge," she murmured. I caught Campbell's look before he dived back into conversation with Johnnie. This made me a little nervous. Was I getting sloppy? I thought back and traced my steps perfectly. No, nothing was left untied. I sipped my drink and wondered what was going through Campbell's head.

Throughout the rest of the night, I observed Seth and Emily trying to catch up with where they were in their relationship. It was easy to see she hated Ronnie, and Seth wouldn't make eye contact with the woman, so I could still use her, but I thought I needed something bigger...

***

"Alex, I need you now! Come home...alone!" Jims's voice rang through my tired ears. These twelve hour shifts were long, and working nights was killing me. I waved goodbye to my partner, hopped in my car, and headed home to see what was wrong with Jims now. I was starting to realize

174

he may have some sort of mental disorder.

Our apartment was quiet, and all the lights were off but the one in his bedroom. "Jims," I called out as I scanned the room. "Jims, I'm here."

"My room," he called. I rounded the corner and froze on the spot. Jims was naked, fully erect, and hovered over a dead woman's body. "I got a little rough."

"Is she…?"

"Yeah, she's dead. I need you to help me get rid of her."

"What?"

He stood and pulled on his jeans and t-shirt. "This is one of the reasons you became a cop, Alex. Don't puss out on me now, boy." He started to wrap a blanket around the woman. I should have been freaked out, but I wasn't. In fact, I didn't really feel anything. I moved to help, and we carried her out of the apartment and put her into the trunk of my car. I didn't speak when we hit the road, and he directed me to a nearby landfill. We traveled a fair distance into the site, and finally he found a spot that satisfied him. We buried her in the trash. I removed my knife and carved the gang sign for the local Crips who patrol the next city over into her arm.

Jims took the knife; he knew I hated germs.

This happened several more times before I found out the main reason Jims got me to join the police force.

I woke with a start when the sound of thunder boomed all around me. I reached for the gun under my pillow and noticed the clock read five a.m. I sagged against my headboard. Since the bar last week, something had been on my mind and I wasn't sure what it was. I felt paranoid. I never felt paranoid. It was something to do with Campbell, the look he gave me. It was like he heard me with Ronnie. Heard me spreading rumors. I closed my eyes and tried to drift back to sleep.

"All right, that's fucking creepy." I laughed and held the clear mask to my face as I peered into the mirror. "So, you just went in and got them to make a mask that looks like your face?"

"Yeah." Jims shrugged and lay on my bed with a bottle of Jack between his legs. He loved his whiskey. "Thought you could fuck with some people for me. They won't be able to tell who you are, but they'll know I'm behind it. Fucked up, right?"

"A tad, yes." I tossed it back to him. "You want to tell me now, or make me wait some more?"

He shrugged again as he took a long sip, then he wiped his mouth along his arm. Jims had zero manners, and it drove me crazy.

"I found him."

The hair on the back of my neck stood at attention. I had been waiting for this moment for almost a year, since Jims found me. "You mean him, him?"

"Yeah." He tipped the bottle back with a grin. "We're moving to California, and you're joining the OPD."

"Holy shit."

***

Seth

The sun was bright, and I wasn't in the mood to deal with the little shits who decided to rob the market on Second Street. Garrett and I dispensed with them quickly, gave them a warning, and headed out to pick up a late lunch.

We parked at the top of the hill and dove into our sandwiches while we watched the city move about with its business. I loved that we enjoyed the quiet together. We both liked to let our minds wander. No awkwardness, just comfort.

"I had a date last night," Garrett said through a bite. "She's a hot little thing."

I grinned with a cheek full of turkey. I loved this side of Garrett. He seemed interested in someone for once. "Yeah, what did you do?"

"Went to dinner then a drive-in." He shrugged. "She's fun." I wrapped up my sandwich paper. "How's Em?"

I sighed. I knew we weren't that great. "All right, I guess."

"The bumps will smooth out soon, just weather the shit until it does." He chucked his water bottle into the bag and handed it to me so I could toss it in the trash can next to my window. "Are we still on for tonight's dinner? Philly is excited to meet everyone."

"Seven o'clock," I confirmed just as a call came through. Garrett rolled his eyes when we realized the two shits we just let go tried it again at the same store. "All right, I'm done with them."

An hour later the kids were in juvie and I was

wiped out. The ratty old chair groaned when I dropped my exhausted body onto its four rusty legs. "Ice!" Riggs chucked an ice pack at me as I let out a sigh. I just wanted this day to end. I held the ice to my shoulder where one of the kids decided to drive a pipe into it while the other attacked Garrett from behind. Needless to say, they were behind bars for a while. "What did the medic say?"

"Just bruising, nothing major."

Campbell made a show of looking all around, then stepped a little closer. He opened a file for me to see. "Look, I don't wanna start anything, but I have a bad feeling Avery may be pushing Ronnie at you."

I glanced up and saw we were mostly alone. "Why would you say that?"

Campbell rubbed his face. I could see this bothered him. He looked uncomfortable to even talk about it. "Just something I saw at the bar last week. I don't know, it was strange, call it a hunch. I'm just giving you a warning because I know you and the missus are going through a rough patch." He cleared his throat. "We all know the truth about Ronnie, but she's a crazy one, and I honestly don't think she's going to back off just yet."

Avery came up behind us, and Campbell snapped the empty file closed. "Just once I wish someone would come up with a better answer than 'it wasn't me,'" Avery complained, then looked at Campbell. "Well, see you guys later."

"The dude sneaks up like a snake," Campbell hissed as he rubbed his chest. "Christ! Anyway, I'll see you later. Just keep what I said in mind. "

"Yeah, thanks." I headed over to Garrett, who was still in the locker room.

"Everything all right?" He pulled a green t-shirt over his head. I shook my head to let him know I wouldn't talk about it here. "Tonight, then." I nodded and hurried to change.

***

Emily

"This is pretty amazing, Emily." Jake looked out my patio doors. "Don't get me wrong, I love Montana, but this is something else." Jake pointed to the water when Graham came out of the bathroom. "Private access to a beach!"

"Different from our mountains, that's for sure." Graham hugged him from behind. "You wanna live here?"

"Maybe." Jake sighed.

"You wouldn't be able to leave Savannah."

Jake shrugged with a grin. "Or Liv. Her pretty little eyes have me under her spell."

I grinned at Pete. I knew he felt the same way about me. If you had me, you got Pete. It was just how things were.

"How are Savannah and Cole doing?" I asked while I washed my hands.

"Really great. Though Cole has become even more protective of her now that she's picked up some shifts at the bar again. She just needs a little break, and work is good for her."

"You mean good for you." Graham laughed and

gave Jake a kiss on the cheek.

"I miss my bestie, so yes, I'm happy she's back. Whatever, she brings in amazing tips, and it draws the Blackstone boys out of the woods. They all come in and check on her."

Graham teased, "Yes, those Blackstone men are something else."

Jake laughed as he stepped outside. "I'm going to go feel the water before I get myself in trouble."

Graham ran to catch up. He took Jake's hand and gave it a little kiss as they made their way down to the beach.

"So, my love, tell me who killed Mr. Green in the library?" I bumped Pete out of my way as I reached for the seasoning. He jumped up on the counter and swung his legs. "Come on, spill it!"

I laughed. I found it funny Pete loved my criminal class. "So, Don is found on the side of the road. It looks as though he jumped from the roof of the office building, there's no sign of a struggle, but his glasses were still on." I waited to see if he followed.

"So he committed suicide?"

I shook my head as I sprinkled the salt over the steaks. "Wouldn't you take off your glasses before you jumped?"

He smiled when he saw my point. "Nicely played. So, who killed him?"

"Well," I minced the garlic clove, "after all the evidence was gathered, it turns out he made a bad business deal and lost his company millions."

"Oh, so it was his boss?"

"Can you pass me the green onions?" He did,

and I continued. "Well, actually, no. He was our first suspect, but it was almost too obvious." Pete leaned in and waited. "He had three missed calls from some woman, but not one from his wife. He had been missing for forty-eight hours, and when the police questioned her, she said they were having some problems. Anyway, turns out the dead guy was having an affair, and when his bad deal was realized, he went up to the roof to think. Meanwhile, his wife connected the dots and found out he was cheating, so she went to his work to confront him on it. She found him on the roof, because she knew he often went there, apparently. So after a heated discussion, she ended up pushing him off."

"Oh, so Mrs. Green pushed Mr. Green off the roof." He laughed. "Damn, I'm missing a great class." He suddenly stiffened, and I felt an immediate mood shift. "Your friend is here."

"Who?" I looked over and saw Travis on my patio.

Pete looked unhappy. I knew I wouldn't like what he was about to say. "He makes me nervous, love. I think he might be homophobic."

"Why?" I didn't see that in Travis.

"Just watch." He hopped off the counter.

"Knock, knock," Travis called from the open door. He smiled wide when he saw me, but I did notice it dropped a little when he took Pete in. "Hi, just wanted to see what you were up to today."

"Hey, I have some company coming over tonight. Beer?" He took the bottle and thanked me.

Pete wrapped his arms around my shoulders.

"I'm gonna go check on Jake and Graham." He kissed my cheek. "Be right back."

Huh, I did see something on Travis's face.

"What does Seth think about Pete being so close to you?"

I turned back to the counter and thought about how it never was an issue. "Pete has been in my life a lot longer than anyone. He's my best friend, my brother. I guess he's like an extension of me. When you're in my life, you get Pete too. Seth never has a problem with him, and neither has Garrett."

"Well, I guess it doesn't matter now anyway."

I whirled around to ask what he meant, but Seth walked in with Pete. "Look who I found."

Seth nodded at Travis, then smiled when he saw me. "Hey, baby." He kissed my lips and his hands held my waist. He did this when he'd had a bad day, almost like he needed me to ground him. I stepped back to look him over, but he seemed all right. "What can I do to help?"

"Here." I handed him a beer. "I got it."

He took a seat at across the table from Travis, who eyed him.

"So, Seth, where are you staying now?"

That's an odd question. I heard Seth's chair squeak as he leaned back. "I've been here. I never left."

"Emily?" Travis made me turn. "I saw you that day you were crying, you were packing up his boxes."

Seth turned to me and clearly wondered what he was talking about. I closed my eyes. I didn't need this right now.

"I wasn't moving Seth out that day, Travis."

He looked back at Seth. "But you said you were done, that he can have her. I thought—" He paused as he realized Seth was very much still a part of my life. "Then who?"

I glanced at Seth. "My mother." I sighed and felt the weight suck me down.

"Hello?" Garrett called from the living room. "Just step away from the barbecue and everything will be—" He stopped when he saw Travis at the table. *Oh Lord, here we go.* "Hey Travis, how are you?" My head snapped back as I tried to understand why he was being nice.

"Good, thanks." Travis stood. "Well, I'll let you get to your barbecue."

"You should stay." Seth stood as well. "We have plenty of food." I swore my mouth just hit the floor.

Travis looked at me with a smile. "Yeah, maybe I will. Thanks."

"Well, hello there, fresh meat." Pete bumped me aside when he spotted Philly behind Garrett. Philly's eyes scanned down Pete's front. "And who might you be?"

"Philly."

Pete circled him like a dog in heat. "Em, love, I'm not hungry for steak anymore."

Garrett punched Pete's arm. "Don't touch."

I laughed, and there was no way Garrett was going to stand in Pete's way of a sexy little thing like Philly. He might be smaller than his brother, but he had a smile that would make anyone, regardless of their sexual orientation, stop and take notice. "Come on, Garrett, the meat is waiting for your secret sauce."

Maddy showed up with Riggs, who offered to swing by and grab her on the way. She seemed to be comfortable with everyone. It was always sweet to watch Seth being so protective of her. He even made sure she ate everything on her plate.

After dinner was cleaned up, we sat around the table with outdoor heaters on full blast. Seth wrapped a blanket over me before he sat down and draped his arm around me.

Philly and Pete offered to do the dishes, and we could hear them laughing. It was nice that they were getting along. Maddy snuggled in her chair and sipped a mug of hot chocolate. She just seemed to be happy to be near her older brother. Her phone vibrated, and she quickly picked it up.

"Hi." Her voice was quiet before she glanced at me. Her top teeth bit her lip as though she was worried. "I'm not home, I'm at Emily's." Seth kissed my head to show me in his own way he was thinking about me.

"Everything all right?" Seth asked her.

Maddy gave a small nod, but it was clear it was not.

"So, Travis," Garrett turned the attention to him. "What's your story?"

Travis, who had remained pretty quiet, cleared his throat. "Don't really have one. I have twin nephews and am really close with my sister. My parents are still alive, but live away, and that's about it, really."

"No girlfriend? Ex-wife?"

"I have an ex-girlfriend, but that ended well."

Seth squeezed my shoulder. "Have you ever spent any time in Texas?"

Travis's face dropped, but he quickly recovered. "I visited there once. I'm not really a fan."

I shifted out of my blanket and let everyone at the table know I'd be right back. I went inside to refill my coffee when I heard a noise from inside my father's office. I carefully opened the door and had to cup my mouth with what was just burned into my eyes.

Philly had Pete bent over my father's desk, driving into him from behind. They were both butt naked, while Philly kept a hand on his waist and the other pressed Pete's front flat against the oak surface. I couldn't rip my eyes away from them. There was something about it...it was almost beautiful. Philly reached around and grabbed Pete's erection and gave it a few pumps. Suddenly Pete turned his head and grinned when he spotted me. He looked so happy. The man had no shame.

"Em?" Garrett whispered from the kitchen. My head whipped over to him, and I quickly stepped back and closed the door behind me. "What were you looking at?" I could feel my face was hot, and I had to press my lips together in fear I might laugh. "What?" He tried to reach behind me, but I shifted so I blocked the handle.

"Come help me with the drinks."

He studied my face, then looked back at Seth, who watched us too. "Em, move, please."

"I can't." I braced my arms on either side of the door frame.

His face twisted like he was trying to hide a

smile. "Please."

"Sorry."

"Last warning."

"I'm doing this for your own good, Garrett." He sighed and acted like he was going to give up. He started to move, but at the last moment he dropped down and lifted me up and over his shoulder. "Garrett!" I squeaked in a whisper.

He opened the door, and I felt every muscle in his body stiffen. I sneaked a peek and saw Philly on his knees with a mouthful of Pete, who was directing him with his hand.

Garrett backed out and closed the door behind him, then he started to pace the kitchen. The floor became a blur and my stomach started to turn. I tapped his back and broke him from his trance. "You think you could put me down and then continue to stew?"

"Oh, shoot." He placed my feet back on the ground and ran his hand through his hair. "Sorry."

"I tried to warn you," I whispered. He was pale as a ghost. "But in all fairness to Pete, that," I pointed over my shoulder, "takes two."

"That's not what's bothering me," he said, lost in thought again. "I see that Philly and I have a few more things in common." I blinked a few times trying to understand what he meant. "Not about the whole man on man thing, just something else."

"What?" I asked. I didn't care how nosy I was, I was curious.

He rolled his eyes. "Never mind." He swatted my arm. "Next time, you could say your brother is naked and screwing the biggest man whore you know."

"I'll remember that for next time." Garrett glared at me before he walked outside.

The doorbell rang, and it made me wonder who was not just walking right in. I hurried to the door.

"Hi." I looked over my shoulder and saw Seth come into the living room. "Is everything all right?" He stepped into the house, and that was when I saw his black eye and split lip.

"No, actually, I'm not."

"What the hell happened, Nicholas?" Seth hissed as he reached for his brother's chin to get a better look.

Nicholas glanced at me. "I think we need to talk, Seth. I think it's time you heard what's really going on."

***

Seth

I slipped my arm around Emily's waist and politely asked her to give us a moment alone. She kissed my jaw and told Nicholas to stay for a drink when we were done.

Nicholas wouldn't sit, he could only pace, his fists clenching and unclenching. I could see he was teeter-tottering with emotion.

"Okay, Nicky, tell me what's going on." I folded my arms and tried to act calm, but I was honestly scared as hell to hear this story.

"It's Dad." He let out a long, unsteady breath. "Someone is after him, and I don't think it's a client. He tried to get me to dig into some man who died a while ago, but I couldn't find anything. Then he asked me to deliver a letter, but I said no, no more, that I was done with whatever mess he had gotten himself into. It was his problem, not mine." He stopped to look at me, but he didn't have to say it. I knew.

"You don't say no to Jack." I rubbed my head. "What does he have on you, Nicky?"

"All the shit I buried for him in the past, he could sink me, ruin my career." He started to pace again, and he muttered under his breath.

"All right, look. Do you still have the letter?"

"No, I wouldn't even take it. The man has me scared of my own fingerprints."

I knew that feeling. "All right, is Dad leaving anytime soon? We need to get into his office to see what we can find."

"I've searched it," he said as he touched his split lip. "I thought he was out, but he came back early." I rubbed my face with twitchy fingers. I'd love more than anything to reciprocate the pain my father had brought to Nicholas. "There's nothing there." He stopped to stare at me. "Seth, I don't know what's going on, but whatever it is, it's bad, and it's getting worse."

"Shit…"

"All I can tell you is the letter was for a woman, ah…Tina Upton."

I convinced Nicholas to stay for drinks. I thought he needed to calm down before he went home, whereas I needed to take a moment for myself. I grabbed a beer and slipped out on the front porch.

Something was familiar about Nicholas's story. I took a seat on the stairs, stared up at the cloudy sky, and let my mind wander back.

I looked around the station and saw everyone was hard at work. I wondered what beat I'd get. I saw the sign for the new recruits and headed into the conference room where a bunch of other guys were waiting. I took note of people's names.

Two bigger guys who looked like they were partners nodded at me as I sat in front of them. Off to my left, I saw a newbie like me. His name tag read Davis, and his partner Johnnie was a dead ringer for John McCain.

"Hey, man." A guy a little shorter but just as thick offered his hand. "O'Brian."

"Connors." I pointed to the seat. "It's open."

"Thanks."

The sergeant came into the room and stood at the podium. He cleared his throat and took a quick sip of coffee from his stained mug. A little spilled, and he glanced down at his tie with a sigh like this hadn't been the best morning for him. His neck flexed to prove my theory right. He was pissed off about something.

"Morning, men." He checked his vibrating cell phone, then looked back to us. "We have a few new recruits today. Welcome." Davis, the guy across from me started to clap, but quickly stopped when he saw all of us were staring at him. "Okay, so O'Brian and Connors," the sergeant pointed over at us, "and Johnnie, the clapper is yours."

A low murmur filled the air as the sergeant took

a call, but before he left, he pointed to the whiteboard that showed us which routes we were assigned to.

We all headed outside to our squad cars. I tossed the keys at O'Brian, who seemed happy with this. I, personally, preferred to be able to scan people's faces. I didn't want to worry about driving. Besides, after what I heard about O'Brian's driving score, I felt pretty damn safe.

I was comfortable with O'Brian. He didn't feel the need to talk, he seemed alert, and we found we got hungry at the same time. What more could a man ask?

"You going to Johnnie's party Friday?" he asked me while I hungrily dove in to the world's best sandwich. "Yeah, all the guys are invited, I think. The guy looks just like John McCain." I laughed as I opened my water.

"That was my thought too." My phone vibrated, and I struggled while I balanced my lunch to pull it free. "Shit," I hissed. I didn't want to deal with this now.

O'Brian packed up his food up and started the car. "Where to?"

I was a private guy. I didn't like to share my feelings or my personal life with anyone, but after the text I had to head home, and O'Brian, thankfully, didn't ask any questions.

We weren't even two feet into my parents' entryway when my baby sister jumped into my arms in a full-out sob.

"Why is he sooo mean?" Her big blue eyes peeked out from between my arms. Tears streamed

down her sweet little cheeks. "Why can't me and Mommy come live with you?" I bent down and kissed her head. She had seen way too much for an eleven year old.

I glanced over at O'Brian, who seemed generally worried about my sister. I told my sister to go to her room, lock the door, and wait for me to come get her. She hurried upstairs. I headed into my father's office, where my brother Nicholas was in a chair in the corner, eyes locked on the floor.

Nicholas would be a part of the San Francisco Police Department in a year. I wasn't sure who wanted it more—him or our father. I knew our father hoped I'd be his puppet and do his dirty work, but when that didn't happen, he moved on to Nicholas. My brother didn't have much of a spine to start with, but now he didn't have any. He just jumped when Jack said so. This in turn had ruined our relationship.

"What the hell do you want, boy?" my father snapped at me. He was agitated, the ice in his glass rattled through the silence that filled the room. I headed over to Nicholas.

"You good?"

He slowly nodded. "Yup."

I shook my head and wondered how he could be such a sellout. I saw some pictures tossed about on his desk, along with a letter. Before I got a good look at anything, my father slammed his hand down to cover the face in the photo.

"Get out, boy!" he screamed, which made my sister gasp from the doorway. Why hadn't she stayed upstairs? "Get the hell out of here!" he

191

shouted. Garrett stepped into the room and wrapped an arm around my sister. He tucked her behind him as if to shield her. He glanced at me before he removed her from the room.

I turned to see my father pour himself another drink. He was a drunk, and he was the reason I chose to go into the police department, to try to do something good in life. I would not bend like my brother, no matter how hard he tried.

"Nicholas," I called over my shoulder, "give us a moment." To my surprise, he left.

Once the door shut, I moved to stand next to my father in front of the fireplace. The light flickered off his face, which seemed suitable because he did walk within the flames.

"I need you to take care of something, boy," he muttered, like it killed him to ask me. I nearly laughed. Like I'd ever help the devil. "Someone has something over me that could destroy everything."

"And what am I supposed to do, Jack?"

His eyes flicked over to mine, and I could see him for what he was—evil. "I need him taken care of. This won't only affect me, boy, it will hurt all of us."

Amazing. Just fucking amazing.

I removed my badge. "This," I held it up, "means more to me than you ever have." His eyes flinched. "This allows me to bring people like you down." I snapped it back into place and turned to look him straight in the eye. "Don't ever ask me for help again." He muttered something. I went to turn, but stopped. "If you really care about Mom and Maddy, you need to leave. Don't bring any of this on them."

"Too late," he hissed as I closed the door.

I wanted to punch the wall. My father was always pissing off his clients, and I was done hearing about it!

Garrett was in the kitchen with a plate full of food. Gretchen, our housekeeper, who under no circumstances would allow you to leave without eating, had obviously gotten to him. Maddy flew out from around the corner and wrapped her small arms around my waist.

"Thank you for coming, Seth."

I hugged her and reassured her I would always be there if she needed me, and that she could contact me anytime, ever. She hugged me again and went to look for Mother.

After some food, we headed back out. O'Brian didn't say a word for the rest of our shift. It wasn't until we pulled in and grabbed our bags from the trunk that I decided to say something.

"Hey, man, thanks for today. My father is—"

"An asshole." He shrugged. "Yeah, I have one too. My mother is one as well."

I smirked. "Well, in that case…"

He extended his hand and shook mine. "Partners watch each other's backs, and keep things private. I don't do gossip. I have just as fucked up family as you do, and my time will come." He shook his keys. "See you tomorrow."

Cold hands slipped into my shirt and pulled me from my thoughts as she kissed my neck. "I wondered where you went."

I took her icy hands in mine and kissed her fingers one by one. "I needed a minute."

"You all right?"

I pulled her around to sit on my lap. "Yeah, just need to figure out my father. Something is going on. He's in some kind of trouble."

She moved to straddle me, then took a sip of my beer before she gave me a soft kiss. "Can I help?" My hands slid up her thighs and around to her ass. God, this woman was perfect for me.

"You can do this." I grabbed her head and pulled her back to me. I swiped her mouth and took charge, needing to feel I had control over something. My father's situation rattled me to the core. I knew in my gut something bad was about to happen. She squeaked when I ground myself into her; she nearly panted with need. Christ she was sexy when she was turned on, her eyes wild and her nipples begging to be sucked.

"Wow," he said behind us, "sorry."

I cursed as Emily pulled back and fixed her shirt.

"Hey, Travis," she whispered and tried to regain her composure. She started to move off me, but I held her in place.

"I was just heading home and wanted to say thanks for the invite." He glanced at me. Well, it was actually a bit of a glare.

Emily smiled. "Of course, anytime."

He waved over his head as he walked back to the tree line. I watched Travis until he disappeared into the darkness.

Emily shoved my shoulder, but I grabbed her tightly as I stood and lifted her with me. "Now, where were we?"

"Nothing like a late night workout." Pete grinned from the doorway. *Shit!* Emily shook her head like she wanted him to shut up. "What?" Pete grinned at me. "All I need is a cig and stiff drink."

I looked over his shoulder and saw Philly fix his pants. "Such a man whore," I muttered and sat Emily on her feet. "I should go talk to Nicholas before he leaves. I'll see you in a minute." I tapped her ass before I left.

Pete licked a finger as I walked by. "Mmm...yummy." I heard him yelp behind me, and I was sure Emily punched him.

***

Avery

Flowers, check.
Panties, check.
Package, check.
Letter, check.

I continued through my list three times and made sure everything was in perfect order. The scratching noise from the patio door had me reaching for a steak knife. I had to talk myself down and remember why I still had the fucking mutt. I glanced at the calendar and saw I would only have him for a few more weeks, then he wouldn't be my fucking responsibility anymore. I dumped the shit-smelling food into a dish, slid it outside, and slammed the door in his face. Fuck, his eyes always freaked me out. You would have thought after all this time I'd be over them, but I wasn't. I wondered if they still haunted Emily's dreams. Oh, that thought spread a lovely warmth through me. I made one more quick call, then called it a night. I needed some sleep since, happily, tomorrow I had decided to step up my game a bit.

I showered, changed, washed my hands, and then slid into bed, delighted with the feel of the sheets that were tucked in tightly and the blanket neatly folded so it was snugged under the sheet flap at the top. I stared up at the ceiling, silently enjoying the shadows that bounced over it as the wind played outside. I closed my eyes and remembered.

"So this is it?" I looked over at Jims, who checked the address again.

"Yeah," he squinted into the sun, "24 Victoria Drive."

The house was huge and sat at the end of a lane. We watched as a little blonde girl chatted with an elderly lady who looked to be the housemaid. I could see the look on Jims's face, and I knew what he was thinking. He had money, lots and lots of money.

"But he's only here about ten times a year. His office is in San Fran." Jims pulled out a camera and snapped a few photos of the house and the little girl. "Let's go check out the city."

We drove around a bit and ended up at a nearby beach, where a group of women were in the middle of a yoga class. Jims pulled out a bottle of Jack and continued to drink while the women bent, flexed, and stretched for our enjoyment.

I felt him twitch when he spotted a sexy blonde in conversation with a brunette. Jims quickly held his camera to his right eye and started to snap photos of her.

We spent the next few hours in the chilly car, and Jims watched her every move. He couldn't seem to focus on anything else.

He made me follow her the next day while he made a pickup. I really wished he would lay off the blow. I turned the heat up and sipped my coffee while I watched her return to her car with her date. She seemed annoyed with him. The guy had the balls to grab her head and start kissing her. I didn't feel any compulsion to help, but it was fun to watch what happened. I knew I was probably missing the 'empathy' gene, but whatever. I leaned back in my seat and settled in and hoped for a good show.

Suddenly, her attacker was ripped off of her and thrown to the ground like he was weightless. I sat forward; this was getting interesting. Her rescuer was blond and looked huge as he shielded her with his body, and he made the other guy leave quickly. She didn't seem that scared and was okay about chatting with the blond guy. I could tell by her expression she was relieved, and she was smiling. He led her to his car…wait…I snatched up the camera and zoomed in on his face. "What the hell?"

My fingers felt around the seat for the phone and press redial.

"What?" Jims barked across the line. He hated it when I bothered him when he was high. He got pissed at my disapproving tone.

"She's with him."

"You mean she's with the cop? Are you sure?"

I snapped a few pictures. "Yeah, she's with him, Jack's son."

There was a moment of silence. "Well, well, well, this just got a bit more interesting for us, didn't it?"

The sun shone through my window and woke me instantly. I hurried to the shower, excited to see my plans fall into place and delighted to think how strange the world really was. I was almost giddy when I arrived at work. I saw Riley glance at me funny. I knew I was normally the quiet, aloof white man in the room, the man people should statistically fear, but they didn't. Because I had the ability to play many roles, I could play the 'loss of my partner' role almost perfectly. No one had any idea I was the one who ended his life. Sometimes I surprised myself at how talented I really was. Jims may have been bat shit crazy, but at the end, I controlled him too. Though I missed my brother dearly, I didn't miss cleaning up his mess. He got sloppy toward the end, and that was why they caught him. But I was a mastermind. I didn't make mistakes. I almost chuckled. Maybe I'd better watch myself, then.

I checked my phone and saw the flowers would arrive at the right time. Perfect. I tucked the last piece of my plan into a folder and tossed my jacket on top of it on the back seat as I saw Riley walking my way.

"Ready?" I beamed at Riley.

He nodded and sipped his coffee as he slid into the front seat. I knew he didn't like me, and that was fine. I'd rather not make nice with him either. I'd already placed him; he was nothing but my shield.

Our shift went by fast, and the sergeant asked us to swing by Davis's sister's place in Fullerton since he was MIA now for a few weeks. I nearly laughed out loud at the irony in this, but I pulled on my concerned cop face as we headed on over.

Knock, knock. My fist met with the cool steel. I waited with Riley, who snapped his gum like a fourth grader. Fuck me upright, I wanted to take that little shit out back and deal with him 'Old Yeller' style.

A tall woman opened the door. She looked confused. "Can I help you, officers?"

I gave my very best comforting smile and placed my hand on Riley's shoulder. "Hi, Gloria, I'm Officer Avery, this is my partner Officer Riley. We're with Orange PD and are friends of your brother's. He has been out of touch lately with the station. Ah, that is to say, he seems to have dropped off the face of the earth, actually. We're worried about him, so we were hoping to ask you a few questions."

She studied our badges, saying nothing, then waved us in.

I needed a goddamn drink after that conversation. Who would have thought the chatty Davis would have such a dull sister? If I was alone, I would have offed her myself.

"So, after a three hour conversation, we learned

nothing, but she doesn't see her brother all that much and she likes cats." Riley sighed and sagged into his seat.

I turned the corner and spotted a man smashing in a window on a BMW. Riley called it in as I switched on the lights. As predicted, the man took one look at us and bolted down the alley. I slammed the car in park and we both jumped out and split up to cut the guy off in the front.

Most officers' hearts sped up at this point. The chase, the hunt, it was always fun, but my adrenaline rush wasn't for the same reason. It was just the exercise, more practice than anything, really. The echo from my boots bounced off the brick walls and filled my ears, which made it hard to hear the guy's footsteps. I stopped and listened hard and heard a fence rattle. I ran toward the sound, only to find myself face to face with a dead end. The guy was running full speed on the other side of the nine-foot fence.

I cursed and thought there was no way I would climb that fence. I wasn't that invested. I made my way back to the squad car where I found Riley leaning against his door drinking a bottle of water.

"Good?" I asked with my best friendly face.

He glanced over at me and clicked his seatbelt. He was a moody bugger, so I ignored him and headed back to our beat.

I decided to shower at the station instead of The Brick. I didn't have much time, and I needed a quick fix before I enjoyed the shit storm tonight.

Footsteps caught my attention, and I looked around the corner and freed my towel from the hook. I headed out to the lockers where I heard someone moving about. I hid behind the scale and saw Campbell with a little tool trying to pick the lock on my locker. *What the hell?* He quickly went through my things, checked my phone and papers. I squinted as the anger rushed through me. Who did he think he was? He quickly closed the locker and left. *I see I may have to change some of my plans.*

My eyes were glued to the rearview mirror. I was certain I had seen Campbell's pickup truck. Though I was sure I lost him, I knew he couldn't be far. My hands rubbed along my jeans. I didn't like the paranoid feeling. I didn't enjoy the role of prey. I was the predator. After a mini pep talk with myself, I parked and headed to the front desk.

"You look happy." I grunted and felt a headache coming on.

She rolled her eyes but looked me up and down. "What's wrong with you?"

"It's been a day." A car door closed, and I moved back to the window. She leaned over the desk and pushed her breasts up. She knew she was pretty, but she should know it wouldn't work with me.

"Well, she's waiting." She shrugged and pretended not to be hurt by me not paying more attention to her.

I scanned the parking lot and saw no one. I gave a small wave as I headed inside.

***

"Alexander," she called out as I was about to

leave. My back stiffened, as I didn't like that name anymore. I turned to find her looking worried. "Avery," she corrected herself. "Someone came in asking questions about you."

"Tall, dark hair, big, beefy-looking guy?" She nodded as I came closer. I stopped in front of her and grabbed her chin. "Tell me everything."

"He just wanted to know what this place was and how long you normally stay."

"And?" My grip tightened.

Her eyes watered and her breathing picked up, but her eyes stayed locked with mine. "I said nothing, Avery." She stepped back and tore her face from my grip. Her hands were shaky as they smoothed her skirt. I sighed and realized I went too far. I started to move toward her, but she held up a hand. "Just go."

"Fuck." I couldn't deal with her right now, so I hurried outside. I had something bigger to deal with.

CHAPTER SIX

Emily

"You don't think that was a little extreme?" she barked at me from the other side of the world. I jammed the laundry into the drier and slammed the door so she would hear it. "Don't get angry with me, Emily Grace. What you did set me back a month!"

"Mother, your belongings are at Gary's office. If you have any problems, take it up with them. As for the buyer, you can tell her that my lawyer will be getting in contact with her, letting her know that it is being illegally sold, as I am the rightful owner. As for us, we're finished. I want nothing to do with you anymore. If you do decide to return, I will get a restraining order. If you try to communicate with me in any way, I will get a restraining order. In other words, Mother, goodbye." My finger trembled as I hit the end button.

I sank against the counter. To say I was exhausted was an understatement, but I promised myself no more Jenny. My nerves couldn't take it. I closed my eyes. I just needed a moment to clear my head. A knock at the door forced a string of curse words out of my mouth.

"Good evening, miss," the delivery man said, standing there with a bouquet of twelve red roses. He handed them to me and asked for my 'autograph' on the dotted line. I thanked him as I brought them into the kitchen. Nestled inside the flowers, I found a card. Just what I needed right now. I grinned like a fool. Seth had never bought me flowers before. He claimed he did when I stayed at Pete's, but I never saw them.

Last night was amazing.

I'm glad you changed your mind.

Ronnie

I hardly heard him when he walked into the kitchen. He spoke, but I wasn't listening. My eyes were glued to the table, trying to think of a way to ask without freaking out at him.

He cracked open a beer and leaned against the fridge as he eyed the flowers. "Who are those from?"

I pushed the anger down. "Well, they're not from you."

His bottle was tilted up when my words hit him, and he quickly rounded the table and plucked the card from my grasp. His expression was scary. It looked like he was going to explode as he grabbed the flowers and tossed them into the trash, vase and all. He hurried upstairs and left me to wonder exactly what I missed.

***

Avery

This was not how I had my night planned. As it was, I missed Emily getting her flowers. Though I knew she might not fall for it, it would still plant a seed and piss Seth off further. It really was all rather entertaining.

I waited for Campbell to leave the market and head home. I beat him there and slipped in through an open window on the second floor.

I cringed at the deer heads that were mounted on the walls. Camouflage vests hung on hooks, and a compound bow rested in the corner. I never saw the appeal in that sport. Where was the fun in killing animals when there were humans to be hunted? At least humans had a delicious reaction to fear.

I traveled down the stairs and into the small closet, where I waited for Campbell to appear. He did, with a load of groceries. He dropped them on the kitchen table, moved about, and tossed things in cabinets. He turned on the stove and started to prepare dinner.

The sound of the leather as it flexed over my knuckles, now that did make my adrenaline pump for all the right reasons. I loved this part. I pulled my mask down and pushed on the door so it made a tiny creak. I stepped into the light of the kitchen right behind him. He sensed something. I could see it in his shoulders.

"What do you want?" Campbell asked. His voice was brave, but I knew him too well. I pulled out a thin cord and wrapped it around my gloved knuckles in a flash, whipped it around his neck, and twisted hard. Campbell was a big man, but I was much stronger. I balanced my weight as he jumped around, fighting to break free. Campbell suddenly leaned back and tossed his weight into me, which sent me into the island. My grip loosened as he sprang to his feet, twisted, and kicked his foot into my ribs. I grabbed his ankle, bucked to the side, and kicked his knee, and he went down hard. *Shit!* I scrambled to get on top of him and managed to block a punch he sent my way, but another came fast, and I missed it. My ears rang and my vision blurred momentarily. My head bounced off the floor as he tried to catch his breath.

A scream from the doorway had me on my feet and my hand in my pocket for my knife. I slashed out at him.

"Campbell!" Vanessa shouted.

"Run! Call 911!" he screamed and covered his bloody neck. Her horrified expression moved to me, then she ran back upstairs. I was torn, but decided I should finish what I came here to do. I saw him stand and hold the wall for support, and his face suddenly dropped as he squinted at me. Then it clicked. My hand flew to the mask that had shifted from our struggle. I glanced at a framed photo and saw my reflection in the glass. My mouth was showing. *Fuck me.* I quickly fixed it, but I couldn't tell if he knew it was me or not. My attention was pulled to a loud click behind me. My eyes focused on his reflection, and I saw him pointing a shotgun in my direction.

Shit…

***

Seth

I was jolted awake by the wind as it scraped a branch against the window. Emily was tangled all around me, just the way I loved her to be. Mind you, it took a bit to convince her to come to bed with me after those fucking flowers were delivered. Of course Ronnie denied sending them, and the flower company said it was purchased with a prepaid gift card ordered from some random email address.

I rolled Emily on to her side and buried my nose into her neck. She stirred a little and wiggled her greedy hips. She was always interested, even when she was dead asleep. Just as my hand was about to dip between her legs, my phone started to vibrate.

Garrett: Get dressed! Be outside in ten. It's Campbell.

I didn't question it. If he sent me a text at three in the morning, it was something important. I kissed Emily one more time and headed for the shower.

"Baby," I whispered, and her eyes fluttered open. I heard the sound of Garrett's Jeep already pulling up, and I cursed. "I have to go. Something happened, but I'll call you when I'm on my way home."

She nodded and rolled over on her back. "Be safe."

"Always."

I met Garrett in the driveway and jumped into the front seat. He didn't say a word until we pulled onto the main road, which had a sheen from the morning dew. "Campbell was attacked in his home tonight. He's alive, but the attacker made a mess of his neck."

My head was in a spin. Who would want to hurt Campbell? "Does he have any idea who it was?"

Garrett looked at me funny before he focused back at the road. "He saw his mouth at one point, but…" He stopped as if he were deep in thought. "He was wearing a mask."

"Okay?"

"He said the mask looked just like Jimmy Lasko."

Everything inside me went still. That name made my skin burn.

The hospital was quiet. Riggs's head was in his hands, while Riley and Johnnie leaned against the wall. Detective Michaels was off to the side with Vanessa, and she looked as if she were in total shock. Poor thing.

I couldn't get a grip; the memories of Lasko made it hard for me to think. The last time I was in this situation was when Emily was found in the woods after Jimmy took her. My gut had been telling me something was wrong, and I hated the idea of Emily hearing about this.

Detective Michaels signaled for us to meet him over in the corner. "All right, guys, here's the description from both of them. 6'3", dark hair, dark eyes, built, and knew how to fight. They both agreed the mask looked just like Jimmy Lasko. I don't know why he was wearing it, but it was nuts, and I don't like where this may be leading. We're working on a sketch now, but it seems ludicrous since we know what Lasko looks like. Campbell was damn lucky his girlfriend distracted the perp long enough for Campbell to grab his gun, or we would be following a different protocol right now."

"How did the guy get away?" Garrett asked.

"Campbell got distracted for a split second, so the guy kicked him in the stomach and bolted."

Garrett gave me a look. I knew...I felt it too. I had to make sure she was safe.

I excused myself and headed outdoors. I needed a moment to think.

"Hello?" Her voice was sleepy. I closed my eyes and reminded myself she was safe and sound at home in our bed, perfectly fine. "Seth? What's wrong?"

"Nothing, baby." I fought the urge run home to her. "I just needed to hear your voice."

I heard the blankets muffle the phone and pictured her wiggling around to sit up. "You wanna tell me what's going on?"

Garrett tapped me on the shoulder and let me know we were allowed to go in and visit Campbell now.

"Campbell got hurt."

"Is he all right?"

A pounding throb started behind my eyes. "Yeah, someone attacked him in his home."

There was a long pause before she spoke again. "Do they have any idea who it was?"

A cab came flying up to the front doors. Avery jumped out and shoved a chunk of money at the driver. He looked tired as he spotted me.

"Is he all right? Can we see him now?" I nodded and pointed to the rest of the guys who waited their turn to see him. As Avery headed inside, he gave me a pat on the shoulder.

Clearing my throat, I continued. "Yeah, he's alive. The attacker tried to strangle him, but he managed to get free. Umm…" I stumbled to find the right approach. "Look, baby, Campbell said the attacker had a mask on that looked just like Lasko's face." I waited and let her process that. I could only imagine her face. "Are you all right?"

"Yes…" she whispered. "Seth…I think I saw that same masked man in your mother's haunted house."

I glanced back at the guys inside and wondered what the hell I should do. Squeezing my eyes shut, I decided to go with my gut. "Emily." I swallowed hard. "Please do something for me?"

"Okay."

"Go to my mom's." I waited for her to interrupt, to argue that I was paranoid. "Please just do this for me. Now."

"Okay," she repeated. She didn't argue for once, and I sagged with relief. "I'll pack a bag and head over in the next hour…well, as soon as I can get my things together."

Bending down, I closed my eyes. "Thank you, baby, thank you. Please don't waste too much time."

"Seth," she sniffed, "come home to your mom's tonight then, okay? I need you to do that for me."

I knew she was scared. I could hear it, and so was I. "Yeah, Em, don't worry, I plan to. Text me when you get there, all right?"

"Okay."

I tilted my head up to the sky and took a moment before I headed inside.

Campbell was as pale as I'd ever seen him. His neck was wrapped in white gauze, and he looked as though he was off in another world. I pulled up a chair after everyone had their turn. I asked Riley to take Vanessa to get something to eat, because it seemed like she needed a break. She looked even worse than the rest of us.

Campbell's fist came up slowly to bump mine. He started to speak, but stopped and went back to staring out the window. I squeezed his arm, knowing he just needed a few seconds. The clock on the wall ticked, making me remember I *had* been up since the wee hours of the morning.

"When I saw his face," he said quietly, his eyes still locked on the window, "the feeling that shot through me was *he's back*, Lasko was back." He stopped and closed his eyes. "I had the gun, and I knew what I had to do." His eyes opened and he looked directly at me. "I had a clear shot, everything inside told me to shoot, but then I saw his mask had moved and he looked so familiar. That one hesitation gave him the chance to run. He got away…damn it!" He nearly sobbed.

"It's not your fault, Campbell," I assured him. "You're both safe, you are all right, and that's what matters."

He shook his head rapidly. "You're not getting it." He cleared his throat. "I know him." His finger hit his chest hard. "I know the shit who attacked me. It will take some time to place who it is, but I know…I know him. When that time comes, I want answers, then I want to wrap a wire around *his* neck and twist as hard as I can."

"Knock, knock." Avery entered the room with a bottle of water. "I thought maybe you'd like some decent water instead of that." He pointed to Campbell's cup.

"Thanks." Campbell pushed the button to sit upright. Avery opened the water and replaced the old straw with a new one.

"So," Avery shoved his hands into his pockets as if this wasn't easy for him. "Do they have any idea?"

"No," I answered while Campbell struggled to get the water down his bruised throat.

Avery glanced out the window as he spoke. "What were you doing before you got home?"

Campbell started to chuckle, followed by a hoarse cough. "I was actually hunting you down."

"Me?" Avery spun around, and his eyes shifted over to me for a brief moment. "Why?"

"We've been trying to plan a party for your birthday for the past few weeks. But since you're so damn introverted, we had to dig when you weren't looking. Yesterday, I even broke into your locker and followed you for a bit, only to come up with nothing."

The look that passed over Avery's face confused me, but it was quickly replaced with concern.

Avery sank into a seat. "Sorry, dude, just plan something for when you're feeling better. Just the guys in my comfort zone."

"It's fine." Campbell shrugged. "I'm just glad I was home and the asshole came at me first."

I glanced at my phone and saw a text from Emily saying she made it to my mom's all right. I only hoped she stayed put.

***

Avery

Slamming the door behind me, I headed into the spare bedroom still full of unpacked boxes and took out the stress of the last twelve hours on my punching bag.

My sore knuckles fueled my mind, which was going in a loop with the realization that I fucked up big time. Soon my muscles burned and felt like jelly, and my legs developed a painful cramp from lack of water. Three more jabs and I fell backward and hit one of the stacks of boxes, knocking it on top of me.

"Shit!" I chucked a t-shirt off my chest, then stood and started throwing the stuff back in. I grabbed a stack of envelopes and was about to toss them when I saw *her* name. Tina Upton.

Jims was already halfway into the bottle when I arrived home from work. He had on a dirty t-shirt and shorts, and another re-run of Cops *played out in front of him. I locked the door in disgust, then froze as I heard something behind me. My stomach rolled when I took in what was in my chair.*

"What the fuck is that?" I hissed at Jims, pissed off with him as it seemed he had added another piece to our already fucked up scenario.

"A dog."

I waved my arms around. "And why is there a dog here?"

"Security."

Rolling my eyes, I moved toward the pit bull, who stared at me. "Down." I snapped my fingers, only to have the dog growl at me. "I said move, *mutt." Nothing. I went to grab his collar, but he took a snap at me.*

"Kum," Jims commanded, and the dog jumped off the chair and went to sit at his feet.

"The damn dog speaks German?"

"Yup." Jims nodded, his attention still on the TV.

"Rigghhtt." I groaned but tried to maintain my cool. I spotted a small box on the kitchen table. "What's that?"

Jims sighed his frustration with my interruptions. He slowly looked over at what I was referring to. "Oh, Aunt May sent them." He stumbled out of his seat and retrieved the box and set it on the couch beside him, then motioned for me to join him. "This is what it's all about, Alexander, why we are here. This is all the proof we need to go after that selfish motherfucker." He handed me the box and the last of his Jack Daniel's. "You're going to need this." He moved back to his chair.

I gingerly placed the bottle on the table and opened the lid on the box. I saw a stack of letters with my mother's name written in sloppy handwriting. "They're all addressed to Mom?"

"Yeah, look 'em over." He had already gotten sucked back into his show.

"But the address is different."

"Remember the old lady in the brown house?" I nodded. "They were sent there. Guess our prick of a father never found out." How odd they used written letters to communicate. Hello, you're leaving a paper trail.

I quickly opened the first one and stopped at the last sentence. "Wait for me, I'm coming, give me two weeks. Jack." I scanned for a date. August third. Holy hell!

I looked over at Jim and held up the letter. "One month before Mom died." Jims nodded. I knew he carried guilt with him. He loved our mother just as much as I did. Still broke my heart that Julia killed her, crazy bitch.

The pieces began to fall into place one by one as I read the letter. It was like it was playing out in front of me. I always knew there was another man in my mother's life, but this...I shook my head and tried to understand what had happened.

Jims got up and dug through the letters, then he handed me one and pointed to the date. "This was the last one that I know of. The address was different. Not sure why she sent it there, but it came back to her."

I read the date, which was exactly one week before my mother was killed. I clamped down on my inner lip as I realized what I was reading. It was a desperate plea for help.

Dear Jack,

I don't know what happened to you or where you are, but things are not all right at home. He knows, Jack, I know he does! He's made comments and threatened me. He's hitting me even more than normal. Jack, I'm scared. I need to get out, I need to get my kids out. I'm scared he's crazy and is going to kill all of us. He pointed his gun at my baby. He said that if he finds out I've been with someone else, he'll kill me and our kids.

Please, Jack, if you really love me like you say you do, PLEASE come and get me away from this man. I hate him.

Where have you gone? I need you!

Love, Tina

I felt the rage go through me as I tried like hell to blink the tears away. This was my mother pleading for help from the man she loved. Not only was she trying to find a way out for herself, but she wanted all of us safe with her.

"That was my reaction." Jims shoved the bottle

of Jack back in my hand. "Now take that rage and let's plan."

***

I couldn't sleep. My mind wouldn't stop, and my body burned with unexploded anger. I decided to head to The Brick. I needed to calm down. I called ahead as usual to get everything lined up so I didn't have to wait. I paid a lot to have a room there. I did not wait.

I checked the time. It was just past midnight when I hurried in with my bag.

"You look happy," I muttered as I walked past her excited face. She popped her gum and leaned over the counter. She watched me pull out an envelope full of cash. I handed it to her and waited for her to tuck it in her bag. "So, are you going to tell me what has you grinning like a fool?" I had no patience; the anger still burned. She shrugged her tiny shoulders and gave me a wink. I stopped and took a deep breath. "Please tell me it's not a guy."

She came around the counter and placed her cool hands on my shoulders. I hated people in my space, but with her I made an exception. In a lot of ways, I loved this girl. She leaned up and gave me a soft kiss on the cheek. I closed my eyes and tried to push my first memory of her out of my head.

"Go and enjoy yourself, Avery." She brushed my hair back off my forehead. I grabbed her hand and tugged her back to me. I wrapped my arms around her tiny frame and took a moment for myself. She didn't pull away. Instead, she held on tight and gave me what I needed.

"Okay," I whispered, "get back to work." I actually grinned as I backed away from her. Punching the code in, I stepped inside the dim hallway, but just before the door closed, I heard her saying hello to someone, and she sounded excited. I almost turned to go back and see whose ass I would have to kick later, when I saw Sherry undoing her robe from my doorway. She tossed me a riding crop, and I forget about everything else.

***

Seth

The house was quiet. Everyone was asleep, and Mom had left the kitchen light on with a note that said my dinner was in the fridge. I couldn't eat. I was mentally fried from helping Detective Michaels chase down dead-end leads. Grabbing a beer, I headed down the hallway to my father's office. The door was open, which was odd. He never left the house without the door locked.

I pushed the door open further, realizing the room was empty. I leaned back out the door and listened for anyone who might be around, but the house remained silent. I stepped inside and turned on the desk lamp, and my hands were actually sweating. I could feel his presence all around me.

"Did I leave this open?" someone said behind me. I whirled to find Gretchen in the doorway. She looked down at her basket of cleaning supplies. "Oh, would you look at that. I forgot the Pledge."

She came inside and set the bucket next to me on the desk. As she did, she glanced directly at me before she started to sort through the cleaners. "The cameras are turned off, everyone's asleep. If I were you, I'd check underneath the bottom drawer." She turned and gave me a little nod. "Just remember, my dear, a secret revealed often has pain following right behind it. That being said, I think it's time." She patted my hand before she walked out.

I wasn't sure what she knew, but I didn't waste any time. I sat in my father's red leather chair, opened the large bottom drawer, and took everything out carefully. I pulled the drawer out and could find nothing underneath, then I ran my finger around the edges. The tip of my finger found the tiny hole, I pulled upward, and sure enough, the floor of the drawer lifted. Inside was a large folder. I pulled it free and opened it. Fifty some-odd letters scattered in front of me.

It didn't take me long to see they were all from the same woman, Tina Upton. My hands were shaky as I lined up the letters by the date stamped on the top corner.

I settled in, sipped my beer, and read how some woman had fallen in love with my father.

By the sixth letter, I mindlessly dipped into my father's liquor cabinet. I needed something stronger to chase down the sickening gut rot. My father had not only cheated on my mother, but with some woman who was clearly in a bad situation.

"Seth?" I glanced up to find Emily leaning against the door frame in a short silk robe. Her hair tussled from sleep, she looked mighty sexy. "What are you doing? It's two thirty in the morning."

I placed the letter I was holding on the desk and leaned back in the chair to stretch my sore back. "Sorry, the day, and I guess the night, got away from me."

She moved over to my side, ran her fingers through my hair, and leaned in so she could study my face. "What's wrong, and why are you in the Devil's den?" I chuckled at how true her words were.

"It's a long story, but it was suggested I check his desk for a secret that could hurt some people." I pointed to the letters. "Seems my father was busy screwing some other woman while my mother was here raising me and Nick alone."

"What?" She grabbed one of the letters and scanned the words. Her hand flew to her mouth as her eyes flicked over to mine. "Do you have any idea who this Tina is?"

"No." I shook my foggy head.

"What are you going to do with this?"

"I don't know yet." I sighed.

She looked down at me with her sexy blue eyes. "What can I do to help?"

Slowly, I moved my hands to the back of her thighs and ran them over the cool silk. Her hands moved to my shoulders as I spread my legs to allow her to come closer. I rested my forehead against her stomach and wrapped my arms around her waist. She smelled so good, a mix of soap and her favorite lotion. I took her hips as I stood and rested her bottom on the side of the desk.

"Seth, here?" she hissed and looked around like

someone might walk in at any moment.

I had to admit the idea of sex on my father's desk seemed totally right just now. I hiked up her nightgown, knowing she would be deliciously naked underneath. She started to undo my belt as I threaded my fingers into her hair and tilted her back to look up at me. I stilled for a moment and burned my eyes into her. "When you're with me, you're with no one else but me." I felt a wave of emotion take over. I saw her blink a few times, but she nodded. She knew I needed her to understand this. "My love," I pleaded with her, my voice choking, "please don't ever hurt me like this will hurt Mother."

"Seth," she let go of my pants and pulled my lips to hers. "There's no one else I would want doing this," she moved my free hand to her breast and gave it a light squeeze, "or this." She moved my hand over her stomach, between her legs, and let my fingers brush over her wetness. "The feeling you give me whether you're inside me or just next to me is indescribable. I respect you and love you too much to ever go behind your back and sleep with someone else."

I grabbed her face as I slammed my lips to hers, and she met my intensity and quickly followed my lead. She dropped my pants just as I leaned her back and pushed up her nightgown. I kissed her neck, between her breasts, fingered one of her nipples, down along her smooth stomach that flexed under my touch. My lips brushed over her hip bone, making her squirm. Moving to her inner thigh, I licked and sucked here and there to get her nicely wound up before my tongue slipped between her seams. She cried out softly and arched her back. This had to be one of my favorite views, my head between her legs, looking up at her hands as she fondled her breasts, and I adored her little moans when I licked the length of her opening. Her taste was intoxicating. I loved to pleasure her that way, and could usually outlast her before she wanted something more.

"Seth," she moaned as her chest rose and fell, "please, I can barely take it."

I grinned and pushed in deeper. My fingers gripped her thighs as I buried my head further. She bucked and grabbed my hair, tugging hard. Fuck, this drove me crazy. I stood without warning, lined up, and sank deep into her tight velvet hole. She cried out, which fueled my lust even more. All that could be heard was the sound of our skin and Emily's little squeaks every time I hit her walls.

"You're mine, Emily," I grunted in between thrusts. "All mine to worship, to own, to love forever." I glanced down at her face, held her gaze as I felt her shoot off screaming into the night, filled to the max with me.

***

Emily

My head leaned heavily against the cold window as Seth drove me to school. He was lost in thought and was pretty quiet this morning. I was worried about him. He had always had a difficult relationship with his father—a bad one, in fact—but this was worse and affected them all.

"Hey, baby." Seth shook my leg to bring to me back.

"Oh." I felt exhausted. "Sorry, I didn't mean to fall asleep."

He grinned, which made his eyes light up. Lord, this man had a one-way path to my heart. "Here." He handed me a coffee. He must have stopped at a drive-thru. I took the wonderful smelling brew and granted him one hell of a kiss before I headed off to my class.

***

I glanced over at a very nervous Scott. I had waved at him to take over his part of the presentation, but he just shook his head.

Taking a step forward, I kept going, filling in for him. "So if the man was found here and given the evidence we have provided you with, who did it?"

Professor Dean squinted at the projector that showed the crime scene and the list of facts on the screen. I could see he was trying hard to piece the puzzle together. I saw the moment when he spotted the twist we had tossed in. He looked over at me and winked with a thumb up. I looked back at Scott, who was still stuck in his frozen state, his eyes glued to the floor. *Come on!*

"Emily, since you seem to have stumped the class, would you please explain who the murderer is?"

"If you look at the man's shoes," Scott broke in

as he finally moved up next to me, "that's where all the answers lie."

I grinned and let him take over. He needed the credit, and he was doing a good job now that he had come back to life.

"Great job, Emily." Professor Dean hurried to catch up with me in the lobby. "I think the fact that you stumped the class gets you a well-deserved A." He held the door open so I could walk into the library first. The place was dead, no one in sight. Even the cranky librarian who worked the floor wasn't at her desk. "I wanted to propose something to you. Can you spare a moment?"

"Sure." I shrugged and followed him to his office in the back of the library. He closed the door behind me and motioned for me to take a seat.

"Emily, I have to say, the work you did on this project was over and above, even more than I expected you were capable of."

"In all fairness, Scott helped too." I felt I needed to point this out.

He smiled and leaned back in his chair. "How have you been?"

My phone alerted me to a text, but I silenced it so as not to be rude. "I've been pretty good, thanks."

He shifted some paperwork around on his desk. "You know, I was a little worried about you last year." I nodded, not really sure what to say. "Are you working right now?" He shifted the subject.

"No."

"Okay," he leaned forward. "Would you be interested in becoming a TA for me?"

"Umm," I stumbled and wondered if now was the right time for that.

"You'll be working long hours." He pointed to a desk off in the corner. "That would be your spot. It will look good on a job application."

He had a point, but things were a little stressful in my life again. I really wanted to be there for Seth, and right now he needed me more than anything. Professor Dean's office phone rang, and he held up a finger while he answered it. I took that moment to check my text message.

Seth: How did the presentation go?

Emily: Got an A, and just got offered a TA position!

I fiddled with the phone, nervous of what he'd say.

Seth: Amazing! That's my girl.

My lips fought the grin that pulled my attention away from the fact that Professor Dean was behind me.

"Will your boyfriend be all right with you working long hours?"

"Yes, he'll understand."

I turned to see him pull a book off a shelf. "So is that a yes?"

"Yes." I forced down my excitement as I jumped to my feet and offered a hand to shake on it. He gave it an odd squeeze. My eyes moved up to his to

225

see his facial expression had softened.

"I think we'll work well together, Emily." He twisted a piece of my hair between two fingers. "You're a beautiful woman."

I stepped back and saw all the warning signs why this would be a bad idea. Disappointment followed as quickly as my excitement had built. His hand dropped, and I knew he realized he had crossed the line.

"Actually, Professor Dean, I don't think it would be a good fit for me. Thank you for the offer, though." I grabbed my bag and headed toward the door.

"Emily," he called out after me, "I'm really sorry."

I didn't stop, and my nails drove into my palms as the last ten minutes played in a loop in my head. Scott caught me at the coffee cart, but I didn't want to see anyone right now. I tried to flag down a cab while I sent a quick text to Seth.

Emily: Not feeling the best, heading home.

"Emily." I heard my name and saw Avery pull up next to the curb. He leaned over Riley, who looked irritated. I bet they wouldn't be partners for much longer. "Hey, how are you?"

I rubbed my head and wished I had my car. "I'm not feeling that great. I was just going home."

Avery's face dropped a little. "Umm, why don't we drop you off at Connors's mother's place? It's not far, and with that guy on the loose, you know Seth will feel a lot better if you're at his mom's."

Closing my eyes, I let out a long, deep breath to steady myself. "Yeah, all right, if you don't mind."

Riley opened the door and gave me a tight smile. I raised a questioning eyebrow, but he just shrugged. I wondered what was going on with him.

"Thanks, guys," I said as Riley helped me out of the back seat.

"Stay here," Riley whispered in a low voice. "Please don't go anywhere."

"Okay," I responded as I searched for my phone. I felt his hand touch my elbow. I looked up and saw he was worried. "What's going on?"

He glanced at Avery, who was watching us in the side mirror. "Feel better? I'll send Seth a text so he knows we dropped you off safely, and tell Martha I'll drop off my mother's samples later on this evening."

"Ah, yeah, cool," I replied, confused. I wasn't aware that Martha knew Riley's mother, but I didn't press it. "Thanks again, guys." I waved and headed up the stairs where Gretchen greeted me with a smile.

"Hello, dear." She wrapped a warm arm around me. "How does a cup of tea sound?"

"That sounds lovely, thank you, Gretchen."

Between Professor Dean, the fireplace, the homemade pumpkin soup, and the cozy blanket Gretchen gave me, it was only a matter of minutes before I drifted off to sleep.

"Are you fucking kidding me?" a voice shouted, and my eyes fluttered open. "I pay you a lot of money to find people, but you can't find her? How does this make you the best there is?" I recognized

Jack's angry voice. *Oh no, oh no, oh no.* I knew he didn't know I was there, and he would get angry if he saw me. "No," he shouted again, "I don't care how fucking much it takes, you need to find out who the hell is sending me these letters. Just fucking do it! And do it soon or you can say good-bye to your hefty new income!" My hand found my phone, and I sent a text to Gretchen to help me.

"Mr. Connors?" She quickly appeared and kept her eyes on him so she wouldn't give me away.

"What?" he snapped.

"Could you help me with the sink? Something seems to be wrong with the hot water."

"Do I look like the help?" He was such an asshole.

"No, sir, you don't, but if you want the kitchen to be clean as per your request, I need hot water."

"Fine, whatever!" His shoes clicked on the marble as he hurried out of the room. I jumped to my feet and made quick work of getting out of the living room and up the stairs to the safety of Seth's old bedroom.

***

Seth

I headed down the hallway to make a quick call and hated that Ronnie followed my every move. I rolled my eyes when she grinned at me. Three rings later, and Emily finally picked up.

"Hey." Her voice sounded a little off.

"Hi. Avery tells me you're at Mom's."

228

"Yes."

"I'm glad he was there to stop you from going home. It makes me feel better that you're safe."

"Umm…" I heard a door close. "When are you off tonight?"

I rolled my wrist to check my watch. "I should be off in an hour. What's wrong?"

"I just need to talk to you, and ah…" she lowered her voice, "your father's here."

My stomach sank. I didn't want her there with him. He was capable of so much damage. "I'll be there as soon as possible."

***

Something seemed off, although it always did when my father was home. I rounded the corner to find Gretchen waving at me. She pointed to his office. I hurried over and pushed the door open to find my father in conversation with Emily, sitting in chairs in front of his fireplace. He never moved his furniture, so this was new behavior for him.

"Oh, hooray, you're home," my father muttered and set his scotch down. I headed over, noting that Emily was stiff as a board. She gave me a nervous glance.

"Hey, baby," I offered her my hand and helped her stand. "Can I borrow you for a moment?" She squeezed my hand as if to say thanks.

"Thanks for the company." My father grinned at me. He knew it must have killed me knowing she was here with him alone.

"Sure, Jack." She followed me out the door.

The moment we were out of sight, I pulled her into my side and kissed her head before I checked her over. "He didn't do anything, Seth."

"What did he want, or what did he talk about?"

"Just about school and my mother." She cleared her throat, and I could tell he made her nervous.

"All right." I let out a breath. "Anything you want to tell me?" She wasn't forthcoming, and being familiar with Emily's ways, I decided to be patient, knowing she would come out with it in her own time. I tried a new tack. "You hungry?"

Emily wasn't hungry but sat with me while I ate a late dinner. I could tell something was bothering her, but I didn't know if she was withholding something Jack said, or if it was something else.

"So when do you start your new job?" I asked as I rinsed my dishes in the sink.

"I decided now isn't the time." She fiddled with her napkin.

"Not the right time? Emily that would be amazing on your resume. I think you should rethink your offer."

"It's not for me—"

"Em, you love that class."

"Honestly, Seth, just let it go." She rubbed her neck and I studied her movements. Then I knew.

"What did he do?"

She closed her eyes and I sat back down at the table. "Nothing, really, he just made me...uncomfortable." She looked up at me. "He played with a piece of my hair and told me I was pretty." She folded her arms. I was sure she was waiting for me to blow up. Instead, I leaned over and pulled her onto my lap.

"What did you do?"

"I told him I thought it was a bad idea for us to work together and left. I know he realized he went too far, but it doesn't matter."

I brushed her hair out of her face and gave her a quick kiss. "I'm sorry, baby, I know you really liked him as a professor."

"I did." She leaned her head on my shoulder. "It's pretty disappointing." Her head came up. "We should go upstairs and talk. I overheard something tonight you might be interested in.

There it was.

***

Avery

Things could not have worked better if I had held the strings myself. The professor was such an easy puppet to manipulate. His interest for Emily was always on the surface. With a shove in the right direction, he made his move, and now McPhee and Connors were at his mother's house via my suggestion. I wanted both of them out of the house so I could have free rein when the buyer came back. I would be the boyfriend who lived there.

I twisted on the blond wig and checked myself in the mirror. Besides the fact that I looked rather like one of the members of One Direction, it looked fairly good. I answered the door on the second knock.

"Hi, welcome to my home. My name is Seth

Connors." I grinned and let the couple in. "Please look around. I'll be in the kitchen if you need anything."

"Thank you." The guy extended his hand for a shake, while the woman's eyes were already scanning the room.

I headed into Mitch's office and faxed off Emily's 'signed' papers to her mother, along with a letter apologizing for *my* rudeness and saying *I* agreed the house should go.

The buyers seemed more than pleased with the deal we had made for the house. I told them I would be in touch with Dr. McPhee, and that everything should be completed shortly.

After they left, I helped myself to a beer and floated around the house. I felt like I was on top of the world right now. Just for a *touché,* I tucked a pair of Travis' boxers in with Seth's laundry. Oh, how I loved to fuck with my puppets. I sank into the couch and turned on the TV to some stupid sitcom. I looked around and felt like under different circumstances I could have been good friends with Seth and Emily. Maybe in my next life. I closed my eyes and smelled the house, or rather smelled my success.

"So that's him?" I asked as Jims got back into the car after he had scoped out the coffee shop.

"Yup, and that's his perfect little family." He pulled out a pack of smokes and started puffing away. It made my nostrils sting. "Three kids and a perfect little wife." He shook the pack at me.

"No." I made a face. "I wasn't aware that you

smoked either." I rolled my window down. I just needed some fresh air.

Jims jumped when a text came through on his phone. "Holy shit." He looked over at me, and his eyes were lit up. "I got her address."

I snatched the phone and scanned over the text. "Ahh." I was lost for words. We'd waited for this moment for a long time. "Should we?"

"Fuck yeah, let's do this!"

I slammed the car into drive and left the Connors family to continue their Sunday brunch.

We pulled up to the 'Norman Bates' looking motel in the heart of Englewood, and I could already smell the filth from where I was. Sirens and screams filled the air with the promise that this wasn't going to be a positive outcome.

"What's the number?" I asked as I scanned the numbers on the doors.

"Twenty-nine B." Jims dropped his cig on the ground, but didn't bother to snuff it out. I couldn't deal with it, so I stepped on it myself, only to have him snicker at me.

"Up there." I pointed and rushed up the stairs and down the long, stained balcony. Pulling my gun, I knocked on the door. Jims shook at my side, his fingers rubbing his nose. I knew he could feel that this place was ripe with cocaine; his addiction was getting worse.

I knocked again, but no answer. Taking a step back, I kicked in the door and rested my flashlight on top of my gun and stepped into the dark room that reeked of stale smoke.

It took only a moment for my eyes to adjust. I

scanned the room and heard a small sound from the far back corner. I had to breathe through my mouth because the mix of blood, semen, and rotten food made my stomach turn. The beam from my flashlight fell on a mound, and I squinted to take in her tiny, badly beaten body lying on an old, soiled mattress. I almost gagged. I turned back to Jims, who was kicking a box out of his way.

"Jims," I whispered before I turned back and dropped to my knees next to her. "Look, it must be her."

"Shit," he hissed and rushed to my side.

I held up a hand to show her I meant no harm. She hardly moved, but I saw her eyes open and look vaguely at me through strings of oily hair.

"Three hundred for the night," she offered in a sloppy voice, "but I don't do orgies, so your buddy will have to wait."

A sound outside woke me, and I grabbed my gun and looked around. "Jesus!" I cursed when I realized what I had done. Jumping to my feet, I listened carefully to see if I was alone. I ran to the top of the stairs. I pulled down the attic stairs, and just as I pulled them back up, I heard the front door open. That was way too close.

***

Seth

The next morning, we were awake early, so we decided to head home even before breakfast. I knew

Gretchen would be upset with us, but we both had the day off, and I needed to get a handle on what my next move was going to be.

"Coffee?" Emily asked as she removed her shoes.

"Sure." I headed upstairs, wanting a shower. "Just give me—" I stopped when I saw the attic string with the little red ball on the end swinging back and forth. I froze momentarily, listening, and then stepped into our room. I hesitated to tell Emily to leave the house. She didn't need any more fear right now. I quietly removed my spare gun from its hiding place, as my work Glock was in a locked box in my car. My thumb cocked it, but something sounded funny. The chamber was empty. *What the hell?* I twisted at a creak behind me, and I raised my gun and scanned around. Nothing.

Every hair on my body stood at attention. I checked each room carefully, avoiding all the squeaky parts of the wooden floor. I moved into the last spare room. Everything looked to be in order other than the wide open window. I knew better than to turn my back to the room to check outside, so instead I backed out and waited to see if anyone emerged from the closet. Nothing, no one was there, but I would bet my life that someone had been. I stopped outside the room and stared at the little red ball. With a hard tug, I pulled the stairs down and slowly climbed the old boards to the top.

I turned my flashlight on from my phone and scanned the attic. It was empty. With a sigh I headed back down, but something still didn't feel right.

"Em?" I called out and heard her moving about in the living room.

"Yes?"

"Come to the bottom of the stairs." I tried to keep my voice neutral when she came into view. "Can you set the alarm for me?"

"Sure." She set it, then looked back at me. "Why?"

"Just makes me feel better with all that's going on." She looked at me, but didn't argue, and went back to the kitchen.

Later, I found Emily in her father's office with a textbook in hand. I knew she had a lot of work to catch up on, so I kept busy with my own errands.

The day went by quickly, and I got a lot done outside. I wished I could say I felt better, but I couldn't seem to shake the feeling someone had been in the house. After an hour more, Emily brought me out a beer and told me she was close to being finished, then she'd start dinner.

Resting the shovel at my side, I sat and enjoyed my drink. I tuned into all that was around me. An odd noise caught my attention, and I scanned the perimeter while I reached for my gun and checked the forest line. Something moved in the bushes, and I focused in that direction. Whatever it was stopped, but the branches still moved slightly and it gave away its location. I checked everywhere but found nothing. It only proved my theory; something or someone was out there.

Every piece of my training came roaring back to me as I studied the shape in the woods. It had to be human. The black figure was much too large to be an animal.

"I know you're out there," I whispered. "I can smell you, feel you, hear your breath shooting out past your teeth as you narrow your sights on me. I might be your target, but right now you're prey and I'm the *fucking* predator."

The black figure sank backward into the darkness. I almost wondered if he wanted me to know he was there.

I locked the door behind me and reset the alarm. Making my way into the laundry room, I started a load, separating Emily's things from mine. I stopped when I come across a pair of male underwear...and they were *not* mine.

"Em?" I called. "Em?" I called again. I hoped to hell these were Pete's. She didn't come to the laundry room, so I poked my head out and found her on the phone. She glanced at me, and I could see she was crying. I mouthed 'what's wrong?' The look on her face told me I was in some kind of trouble. I waited for her to hang up before I asked again.

"So is that why you were late last night?" she whispered.

"What are you talking about?"

She tilted her head back to stop her watery eyes. "You don't like living here, do you?"

I shrugged and wondered where this was coming from. "There are things I don't like, one being we are surrounded by three quarters woods, and given our history, it doesn't make me feel overly easy, but I—"

"Fine!" she suddenly snapped. "But how could

you, Seth? This is my home. You had no right!" She came at me as sobs ripped from her throat, and her fists pounded my chest. "My only memories of my father are in the house!" I grabbed her hands and hauled them above her head so she couldn't move. "How could you do such a thing?" she repeated. I turned her around and wrapped my arms around her middle.

"Instead of yelling and hitting me," I hissed in her ear, "tell me what the hell I did."

She bucked under me but didn't break my hold. "You signed my house over to my mother, and now the paperwork is going through! She's selling my house!"

"What?" I let go, completely stunned by her news. "You think I'd do that to you?"

"The buyer said she met you, she described you to me, you were here. What else is there to say?"

"Look," I held her shoulders so she'd look at me, "I don't know what the hell is going on, but I'd never do that to you. You should know that. You are just reacting with emotion, so stop with this shit and think."

She wiggled out of my hold and rubbed her stomach. "I really don't know what to think anymore, Seth."

I tossed the random pair of underwear at her feet. "Yeah, I guess I could say the same."

She glanced down and back up at me. "Whose are those?"

Shaking my head, I went back into the laundry room. "Seeing that we're not trusting one another anymore, I'd say you have some explaining to do too."

"You think I slept with someone?" she huffed back at me. "Or maybe I just kissed them and 'pushed them away'?"

My blood boiled as I turned around to see her bloodshot eyes. "You know what, Em, I think we should just cool off a bit before one of us says something we'll regret."

"I'm going to Pete's," she tossed back.

My hands flexed at my sides. "Or you could stay and not run to Pete's whenever the going gets rough."

"We're way past rough, Seth." She picked up her keys. "I think we really need to decide if all of this is worth it."

"Stay," I whispered. "Let's figure out what's going on." I showed her a raw moment inside my heart. I needed her to see how much I *didn't* want to do this.

She shook her head, and I could see she needed more time. "I'm just going to go to the store. I'll grab us something for dinner."

With that, she left. I knew better than to force her to stay. She'd come back, and maybe she'd have calmed down a bit so we could get to the bottom of whatever she was talking about regarding her mother and the house.

The attic door was directly above me, and I yanked on the string and pulled down the stairs. Now that I was alone, I wanted a better look.

Slowly, with my gun drawn, I headed up into the dimly-lit attic. Once at the top of the stairs, I found the light switch, which revealed trunks, buckets of old vinyl records, a box marked 'wedding dress,' and other boxes that were labeled 'baby clothes' with various ages indicated neatly on each one. I pulled out my phone to use as a flashlight again and panned it around the further corners of the room. It wasn't until I moved a few boxes that I found a sleeping bag tucked into a corner. Squatting down, I examined the bag. Nearby, I found a crumpled wrapper for a Mars candy bar. I turned off the light and sat down where I thought someone would sit and listened, trying to get a sense of the person. It was eerie to think someone could be here and watching and listening to everything that went on in our private life. Or maybe this was nothing? Maybe this was Emily's. Perhaps she came up here to get away from her mother when she visited. My sense, however, was that this would explain everything I had been feeling lately.

The doorbell rang, startling me. I reached for my gun and headed back downstairs, but not before I noticed the attic window was wedged open. What really had my skin uncomfortable was the markings in the dust. Someone has recently been up here, and my guess would be it wasn't Emily.

"Oh, hey, Riley." I tried to shake my paranoia as I looked him over carefully. I stepped back to let him come inside. "How are you?"

"Umm, not so great, actually." His posture agreed with him. "I really need to talk to you about something. I planned to come by last night, but then this happened." He handed me a piece of paper. "I found this the other day, thought you might want to know." I scanned the page and felt like I just got punched in the stomach. At the bottom of the document was my name, signed in handwriting that wasn't mine. But it was familiar.

"Where?"

I sent a quick text to Emily to ask to her to come home right away. A moment later my phone vibrated.

Emily: Just ran into someone, be back in a few.

Seth: Who?

Em: Avery.

Shit!

Seth: Call when you get back into the car. It's important.

***

Avery

I tried listen to her words, but my mind drifted off as she continued to ramble on about apples, and I didn't give two shits about which fucking apple tasted better than the other.

"Any plans this afternoon?" She glanced in my direction. I wished she'd tell me what was wrong. I wanted to know if I'd missed something good.

"Nope." I tried not to smirk when I said my next line. "I was going to swing by Matthews's grave and leave these flowers." That sounded good. I had a nice little catch in my voice.

Her face softened and I thought I saw her eyes moisten. *I am good.* "That's so sweet, Avery. Look, feel free to come over tonight if you'd like…you know, if you don't want to be by yourself. Seth is grilling some chicken."

"I'd like that, thanks." I smiled, then headed down the opposite aisle, dumping the flowers in the trash on my way out of the store.

Starting the engine, I settled into the seat and watched the rain as it bounced off the windshield.

This wasn't the plan, not at all, but life sometimes threw you a bone. It was exciting having Connors moments away from discovering me. The thrill that came over me when I narrowly escaped being caught in the house, or our encounter outside near the patio, was stimulating. He never stopped surprising me. The man really was born to be a cop. I knew he knew I was there. We looked right at each other. He may have had great instincts, but I was smarter. This cat and mouse game was becoming entertaining, and I loved it.

I was pissed that I missed the fight over Travis's underwear. I was almost sure that was what had upset Emily. However, I hoped I didn't miss the phone call from Jenny about the house. After a quick visit to The Brick, I wanted to be back in time to see it all unravel.

My neck twitched as I sat and watched the men come and go from the sex house. I hated the way the clients looked at her like they all wanted a piece of her. I let my mind float back.

She hadn't said much since we brought her to our apartment over three weeks ago. She mostly just sat, usually on the opposite side of room, and nursed her favorite diet cola. She was a tiny thing, very thin, and her skin was an odd color, most likely from all the drugs that were hopefully leaving her system. She was young, so her body should bounce back fairly quickly.

I handed her a set of keys and a bag from Forever 21 and hoped something would fit her.

"What's this?" she asked cautiously as she peered into the bag. "I don't have any money for this, Avery. Harry took all of it."

The name Harry made me want to hunt that fucker down and slice him from dick to lip.

"I'm not looking for you to pay me for this, it's a gift. Besides, it's time for you to get back into the world you were meant to be in." She gave me a little grin before she pulled out the clothes. "Try them on and be ready in twenty minutes. I'm taking you to meet someone."

A short time later, we stood in front of the building. "It's not a job I want you to have, but it will do for now. I know the owner well, and you'll be looked after here." She read the letters on the sign.

"The Brick?"

"Yes, it's a gentlemen's club." Her head turned to me, her eyes suspicious, but I rested my hand on hers to reassure her. "No one will touch you here. They are very strict, and there are rules. This place is very upscale, and people pay a lot of money to remain anonymous." I saw her shoulders relax a *little. "I know it's scary, but trust me, you will be okay here. I wouldn't let anything happen to you." I opened the car door and headed over to help her step out.*

"Thanks." She leaned up and kissed me on the cheek. I knew she wasn't used to such good manners. I smiled and thought how strange it was to let someone touch me with affection. I followed her inside and observed her as she took in the exquisite décor. I could see she was impressed. She lost some of her nervousness.

My friend Jezz was there to meet us and hurried over to extend his hand to her. "Welcome to my home, my dear. I am Jezz Ebel." He looked her up and down and raised a perfectly manicured eyebrow. "Well, well, aren't you going to be a lovely little thing to have behind the desk." She glanced over at me briefly.

"I know I'll do a good job for you," she said with a smile. Touching my arm, she gave me a look, then she slipped her arm through his. "How about a tour, Jezz?" She smiled up at him. I almost laughed at her sudden change in demeanor, though I didn't really like the idea of her touching him.

I ran the strands of the leather whip through my fingers, glad that my cotton pants allowed my erection to grow to full length without discomfort. My chest was already sweaty with what had just gone down. She lay panting, her ass red as a cherry, stuck up in the air and waiting for my next command. I liked to watch this part very carefully. It could go one or two ways. Either she'd take my next hit and pass out, or she'd come. It was all about where the whip hit first. I palmed her ass, which made her moan. Sherry peeked over at me and licked her lips.

A slow smirk ran across my face as I pulled back and cracked the whip right on the inside of her leg. She fell screaming forward. I chucked the whip, took her hips, and sank in while she orgasmed all around me.

***

I felt better, more relaxed and focused about what I had decided to do when I pulled up to the house. O'Brian's car was already there. I popped the trunk and scooped up a case of beer and some chicken breasts and hurried up the stairs.

I could hear people in the kitchen, and I wasn't surprised that Johnnie was at the kitchen table.

"Avery." Garrett greeted me as I walked over to the fridge. "Did you hear about Davis?"

"No."

"He is officially pronounced missing and assumed dead." Garrett glanced over at Johnnie, who looked moments away from losing it.

I hid an eye roll by rubbing my face and looked at Johnnie. *Suck it up, you fucking vagina!* "I'm really sorry, Johnnie."

"Thanks, man." He jumped to his feet. "Fuck, I really need a drink."

I couldn't agree more. I jammed my box of beer into the fridge and headed out to the patio where the tension was building at a rapid rate. I was nearly giddy.

"Hey, everyone," Emily said in a quiet voice as she struggled in with three large bags.

Garrett helped and set them on the counter. "Are you just getting home now?"

She nodded. "Pete called. He needed my help, and I needed some space to think."

I was on the edge of my seat waiting for the ball to drop. "So you've been out since I saw you this morning?" She nodded, then froze when she saw Seth.

...and go!

"I was beginning to think you weren't coming home."

She shook her head and roughly placed the peanut butter into the cabinet. "It's not like it's my house for much longer."

Oh wait! Did Jenny already call? Fuck me!

"Don't blame people for things when you don't have proof, baby girl," Seth snapped back. His stance dominated the space over her. "You should know me better than that."

She put her hands on her hips. "Maybe I don't know you at all, Seth."

Garrett and Johnnie slowly got up from the table and headed outside. I followed but stayed close to the door so I could hear everything.

Emily handed Seth her cell phone. "You tell me why my mother would text me this if it wasn't true. I get she's a shitty mom, but she apparently has papers with my 'signature' on them granting her the deed to my house! You know how much I love this place. I've been fighting for it for years."

"Exactly, Em!" Seth shouted. "I know you, I know you love this place, that's why I never suggested we live somewhere else. To be honest, yes, I'd love to have the option to move, but *only* so we can get a place that's ours, not just yours."

Garrett bared his teeth. I could tell this was hard on him. He loved team Smiley. *I fucking hate that name.* I, on the other hand, hid the grin that was threatening to burst the seam of my mouth.

"Okay," she whispered. "Honestly, Seth, this is where I belong. I need to live here. I never thought it was a problem, but I can see now it is." She cupped her mouth to stop her cry. "I'm so tired of this."

I'm not!

"Me too," Seth sighed.

"I'm tired of fighting for something that just doesn't seem to work. Square peg, round hole." Her head dropped as mine raised. This was an epic moment. "I think we need to step back. Maybe take a breather. Take a break from us. Who knows, maybe we'll be happier apart."

"Wait," he grunted like he heard her wrong. "You want to break up?" She nodded and kept her eyes glued to the floor. "No."

"Not just your decision—"

"Clearly it's not!" Seth's jaw flexed. "Please, Emily, I love you."

"I know you do, Seth, and I love you, but I'm not sure it's enough anymore."

Seth looked over at all of us. "Does this breakup have anything to do with the guy's underwear I found this morning?"

The idea of making popcorn and pulling up a chair was tempting me.

"Are you fucking kidding me?" Emily grabbed her keys. "Look, I'm going to stay at Vanessa's tonight."

"Run," Seth flicked his hand toward the door, "like always."

Emily looked over at us. "I'm sorry, guys."

"Emily?" Travis said behind me. *Oh, hell yeah!* I wanted to rub my hands together in excitement. Travis was the fucking cherry to top of this night. I noticed Garrett shook his head at Seth. I hoped he told him to back off. "I heard some yelling, and I just wanted to check in on you."

"Thanks, Travis." Emily smiled. It was forced, but she meant well. *God, I love this.*

"Yes, your timing is great as always, Travis." Seth snickered.

Garrett moved to block his path. "Thanks for checking in, but we got this."

Travis glanced at me. I just shrugged and acted like normal.

"Emily, do you need help?" Travis stepped around Garrett's massive frame. Seth leaped forward and out the door.

"You think I would ever hurt her?" Seth yelled inches from his face. Truth be told, Seth could seriously hurt someone, but he wouldn't. He wasn't like me. However, when it came to Emily, who the hell knew. "Do you?"

"Seth!" Emily cried and grabbed his arm. "Please, Travis, go home. He would never hurt me. Thank you for checking in, but honestly, it would be best for you to go back home."

"Okay." He turned back to Seth. "Only looking out for her, that's all, man."

"And if I thought that was all it was, I'd be cool with it, but the fact that you've been flirting with my girlfriend since you moved in proves otherwise."

He shrugged at Seth, and I could see it coming. *Come on, say it, say it.*

"Have a good night, Em." He stepped back, and I wanted to yell at him. *You had your moment, Travis, and you didn't take it! You stupid shit, be a man!* "My door is unlocked if you need somewhere to go."

Good to know.

"Thanks." Her breath came out in a hurry. She still had a death grip on Seth, who looked down at her. Travis hurried back to the path.

Coward.

Emily turned back inside. "I should go." Seth rubbed his head and muttered something.

After Emily left, I sat back and had to listen to Garrett try and talk Seth into stopping her. Seth wouldn't go…interesting. *Oh hell, this is just perfect.*

"What happened with the house?" I asked and noticed Seth texted someone.

"My sister." He held up his phone. "Wants to come by." Poor perfect princess wanted to spend time with her brother. I was sure they would probably have a car service drop her off. "Umm," he rubbed his face again, "somehow Jenny forged Emily's signature and has a buyer for this house.

249

Problem is Emily thought it was me who tricked her into signing them."

"Oh, shit." *I don't give a shit.* "I wonder what happened."

Seth stood. "Do you guys mind if we do this another night?"

Yes, I'd rather like to bask in this moment alone.

CHAPTER SEVEN

Emily

Campbell had a nice house. You sure could tell he loved to hunt...animals stared at me from the walls, and it was creepy. I thought the deer just hissed my name.

Vanessa showed me to the guest room, where I placed my overnight bag on the floor then sank onto the bed, exhausted.

"How's Campbell holding up?" I asked.

She gave me a worried shrug as she sat down next to me. "He's like Seth, so I don't know. Um, he's worried about me being here on my own." I nodded, understanding that feeling all too well. "I'm just glad he's okay."

"Me too." I gave her a long hug. I really loved Vanessa. She was always so caring. I was happy to be able to return the comfort she had given me in the past.

"I'll open some wine." She pulled back and stood.

"Okay." I watched as she closed the door behind her.

I pulled out my phone, sent a text, closed my eyes, and wished so much that today didn't happen. I was so confused. My mind drifted off.

"Come on, come out with us," Erin begged from my kitchen counter. "Please don't leave me alone with Pete. I can't control him like you can." I rolled my eyes at her but knew she was right. He needed a very short rope. "You've been moping around here for weeks, and you won't tell me why. At least come out with me. You owe me." I never wanted to tell anyone about kissing Seth. It hurt way too much.

"For what?"

Her hands shot to her hips. "Seriously?" Her eyebrow raised. "You left me alone at The Goose with Ronnie the hot bartender last month. My wingman just up and left."

"First of all, you needed that push because you wouldn't have ever said three words to him if I didn't up and leave. Second, if I didn't free up that chair, you would have never met Alex. So really, you owe me."

She thought for a moment, then waved her arms around. "Okay, well, whatever!" She hopped off the counter. "I'm calling Pete to come over here. I can see I'll need backup with you."

Two hours later I was in a booth, drink in hand, while the beat from Thrift Shop *vibrated through my rib cage. Pete was loudly singing all the words, while Erin grinned at her phone. I was sure Alex was responsible for her annoying glow.*

"I like." Pete pointed to my little tan dress he had picked out for me. He said the color complimented my skin tone. I winked as I downed my martini. I was a partier as a rule, that was no secret, but I'd been feeling off...since that night.

I ordered another drink and felt more relaxed. Erin whispered something in Pete's ear, and before I knew it, I was pulled onto the dance floor. Pete danced behind me as the song changed to Bruno Mars's Gorilla. *The dance floor wasn't busy. It was just us and five others. I sensed someone watching me and glanced over at a man approaching me. He was tall, in a blue polo shirt and jeans, and there was a bit of a limp to his step. He nodded at Pete, who leaned over my shoulder to see if I was all right with it. With a pretend grin, I took my new friend's outstretched hand and let him spin me around. Then his hand landed on my hip and he started to grind into my back. I looked over and saw Pete dancing with some other poor girl, who would be disappointed when he wouldn't take her home.*

"I'm Tim," the guy grinding me from behind shouted in my ear. I shouted back with mine. For some reason, he took that as an invitation to let his hands wander. I played it off, as I was all right with it until I looked across and locked eyes with Seth standing a few feet away at a table with some other guys.

He stared at me. He wasn't shy about the fact that I caught him. He just watched me, and me alone. As much as I'd missed him these past few weeks, I was pissed that he left me at the door after the hottest fucking kiss I'd ever had, never to be heard from again. So I decided to play a little, make him feel as I did. Used and hurt.

My arms reached back over my head, where I slid my hands around Tim's neck and added an extra roll to my hips. Tim's hands ran down my sides, and I leaned my head back, closed my eyes, and moved to the beat. When I opened them again, Seth was gone. I felt disappointed. I looked over and saw Pete solo dancing, singing the words loudly just for himself. Pete was incredibly comfortable in his skin, and it was contagious.

"I'm going to get a drink," I shouted as the song ended. Tim snatched my hand and pulled me to the bar, then he pushed me in front of him.

"So, Emily, what is it you do?" His finger dragged from my collarbone to the top of my breasts.

"I'm a student at Orange." I glanced over my shoulder and saw Erin heading for the restrooms. "Tim, would you mind ordering me a dirty martini?"

I headed to the restroom, but somehow I missed Erin. I fixed my makeup and popped a mint. I beat the long line that formed while I was in there. The hallway was dark and narrow, with little red lights to guide customers back to the club. Suddenly, Seth blocked my path. I stopped when he took two quick steps my way.

He shoved his hands in his pockets and leaned against the wall. He looked good in his red t-shirt and jeans. His hair was tousled in a sexy-messy way.

"Hey," I said quickly as I went to walk by.

"Hey, can we talk?" He put a hand out to stop me.

"Sure." Oh, this was not good. Why did it have to be so dark and cramped there? I resisted the urge to run my fingers along his arm muscle.

"I'm sorry I kissed you like that and left. I just—"

"It was a mistake, I know, it's okay."

Lies.

His head shot up. "No, no, it wasn't a mistake. It was…" He shut his eyes briefly. "Can we start over?" His hands flew in the air when he realized how stupid that sounded. We were too sexually attracted to each other. "Not like that, but can we just try this out as friends?" Friends? That stung, but it also meant I'd see him again. I thought I would be willing to try that. "Please?"

"Why?" I needed to know.

"Because I need to be around you. Call me crazy, but there's something about you that makes me feel right inside."

"But you don't know me that well."

"I know, that's why it's crazy." He laughed, and his whole face lit up. I saw a carefree fun-loving, incredibly sexy man who appealed to me in many ways.

"Okay, Seth Connors." I gave a shy smile. "Let's give this a shot."

He leaned in to give me a kiss on the cheek when I heard my name. I went to turn, and caught his lips with mine in the process. I leaned back and looked up at his expression. It was pure hunger.

Oh shit.

My back started to feel hot, like someone turned on the heat. I felt around the bed, but it was empty, and the sun shone in from a different direction. Wait, where was I? For a brief moment, I slipped into panic mode, but then I heard Vanessa downstairs and it all came back to me. *So much for our girls' night.*

After a hot shower and some fresh clothes, I headed downstairs to find Vanessa and Campbell at the kitchen table. I couldn't help but stare at the bandage around his neck, and I could only imagine what the scar would look like.

"Hey, Em, I'll get you some coffee." Vanessa headed over to the coffee maker.

Campbell held up his cell phone and showed me five calls from Seth. He made a strange face, then I heard the front door open.

"Hello?" Seth called out, and Campbell mouthed 'sorry' to me.

"Kitchen," Vanessa called out while she handed me my coffee. "I don't care what's going on, you just need to talk. You have too much history to leave it like this."

"Hey." Seth came in looking like he hadn't slept at all.

"You look like shit," Campbell muttered in his strained voice.

"Yeah, well, I had a lot to think about." He glanced at me "Em, walk with me?"

"I have some things I need to do—"

Seth blocked the doorway. "Fine, but first we're going to talk."

I slipped off my shoes and left them by the

wooden stairs. Seth did the same, and we walked down the beach until we were out of sight of the house.

"Do you think he bought it?"

"I do." He nodded. "Johnnie doesn't need this right now, but he'll understand later. You can deal with Pete."

"I hate to lie to our friends."

"Me too, but this is our mess, and if we can protect them right now, then that's what we have to do. The less who are involved, the better. Garrett and Riley are the only ones who can know, okay?"

"I'm sorry I didn't believe you about the house."

Seth ran his hand along the back of his neck. "Avery is playing a dangerous game here. I'm just glad Riley found those papers for proof. Or I may have lost you for good."

"No, Seth, I just reacted with my usual emotion, not thinking. I would have figured it out. I just don't get it; why is Avery doing this? What are we missing?"

"I don't know." Seth checked his phone. "But we need to be very careful right now."

"I want to go home." I felt like I needed to be in my own space to re-group.

"I don't know, Em, I—"

I turned to face him head on. "Seth, you can't keep me from my home, you can't—"

"Yes, I can, and I will. I made a promise to your father that I would protect you to the end. I will keep my word."

"Wait." I held up my hand. "You visited my father's grave?"

257

"Yes."

"Why?"

"Why not?"

"I just didn't know. I didn't think you would do that."

"He is important to you, therefore he is to me. I wanted him to know that someone loved you, and will protect you no matter what the cost is."

I lowered my head to shield my emotion. Seth moved closer, and both hands moved my hair out of my face, and his thumbs brought my face up to look at his.

"We have a sloppy history, but it's our history. We're young and have a lifetime ahead of us, and if I thought it was the perfect moment, I would get down one knee and propose the hell of you." He stopped to read my face, but I was so stunned by his confession that I just stared up at him. "But now isn't the time. We need to get through this first. I need to make sure you are safe so when I ask you to marry me, we can move forward and not get sucked backward in this bizarre hell."

I nodded and closed my eyes to think about how wonderful that would be.

"Do you believe me?"

I took a moment to push Ronnie, the fake house sale, the flowers, and everything negative out of my head. Seth must have thought I was questioning him, because when I opened my eyes, he was below me on one knee.

"This has been a crazy rough go for us with Jimmy Lasko and now Avery. Why he's messing with us now, I don't know, but I'll find out. I know everything seems to be against us being together, but damn it, Emily, I can't breathe without you in my life. I don't know how to live without you. I don't have a romantic line to use to sweep you off your feet. I'm just madly in love with my best friend. I would take a bullet for you. I'm not perfect, I know I'm protective, stubborn, but it's because I love you. I have a ring, but not on me." *What? When?* "But, Emily McPhee, will you—"

"Don't." I stopped his rant. I couldn't do this right now. "Please, not here, not now." I had a sudden rush of emotion. He opened a whole new level of mixed feelings.

He rose to his feet, grabbed my hand, and led me into the cover of the forest. Thankfully, it was mostly pine needles under our bare feet. He stopped me in front of a thick tree trunk, where he guided me until my back hit the bark.

"Am I alone with how I feel?" His face scrunched, and I could see he was concerned.

"No, Seth, no!" I nearly cried. "I chased you for two years. I think I wanted you before you wanted me. It's just this never-ending story with death, pain, kidnapping, basements, and I just feel like it's all sitting right here on my chest." My mind started to fire off all my unfinished business I had with Seth. "You kissed me, like a reach for the stars over the moon kinda thing, then you left me, and I think part of me flickered out that day. You just left me to wonder was it a girl calling, or was it a better offer—"

"My father," he interrupted. "It was my father. He threatened to mess with you if I didn't keep my distance. That day I left you, it was because my father came home with a visitor who harassed Mom and Maddy." His body pressed into mine and his head hovered over me. "I regretted leaving you there, but despite what my father said, I couldn't stay away. I thought about that kiss every single time I was around you. Every time you'd look at me, I got excited. Then you moved on, and started talking to other men, and I couldn't take it. I'm selfish, I know, but I had to have you. Then I gave in, and I haven't stopped falling ever since."

"Yes," I said quietly.

"Huh?"

"I will say yes when you ask me, Seth. Now isn't the time." I cupped my hand along his cheek. "I will marry you. I would have married you the day I met you. We have a lot to get through, we have to pull off one hell of an act, but if you love me even half as much as I do you, then my answer is yes."

He grinned and caught my lips with his. I leapt into his arms and wrapped my legs around his waist.

"Okay, but first we need to break up," I joked, but it was true. If we were going to pull this off, we couldn't be together. Avery needed to think we were done.

Seth hiked up my dress. "I need to say goodbye first."

"You read my mind."

***

Avery

The high I had was slowly fading out. I needed to know they were broken up for good.

Avery: You good?

I waited as I pulled my keys free from my pocket. I balanced my takeout food on my thigh and pressed the key into the hole.

Seth: Yeah. Em and I are done, probably for the best anyway.

Perfect.

Avery: You two will be fine, you always are.

Seth: Not this time. Travis can have her. Not worth my time anymore.

Oh, ouch. I grinned at his crass words.

Avery: Crazy to hear, dude, but you're a free man. Live it up.

Seth: That's the plan.

The adrenaline shot through me as I opened the door, but I stopped dead in my tracks. The TV flickered with a drama, and an open beer had a water ring along the bottom. *Who the fuck was in my house?* Whoever it was had been here for a while. I slowly drew my gun and closed the door behind me. The living room was clear, the kitchen was clear, then I heard a strange clicking noise. I turned and came face to face with that goddamn dog. Suddenly, she came into the kitchen in one of my t-shirts.

"Hey." She grinned as Adler trotted over to her legs and brushed lovingly against them. "Sorry, but I won't give a blow job to my landlord, so I had nowhere else to go, and, well…you gave me a key."

Fuck me. I wiped a bead of sweat off the top of my lip. "I could have shot you."

"But you didn't." She shrugged and rubbed Adler's ear. The dog had the balls to roll over and get a belly scratch. I had *never* seen him act so much like a pet before. "Are you hungry?"

I sighed and went back into the living room to retrieve my Chinese takeout. I wasn't sure how I felt about having her in my house alone. Not to mention the fact that she let Adler inside. I quivered at the thought of him on my bed. I nearly gagged.

"Beer?" she asked as she opened herself another one. I nodded and tried not to think of the water ring embedded into my wooden table.

"You can have the spare room," I said as I made myself a plate. Everything was separated so that nothing touched, and the sweet and sour sauce was drizzled in a crisscross over my chicken. My plate sat in the center of my placemat, the knife and fork were horizontal over top of my napkin. I looked up and saw her watching me. "The en suite bathroom has fresh towels, and the bed's linens are clean as well."

"Are you always this prepared?" She laughed as she ripped a piece of pork off her fork instead of using her knife. I had to look away before I said something I shouldn't.

"Where are your belongings?"

She used her fork to point to the hallway. I cringed at everything shoved into three pillow cases.

"Do you still have your car?"

"Yes." She gave me a look. "He wanted a blow job for the price of the broken sink. He tried this shit too many times on me, Avery. I won't do it." Her chest started to heave.

"It's fine, just stay here until we find you a better place. What time do you work tonight?"

"Seven to seven."

I hated that she worked the night shift, but she seemed fine with it. I ate a few bites, but thought I should make conversation. "Are you still seeing that guy?"

She smirked. She knew I didn't like to talk about him.

"Yes." She downed her beer like a collage frat kid.

"So you won't tell me his name?"

She shook her head. "He's great, but we want to keep it low key. We're not looking for anything serious."

"Have you two slept together?"

"Avery!" She laughed as she carried her plate to the sink. She returned with another beer and a pint of chocolate ice cream. How the hell did she stay so small? "That's not really any of your business."

"It kind of is," I challenged.

"It's kind of not." She flipped her hair out of her face. "You wanna tell me why you have pictures of a burnt body in your bottom drawer?"

I choked on my rice but quickly drank some beer to help it slide down faster. "You went through my things?"

"Yes." She flipped the spoon around so it curved around her tongue. "Doesn't look like research, so why do you have it?"

"It's personal."

"Personal, like your old partner?"

I went to yell but stopped myself. I had to remember who I was speaking to. "He was someone I knew once, someone who—"

"Got in your way?" she finished for me. She looked at her Hello Kitty watch. "Shit, I gotta go. He's picking me up."

"He's coming here?" I nearly shouted.

"No! God, no." She gave me a look like I was crazy. "I told him to meet me at the diner down the street."

She headed over to her pillow cases and dug out a mini skirt and a tube top. She wiggled the skirt on, then ripped off the t-shirt with her back turned to me and shimmed the tiny scrap of blue over her breasts. Her heels were about three inches high and made her long, slim legs even longer. I stopped her when she got to the door, and grabbed her chin so she'd look at me.

"Be careful, you hear me?"

She rolled her eyes, then brushed my hand away. "Aren't I always?" She grinned before she gave me a quick peck on the lips. "See you later, Avery."

I watched her walk across my driveway and up the street. I didn't have a good feeling about this.

***

TWO WEEKS LATER

One would think Seth was a creature of habit, but he wasn't. His grocery store visits were a mind trip. To try and track him was like chasing the wind. Seth stood in front of the Hamburger Helper section. He seemed lost, almost like he came here because he didn't want to go home. This was a delightful feeling to have rush through me. *Poor Seth.*

I stood next to him. "You're standing in my spot."

"Huh? Oh, hey, man. I'm just searching for tonight's dinner." He sighed and tossed two boxes in his empty basket.

"Why don't you hit up your mom?" I suggested with an evil undertone that he missed completely.

"Ha!" He ran a hand through his hair. "Nah, my…" He stopped himself with a little shrug. "I'm not in the mood right now."

"I was going to head across the street to Rick's BBQ. You wanna join?"

See, I'm a good friend.

He picked up a box and read the ingredients. I bet he missed Emily's cooking. "Yeah, all right."

Suddenly, all my attention was pulled to her. She had earphones in, but she was pretending to read a magazine. She seemed to be watching someone. Seth was rambling on about something while I nodded. What the fuck was she doing here? This was not good.

"Someone you know?" Seth's voice ripped through my mini freak-out.

"Huh?" I tried and recalled his words. "No, she's, ah…bad one night stand."

I caught Seth's smirk as he glanced over at her. "Umm, seems that way."

She suddenly went wide-eyed and hurried toward the door.

Oh, fuck no!

"So when do you want to head over?"

"Ah…" I picked up a box of Hamburger Helper and smacked it into his chest. "This is my favorite. See you later." I raced down the checkout lane, past the old lady taking her sweet time paying with a check, and out the door to find her quickly walking around the corner. I nearly did a double take when I saw *him* paying for a bottle of booze.

"Hey," I shouted when I got close enough. I dragged her behind a five foot stone wall and pushed her back flat to it. "What the fuck are you doing here?"

Her head and shoulders dropped as she pulled her earphones free. I heard her whisper something. "I just…"

It hit me like a fucking flick to the nut sack. "Are you following *him*?"

She looked up as tears streamed down her face. "I just wanted to see what he was like."

So stupid. I closed my eyes and tried to calm the

adrenaline that pumped into my blood to the point of pain. "You were almost spotted by his son."

"What?" *Oh, did I fail to mention that Jack had a son?*

"I thought he only had a daughter." The look on her face hurt a bit. I could see a little bit of trust flake away. "What the hell, Avery!" She took a punch at my shoulder that was pretty pathetic before she started to cry harder. "How old?"

I tucked my asshole side away and saw this moment for what it was. With a deep breath to settle the nerves, I wrapped my arm around her neck and pulled her into a hug. She let me and held on tightly.

"Twenty-four. We found him first, that's what drew us to California. He has a younger brother as well." I normally kept quiet, as Jims always said we should keep everything quiet until it was time. Problem was, we'd have been done with this shit if Jims hadn't gotten involved with Emily. This whole thing would have been over with six months ago.

After a quick kiss to her head, we walked back to the street and up toward my car. "He's handsome." She sniffed with a little smile. "Jack, he's quite handsome."

I shook my head and pushed my hate for that man aside.

"Stay on your side of city from now on," I warned.

"Always such a Dom," she snickered back and hopped into my car.

***

267

I shouldn't be here, I knew. It was against all my rules. I turned up the music and settled into the leather seat. Radiohead pumped from my speakers as the bottle of Jack warmed between my legs. This wasn't me. I was slipping into old habits like Jims did.

It could be worse. Adler could be in the back panting his nasty breath over the back of my neck. But instead, once she left, I shoved him back outdoors where he belonged.

Headlights blinded me momentarily, and I squinted to see the poorly-lit parking lot. The damn trucker had his high beams on, which made my head ache instantly. I closed my eyes and rubbed the spot above my left eye. I only got headaches when I was stressed. She made me stressed. I wanted to know where the hell she was. Her shift ended forty-five minutes ago, and it only took sixteen minutes to get home. Eighteen if the lights on Second Street turned red.

"I fucking crave her, Alex." Jims leaned over and did a line of coke.

"Don't call me that, Jims."

"Sorry, Avery." He snickered. "Officer Avery."

I rolled my eyes. He was such an asshole sometimes.

"What do you even see in her, anyway?"

He raised an eyebrow at me. "She's Julia's twin, but with less sass and bigger tits."

Jims and I never really talked about him and our sister having a sexual relationship. I didn't want to hear about it, but he did have a point. They looked extremely similar. I just thought he had a type. I hadn't realized he missed or even loved Julia that way.

Knock! Knock! Knock!

I jumped and reached for the steering wheel. I rolled down my window and watched as she folded her arms. She was not impressed.

"How long you been waiting?"

"Long enough to know you're late."

"Screw you, Avery." She flipped me the finger and started to walk away.

I hopped out of my car and raced after her. Grabbing her arm, I forced her to look at me. "Hey! Screw me? Seriously? I saved you from being a fucking prostitute, and this is the thanks I get?" My chest heaved with anger. How dare she treat me like this?

"Yeah, Avery, you did, but you don't own me."

"Where were you tonight?"

She ripped her arm from my hold. "No! We aren't doing this again."

I stepped forward and towered over her. "Where?"

"I was with him," she shouted. "He picked me up, took me out for a drink, and dropped me off here. Not at your place, here."

My hand snapped around her neck, and I lowered my head so my mouth hovered over hers. "Did you fuck him?"

"If I did?" she challenged.

I closed my eyes to calm myself, but it didn't work. "Then I would kill him."

Her face flashed fear, but she kept herself together. "I didn't sleep with him, Avery. We're not like that yet." My gripped tightened. "We're not like that," she corrected.

I steered her to my car and gave her a little shove when we rounded the bumper. "Get in."

She did, and I checked the time.

Fuck! I should have been there twenty minutes ago!

"I have somewhere to be. I'll drop you off at the house."

I left her at the house and hurried to make up for lost time. There he sat in the window of the coffee shop, just like he was instructed to. In his light green dress shirt and jeans. I made sure to tell him to wear certain clothes so he thought I didn't know his face.

I saw the bus boy out for a smoke. My sunglasses made me look like I stepped out of an eighties band. The black plastic frames with neon green arms paired perfectly with my NKOTB ball hat. With the letter in hand, I hurried over and befriended the boy and paid him fifty to deliver it. He never questioned why I was wearing sunglasses when the sun was barely up. Typical teenager, he most likely thought it was a fashion statement.

The look on Jack Connors's face when he laid eyes on that letter and photograph was enough for me to snap a few photos with Jims's camera.

I zoomed in and watched a drip of sweat that traveled from his sideburn to his jaw. *Yes, Jack, you should be very afraid.*

As I pulled out of the parking lot, I saw

Connors's car a few yards ahead. I pulled into traffic and followed at a safe distance. I wondered where he was going.

**

Seth

I felt restless. It had been sixteen days since I'd been able to see Emily. At the moment, she was staying with Pete. Campbell began to suspect something when she started to ask questions about me. We didn't text, call, or even email. It was too risky. Avery hunted around for information, but at this point he seemed to have given up.

As days passed, more questions came into play. Garrett and I had dug into his past, but kept coming up with dead ends. One thing was for sure; Avery's past stopped when he arrived here in California.

"I'm starving," Garrett grunted. "I'm calling in our order now, so we don't have to wait."

"Good plan." My phone vibrated against my leg. I pulled it free and saw Agent Crew's name on the ID.

"Agent Crew." I looked over at Garrett, who appeared worried and quickly ended the call to the sandwich shop. "What can I do for you?"

"Meet me at The Brew in ten, bring O'Brian."

The line went dead. I didn't think twice as I pulled a U-turn and hurried to Huntington Drive.

The Brew was full, but a table off in the corner was empty. We quickly grabbed it and ordered three coffees.

My work t-shirt felt tighter than normal, and my finger ran around the edge to seek any kind of relief.

"There's Crew." Garrett nodded toward the door.

Crew took a seat across from us and slammed a heavy folder down in front of us.

"Good news or bad news first?"

"Bad," Garrett and I both said at the same time.

Crew inched his glasses up his nose with his finger. He opened the folder and twirled a paper around, then he held up a picture of Avery in his uniform. *What?*

"Alexander Avery was born in Chicago. After his parents were killed, he lived with his grandmother in Florida until he ran away and went to live with his brother in Chicago. His grandmother passed away the following year." Crew glanced at me funny, waited a beat, and then kept going. "He joined the Chicago PD, then later transferred to Orange PD. He and his brother lived here until his brother was killed a year ago."

Garrett shook his head. "I don't understand where you're going with this."

"Who is his brother, and why are you looking into Avery?" I glanced at Garrett, confused, as only four of us suspected Avery of something, and Crew wasn't one of them.

Crew held up his hand. "Because of his brother."

"Why? How did his brother die?" I tried to understand.

"Shot."

"By who?"

Crew leaned in over the table. "By you, Seth."

272

My stomach sank and my brain scrambled to catch up as he pulled out a picture and turned it around to show me Jimmy Lasko's face.

"Holy shit." Garrett covered his mouth. "Avery is Lasko's brother?"

"Yes," Crew confirmed as I sank further into my seat. My brain was caught in a loop.

Lasko was Avery's brother. Avery was Lasko's brother.

"So," I said quietly, "the entire time," I closed my eyes in disbelief, "those six days of hell, Avery must have known where Emily was?"

Crew nodded. "Emily is a dead ringer for their sister Julia." He pulled another picture free and held up Emily's twin. "Julia." He made a face. "It's sad. She must have been at the wrong place at the wrong time to catch his attention."

I glanced at Garrett while my stomach rolled. Crew put the picture away and continued.

"Lasko and Avery lived together. After some psychiatric evaluations, they were sent to other family members in Germany and Florida, where they must have changed their names. Lasko must have come back after Julia passed away to find his brother."

"Why California?" Garrett asked, and I could tell he was still trying to process this crazy shit.

Crew leaned back in his seat. "After a lot of digging, we realized they were watching you, Seth."

"What?" My head snapped up to look at him. "Me?"

"Yes." He pulled some more papers from the file. "Looks like your Emily may not have been the original target."

"Wait, wait," Garrett held up a hand. "How in the hell did the FBI not know any of this a year ago?"

"After Lasko was killed and a possible lethal injection was put to Hank Wallace, he started talking. He spoke about how Lasko had a brother, but he never met him. Hank mentioned that he bragged once that he could get away with murder because he had someone to cover it up. We started to dig, figured it could be a cop, but it was a stretch. I know every cop has their DNA on file, but it took time before we connected the dots." Crew hesitated, then seemed to make a decision. "Seth, the brothers were close, and they were after something. I don't know what yet, but I'll keep digging. My advice, if you want it, is watch your back and watch your family. Just because Lasko is gone doesn't mean Emily is out of trouble either. I think you are the target, not her, but if he wants to hurt you—"

"Hurting Emily is the best way," Garrett finished for him with a grim expression.

What the hell would Avery and Lasko have against me? I wanted to kill Avery with my bare hands. I couldn't get past the fact that he had known where Emily had been taken...fuck, he had even had a part in it.

"Jesus," I blurted out, "it was fucking Avery who planted that camera in our hotel room. The one Emily mentioned she saw right before she escaped."

Garrett cleared his throat. "Anything else you want to share, Crew?"

"Not yet, just that we have two agents tailing

him. He'll slip up soon, and we'll nail him."

"Slip up! You know Avery is Lasko's brother, go arrest him." I banged my fist on the table.

"On what?" Crew shrugged, unfazed by my outburst. "Can't arrest someone for being related to a psychopath." He held up his hands. "Look, we don't have any proof right now that Avery is guilty of anything. He's good, he's careful, he covers his tracks well. If he is up to something, well, everyone slips at some point, and when he does, we'll book him. But, guys," Crew rested his elbows on the table, "we have to play this carefully and by the book. We're talking about bringing down a cop. One fuck up on our end, one leak, one suspicious glance at him, and we're over. This case will be thrown out. So stay calm, but stay alert."

"So, what is the good news?" Garrett asked as Crew started to put the papers back into the folder. He stood and pushed in his chair.

"The good news is you know who Avery is and can keep an eye on him. Let's keep it that way." He glanced at his watch. "I'll be in touch. Keep in mind, your phones, computers, anything electronic can and will most likely be tracked. He's smart, so be smarter."

With that, he was gone. Garrett and I sat in silence for a few moments. The idea that a trusted friend was connected to our nightmare was a hard thing to comprehend.

***

Avery

Blood drained from my face, my skin prickled, and my heartbeat pounded in my head. Why the fuck did Agent Crew have a photo of me? Did they connect me to Jims? My hand reached out as I felt like a vice was tightening around my neck. Black spots appeared, and it tainted my vision. I slowly backed up to my car and sank into the seat.

If Agent Crew dug hard enough, he could match my brother's DNA with mine, but he'd have to have a reason to. Then it hit me, and a layer of sweat broke across my upper lip. Hank-motherfucking-Wallace must have rolled over. Jims must have told him he had a brother. I never met the man, but if Jims was strung out on drugs, who the hell knew what he'd spill.

Fuck! Fuck! Fuck!

My wrists banged on the steering wheel until the pain shot up to my elbows. I grabbed my phone and called her.

"Hey." Her cheery voice didn't go with how I felt today.

"We need to do this tonight."

There was a pause.

"What's going on, Avery?"

"I think I was made—"

"How?" she interrupted.

We didn't have time for this. I'd explain later. "Grab your shit and be ready for me in one hour. You remember the plan?"

"Yes."

"Well?" I sighed. She knew I needed her to

repeat it like always. I needed to know she knew exactly what to do.

"We out Jack and demand the money. "

"Right."

"No one gets hurt, right?" she whispered. I could tell she was nervous.

"Interesting you'd ask that, considering—"

"I'm not like Jimmy. I couldn't live with myself if I hurt someone."

I pulled into a gas station and hopped out of the car. "Only in it for the money, nothing more than we deserve," I reassured her. "Now pack your shit, 'cause we're not coming back."

Opening my trunk, I pulled out three gas cans and filled them to the top. Time to make things right.

***

Seth

I pulled into Garrett's driveway and turned off the car. We both got out with our food in hand—not that either of us felt hungry—and went inside.

"So the camera in the hotel room was planted by Avery." Garrett handed me a beer and unwrapped his sandwich. Now that the shock had worn off some, we started to connect the dots to everything, and it was fucking mind-blowing.

"Most likely killed Matthews," I added and swallowed back the loss of my friend. "I wouldn't be surprised if he was connected to Davis somehow."

Garrett's face went white. "Campbell." I nodded. "I bet he saw Campbell poking around and thought he was onto something."

My phone vibrated on the table, and a quick glance had me typing away a quick response.

Maddy: *I have a surprise and I need you ALL here to see it.*

Seth: *Now?*

Maddy: *Please, Seth, I wouldn't ask if it wasn't important.*

"Shit," I muttered, "I gotta go."

"Everything okay?" Garrett popped two chips in his mouth.

"Maddy has a surprise and wants us all there to see it. She said it was important. I'll call you later."

My head spun as I drove over. How could Avery be related Lasko? How could I have not known? I cringed at all the times I left him alone with Emily. Why did he never hurt her? Was I the target? If so, why? This was insane.

I nodded at the guard as I drove through. "Have a good day, Mr. Connors. Your company arrived about twenty minutes ago.

"Company?" I whispered and wondered what the hell Maddy was up to.

"Hello?" I called out as I stepped into the entryway. Chatter came from the other room.

"In here," my mother called out from the kitchen.

Nicholas sat with Mom, and my father was off in the corner with a pissed-off expression. Gretchen was preparing coffee and cake. The only one missing was Maddy.

"Drink?" Nicholas asked. I gave a quick nod as my phone vibrated again.

Emily: *Any idea where Maddy is? She missed our lunch date.*

Huh. Normally I'd give her crap about texting my phone right now, but it was an innocent text.

Seth: *No, she told us to meet her at Mom's for a surprise. Teenagers.*

Dammit, Maddy. I rolled my eyes at the thought of Emily being stood up. That wasn't typically something Maddy would do.

"Here." Nicholas handed me a beer. "Any idea what's going on?"

"Did anyone try her phone?" my mother asked as she pulled hers free from her purse.

"Went straight to voicemail earlier," Nicholas answered, then studied my face. "Care to share?"

"Later."

A loud ring echoed down the hallway. I looked at Mom, and we all started to move in the direction of the sound. I was the first to round the corner and see my baby sister tied to a chair in the center of the living room. She was crying, but her sobs were silent since a wide piece of duct tape covered her mouth.

279

"Mads!" I shouted as I ran to her side. She started to panic, her hand pointing behind me. One moment I was looking at Maddy, the next I felt a jab to the ribs. I whirled around to find Avery pointing a semi-automatic rifle in my face.

Oh shit!

"Sit," he commanded. I looked over his shoulder to Nicholas, who had raised his arm at someone behind me. I glanced and saw a woman standing there. She had light brown hair, a skinny body, and big boobs. My eyes widened at the gun she was pointing at us. *Who the hell is this?* She stared at my father, then at me, her gaze going back and forth. I recognized her from somewhere. *She's the girl from the supermarket. Avery's one night stand. What?*

"Everyone sit down, shut up, and do as you're told." Avery nudged me with the tip of the rifle. Mom pulled my arm so I would sit. Maddy shook in place. I caught her eye and gave her a little nod to tell her I had this.

Avery pulled up a chair and motioned for my father to take the offered seat.

"Jack, would you be so kind as to take this seat facing your family?" he said. His voice had an oddly formal tone to it.

"What is this about?" my father challenged as he crossed his arms and stayed put. His classic asshole move.

Avery gave us a little smile before he swung the gun around and butted the handle of the rifle into the side of my father's head. A loud curse flew out of his mouth as he fell to the floor. Avery dragged him up and threw him in the direction of the chair.

"You don't get to ask the questions."

I took this distraction to pull my cell phone free.

Seth: 31/32

Garrett: 4

Avery looked away from my father toward the nervous girl and ordered her to remove our cell phones. I had quickly slipped mine back in my pocket. Her hands shook when she collected them. Who the hell was this girl?

Mom let out a little cry as Avery pointed the weapon at her. "Trust me, Martha, you'll want to hear this."

My father crawled into the chair and held his head where the blood dripped.

"Now," Avery stood behind my father, "it's time for you to confess your sins."

I glanced at Nicholas, who had the same 'oh shit' expression as I now wore.

The letters, shit!

"Forgive me, Father, for I have sinned. It's been…" Avery started for him. When my father didn't speak, Avery rolled his eyes. "I've got all night, Jack." Avery looked at the girl. "Maybe he just needs a little reminder. Tina Upton." My father's head snapped up to look at Avery. *How the hell do they know that name?* I felt my mother shift next to me. "There it is," he said to the girl, "the recognition."

"This has nothing to do with you, boy!" my father snapped. Rage flickered across his face.

"This has everything to do with me," Avery shouted at him.

My mother spoke up. "Who's Tina Upton?" This was going to kill her, and I felt a pang of hurt for my mother and my sister.

Avery whirled around. "My mother."

"What?" I blurted without a thought. "Tina Upton was your mother?" I didn't get to read all the letters. Fuck, in hindsight, I wished I had. Maybe I would have seen this coming.

"Yes." Avery gave me a hard look, but I could see the wound was raw. "You see, your father met my mother on a business trip." He turned to my father. "Did you think of Martha while you fucked my mother, Jack?"

Jack's gaze shot over to Mom's, as did mine. Her face was shocked, and her eyes filled with tears. I took her hand in mine and held on tight. *My poor mother.*

"Did you tell her you had a family?" When my father didn't answer, Avery pointed the gun at his hand on the armrest and pulled the trigger.

Everyone screamed, *including* the girl who came with Avery.

"Shut the fuck up!" Avery pointed the gun at all of us while my father cried out and held his bloody hand to his chest. "Christ, Jack, all you had to do was answer the question. How will you be redeemed if you don't wash your soul clean?" Avery shook his head impatiently. "Right, so where were we?"

"No," my father grunted, "not until the end."

"But you knew she did."

When my father didn't answer, he went for his other hand, but this time the girl stepped forward.

"Alexander, no." She held up her hand. "You promised."

"And so did he." Avery aimed the gun, but not before he shot her a dirty look.

Interesting.

"Yes, I knew," Dad cried. "I knew her husband beat her, and I knew he beat his kids too."

"Then why?" Avery grabbed his face so he would look at him. "Why did you promise to save her, then leave her to die?"

I knew my father was a terrible person, but to know all this and do nothing about it…he was nothing but a waste of human space.

"Because she was crazy," my father blurted. "Because she wouldn't see herself for what she was. A piece of ass to entertain me while I was away."

"Jack!" My mother nearly leapt out of her seat, her expression furious, but I caught her. I didn't want her getting hurt any more than she was.

Avery laughed. "I know, Martha, I know."

"Avery," the girl whispered, and we all looked over. Tears streamed down her pale cheeks. "Stop it; this isn't what you said we'd…"

Avery held up his hand, his expression shutting her down. "Tell me something, Jack, did you leave before or after you found out my mother was pregnant?"

"Oh, God!" Mom's voice was flat. I didn't think she could take much more. My mind was swimming laps—this was insane!

"Oh, please, Martha, Jack has fucked many

women, haven't you, Jack? I'm sure this is the only one who kept the baby."

I looked back at my mother's face. She had devoted her entire life to us kids and her husband. My mother was old school and stood by her choices. She knew my father was not a good person, but she never thought he would cheat.

"Mom," I whispered, "breathe."

"Martha," my father's voice felt like acid to my ears, "it's not what you think, I—" In a flash, Nicholas lunged forward and punched my father square in the nose, then repeated the process. Avery left him to it, enjoying the move, but when he began to step toward Nicholas, I leapt up and pulled my brother back to the couch. Poor Maddy had her eyes closed tightly, sobbing through the duct tape. I knew I would find a way to tear Avery apart piece by piece, like he was doing to my family.

"As much as I love a good, old-fashioned family fight, I need Jack awake for my grand finale." Avery reached for the girl's arm and pulled her to stand in front of my father. "Alyssa, I want you to meet Jack. Jack, say hello to your daughter."

Everything went quiet. I thought we all stopped breathing at that moment. My father's gaze went from Mom, to the girl, then to Mom again. Holy shit, this girl was our half-sister! The fact that it also made her Lasko's half-sister wasn't lost on me either. I felt sick. Then a rage bubbled up inside of me, making my stomach roll.

"Holy shit," I hissed. There was no damn way I could be connected to this fucking freak show of a family. Sweat raced across my hairline. This was not happening.

"Did you know about her, Jack?" My mom suddenly found her voice, and it pulled me off the ledge.

"Don't lie, Jack, the Lord is watching and judging. Plus, I have letters to prove that you did." Avery looked at Mom. "He's known for years. My sister was two months old when my parents were killed. Jack here promised our mother he'd come and take us away. He knew her husband would hurt us. He told her we would be a family, that he would protect her. But that never happened, did it, Jack?" Avery kicked my father's leg, then kneed him in the nose, and blood spurted across the floor.

As much as I wanted to kill my father myself, I needed even more to know what the hell Avery wanted out of all this. "What is it you want, Avery?"

"What I want, Connors, is my goddamn life back. I wanted to have my mother raise me, not my psychotic grandmother, who beat me on a regular basis. I want my brother. I want the life my sister deserved, to grow up with her own mother and brothers, not passed around like a toy through the foster care system, not to end up a runaway and forced into prostitution. What I want is a goddamn payment for all the shit your father put us through!" He dropped a paper onto my father's lap. "A half a million in this account, now."

My father started to laugh. "You stupid fool," his bloody head flopped back, "do you know who I am?"

"A coward." The words dropped from my mouth

without a thought. My father snickered something, but I ignored it. Avery gave me a smile, and I shot him a dangerous look. "You may have the face of my friend, Avery, but you are proving to be the son of the Devil."

"Oh, Seth, you have no idea." He pulled a bag free from behind the couch, then he looked at the girl and nodded. "Tie them up."

Her face fell. "This wasn't the plan."

"Plans change."

"Avery."

He moved to stand in front of her, but made sure he could still see us all. His hand moved to her chin, and he took it roughly in his hands. "Alyssa, you bounced around in foster care, new daddy after new daddy, only to get caught up with Donald. How many men did you sleep with to keep your place at that seedy motel?" Her gaze dropped to the floor. Jesus Christ, he was trying to brainwash her. "Who saved you from that hell? I didn't have to do it, but I did because I loved you."

"No, you're right, Avery." She nodded, but something about her tone made me look over. She took the bag and dropped it by Nicholas's feet.

"Start with him." Avery pointed to me.

"Hands," her small voice demanded. Avery raised the gun, but then moved it over to Maddy, who was now staring at the wall. Moving my hands into place, she started to wrap the rope around my wrists, though she didn't make it very tight. Gretchen, who I'd completely forgotten, was on the other side of my brother, and she started to cough and draw Avery's attention. The girl made a strange knot and slipped the end into my hand. She bent down to grab the other rope, and when she caught my eye she motioned to the bag next to her. A handgun was tucked into the corner. I gave a slight nod so she knew I saw it.

I'm not sure what her angle is, but who the fuck cares? I need to get my hands on that gun!

Avery moved to stand in front of Gretchen and shoved the gun in her face.

That's when I smelled it, smelled the fear that was to come. Nicholas must have caught it too, because his knee pressed into mine and he made a sniff sound. I looked all around to see if I could find it. The girl finished tying Nicholas's wrists, and I noticed she did it the same way she did mine, loose. Then she moved on to Gretchen. I watched as she did my mother's. She was extra gentle, but tied hers differently than mine. I had a feeling Avery played mind games with his sister—our sister—fuck, I wasn't ready for that thought yet. She seemed different than her brothers. She must have more of her mother in her. My impression of Tina Upton, from her letters, was that she loved her kids and would do anything for them. I wasn't blind, though, to the fact that this girl was pointing a gun to my head and those of my family.

Avery pulled a laptop out of the bag and set it across my father's legs.

"Transfer the money," he demanded with a nudge of the gun.

My father didn't move, he just sat there with a sullen look on his face. My guess was that he knew his life was fucked, so he was fine with taking us all down. Good ol' daddy dearest.

"Now!" Avery shouted.

"Screw you."

"Screw me?" Avery grabbed my father's knee and in a flash planted a bullet in his flesh. My mother screamed and held up her bound wrists.

"I can do it!" I glanced back and saw her expression as she pulled herself together. "Please, let me transfer it."

Avery set the laptop on her lap and watched her struggle to type the password. "There." He snapped the laptop shut but froze when he heard a police siren. He raced over to the windows and started to pull the curtains shut.

I glanced at Nicholas, who gave me a little a grin. He knew Garrett would come through too.

"Fuck," Avery cursed as he looked at all of us. "Change in plans, sweetheart." He blew past me, leaving us with the girl who went wide-eyed a moment later.

"What are you doing?" she screamed, and then the unmistakable smell of gasoline met our nostrils. Avery began to splash it over the hardwood floors. Panic spread through us, and Maddy suddenly started her muffled screaming again. Even my father finally had lost the smug look.

I quickly stood. "Avery, please just go out the back way and leave. You got what you came for, and you've managed to destroy my family."

My mother started to pray as Gretchen took my seat and held Mom's hands with her own bound ones. Nicholas started to untie his hands, while Avery poured the second can in a circle around us.

"It's not enough. You must die to cleanse your souls." He sounded like a madman.

I heard her before she burst through the door. I should have known better then to leave her with the text I did—I should've known better. When she ran into the living room, out of breath and in a panic, she had no time to process what was happening. Her eyes widened in horror and she came to a sudden stop, breathing hard.

Avery raised his gun and pointed it at her with a laugh. "Oh, sweet Lucifer, this day just keeps getting better."

One moment she was standing a few yards from me, the next she was wrapped in Avery's arms with a gun to her head.

"Seth," she whispered as her terrified expression locked onto mine.

I held up my hands. Panic coursed through my veins, but I knew I had to keep my cool.

"Mmm, McPhee." Avery buried his nose into her hair. "I've watched you for a year, watched your most intimate moments. Saw you strip naked, watched you fuck Connors like the dirty girl you are, and all the while I never laid a hand on you. Because you were my brother's." He laughed as his hand cupped her breast. I knew I needed to stay in control. "Did you know I plotted your death more times than I could count? Did you know that it was Adler, Jims's dog, barking outside those glass doors when you were at my house?" Emily wiggled in his hold, but Avery had a good grip. "I used to lie down next to you in bed, when Connors worked the night shift. My fingers would creep down your bare thigh, and you'd let out a soft moan—"

"Stop!" she screamed and tried to elbow him in the stomach, but he turned her around and backhanded her.

"Enough!" I barked, sending the room into silence, "Christ, Avery, it's fucking enough. The place is surrounded, and there's nowhere left for you to go. Enough already!"

Avery's face froze. He was not used to someone speaking to him like that.

"Alyssa," he hissed, "pour the gasoline over Emily."

The girl was frozen in place. "No."

Avery cracked his neck and pushed Emily to the floor. He reached for the gas can and looked at me. "All he had to do was take us away from there. An eye for an eye, Connors."

The entire place erupted in fear, and my head swam as Avery tipped the gasoline over Emily, but only a little came out as he had already emptied it. He cursed and tossed it off to the side.

"What about yours?" I suddenly spat out and hoped that if I could keep him talking, he wouldn't light the match. "What about your soul?"

Avery smirked, and he looked like my friend again. "You wanna know my demons?" He tossed the gas can and went for the third. Fuck, this place would be lit up like a Christmas tree soon. The smell of gasoline was so strong we were all beginning to cough and gag. Emily was frozen in place. Avery raised his arms like he welcomed the Lord. "Forgive me, Father, for I have sinned. It's been two months since my last confession." He suddenly poured the flammable liquid over our family pictures as I took a step toward Emily.

Maddy kicked when he came near her, but he just laughed and turned to look at me. My mother went to get up, but I immediately told to her to be still. Avery was unstable, and I needed to keep him calm.

"I killed Matthews, you know," he laughed, "with sleeping pills. I rather liked him, really, but he chose the wrong team, so he had to go. I planted the camera so Jims could watch you all dance while he made Emily his." I moved two more feet. Alyssa watched me but didn't say a word. "Let's see, I used Ronnie and Travis as pawns to tear you two apart. They were both weak, and easy to use." He went back to soaking our memories. "After Emily gave me a black eye at the Halloween party, Davis came over unannounced and found himself," he held up the gas, "well, just like this, actually." I allowed this information to be stored within me. I knew I would need to retain it without letting my emotion get the best of me. One more step toward Emily, then Avery swung around to face me head on. "You know what, Connors?" He dug in his pocket. "I think I'm ready to be free now."

"Avery, no!" the girl called out in a panic. "You promised me you wouldn't hurt anyone. You promised me you weren't like him."

"You promised me you were on my side, but you're not, are you?" Avery challenged, then pointed to my wrists. "You lied; now we must all pay for our sins." He lunged at Emily and grabbed her by the hair. She cried out in a sob as he took a few steps back from me.

"Just let her go." I heard the defeat in my voice. I was so incredibly tired of this game. It needed to end, just not like—

He held up a Zippo and brushed his thumb over the wheel, sending a flame into the air. I looked around the room. Everything seemed quiet, then erupted in motion as my family jumped to their feet in a mad panic, and the smell of fear was laced with the gasoline. "Say goodbye to your perfect lif—"

Pop! Pop! Avery's face froze and his eyes locked with the girl, who had her gun raised. Blood poured from his stomach, like a hole in a hose. Terror for Emily burned through me as her screams registered in my brain.

"You once told me Jimmy was the monster. Now I see it's you." Tears fell from the girl's cheeks as she watched him fall to the ground, and he took Emily down with him. I dove for the Zippo, but it bounced from his fingertips and landed in a puddle. I hooked my arm around Emily's waist and pulled her off Avery as flames raced up her sweater. She screamed and bucked as I dove on top of her, smothering the fire between us as we fell to the floor, just missing a puddle of fuel.

"Run!" Nicholas yelled and bolted for Maddy. Mom and Gretchen helped my father out of the chair and raced to the front door.

In a matter of seconds, the living room was engulfed with an orange blaze, the heat becoming intense. Nicholas freed Maddy as the girl grabbed my sister and rushed her outside. Nicholas turned around to see if we were following. I held Emily in my arms and ran for the door, and we reached it just as things started to explode around us.

"Stop!" Emily screamed and jumped from my arms, running toward the living room.

"Emily, come back! What the hell are you doing?" I screamed, catching Nicholas's attention. "Go! Make sure everyone is okay," I yelled at him as I dove for the door where Emily had gone.

She was standing there, crying. I yanked her arm and pulled her backward.

"Are you crazy?"

"No!" she sobbed, her face full of fear and...determination, "I have to know this is over! I need to know he's gone...must be sure!" The roar of the fire was deafening. All our memories were burning, but none of that mattered. I felt her desperation, the need to know that this was finally the end.

"Look," I shouted desperately at her and pointed to Avery's body covered in flames. I was sure I could smell his burning flesh. "He's gone!" The urgency to get out of there made my voice crack. We had very little time left. "He's dead, Emily, it's over!"

Firemen burst through the front door just as the flames engulfed the stairs. Emily yelped as she was suddenly grabbed around the waist by a fireman and rushed outside. I followed, helped by another.

Clean air never felt so good as I sucked it in over my raw windpipe. My eyes felt as though I'd rubbed them with sandpaper, and my skin was covered in soot.

"Where is she?" I barked at the fireman who

looked oddly familiar. His jacket read Firehouse 59.

"She's fine, Seth, they're just checking her lungs."

"I know you," I coughed.

He gave me a little nod. "I took her to the gala. Ethan, remember?"

"Oh, right," I felt the burn shoot up from the bottom of my lungs.

"Here." He handed me an oxygen mask, but I pushed it aside. Ethan shrugged and pointed to an EMC truck about fifteen feet away.

"Thanks." I patted his shoulder as I hurried over to find Emily fighting with a paramedic. I rushed to her side and dropped to my knees.

"Jesus, Emily." I pushed back the blanket and checked her over. "Are you okay?"

She didn't answer, she just buried her head in my neck and sobbed and coughed. The medic who had been attempting to give her more oxygen tried once again, but stopped when I shook my head and held up a finger. We needed a minute.

"I know, baby, I know." I stroked her back to soothe her. "Just get some more oxygen into you, okay? You need it. I'll be right here." She nodded as the guy put the mask over her dirty face. I stood; I didn't want to be here anymore either.

"Seth!" Nicholas appeared at my side and wrapped his arms around me. He bent down and rested a hand on Emily's shoulder and gave it a pat. That was the most affection I'd ever witnessed from him. I grabbed his shoulder and held on while he filled me in. "Mom is with Maddy. They're taking her to the hospital, but she'll be fine. Gretchen is with Dad." He gave a little chuckle in his hyped up state. "I want to kill him."

"Me too." I put my head to his. "Me too." Emily stood, pulling off the mask. I knew she was done with sitting still and needed to stand, so I helped her up. We stood there, our minds struggling to absorb the last few hours. I put my arms around her to steady her.

Then I saw the girl. She was standing on the sidelines with a paramedic, who was wrapping her arm with some gauze. She caught my eye as he finished. She spoke to the medic, then came over to us. I slid Emily to my side, but wouldn't let her leave me. Nicholas stayed close as the girl approached us.

"Here." She handed me a phone. "Umm, it's Avery's phone. He gave it to me before we came in. The password is his badge number. Everything you need is in there." She handed me her keys. "Here are his house keys. He has lots of pictures you might be interested in." Tears left clean lines down her dirty face. She looked at the ground. "I'm...I'm sorry, I didn't know he was going to do that, I really didn't. He said no one was going to be hurt." She looked up at us. "I don't hate your father for what he did, I just hate that he didn't want me."

I didn't know what to say, so I went with the truth. "He didn't want any of us."

"Alyssa?" Garrett suddenly appeared out of nowhere. He looked incredibly confused.

"Garrett?" The girl's face dropped, and her eyes shifted from him to me.

My mind raced. "You two know each other?"

Could this shit get any stranger?

Garrett stared at the girl as she said, "Umm, we met at the mall a while back."

Bullshit. I knew she was flat-out lying, but we were all too damn fried to press for information.

"Stand back!" A fireman called out as they turned on two hoses and aimed them at the house.

Riggs came up behind us and showed me the handcuffs.

"Sorry, but…"

"It's okay," she whispered and put her hands behind her back. "I'm sorry, Seth, for all of it." She looked at Garrett, who still studied her silently as though he'd seen a ghost. "I swear, Garrett, I didn't know you knew him."

We all watched as she was placed in the back of the squad car.

"What was all that about?" Emily whispered.

"That? That was my sister."

***

"I need to tell you something." Garrett pulled the car over and parked in front of an abandoned warehouse. It had been a week and half since we'd spoken about what happened that night at my mother's house. I had many questions but kept my mouth shut. We shared when we were ready.

"Shoot." I opened my water and drank the whole thing. My throat hadn't been right since the fire.

"Do you know what this place is?" He pointed out the windshield.

"Art gallery, though I've heard rumors."

"It's a gentlemen's club." He sighed and closed his eyes. "It's more aimed at men who like to be in control." He glanced at me out the corner of his eye. "It's where Alyssa and I met."

Wait?

"Why were you—oh." I shook my head, surprised I hadn't known this.

"I've been a member for seven months. I just wanted to try something that interested me."

Huh, I wouldn't lie. This place now piqued my interest.

"I swear, Seth, I had no idea who she was. She was just a friendly face who worked the front desk."

"I know," I reassured him.

"Nothing ever happened, we just went out for dinners and whatnot. We kissed once, but never got far. We both wanted to take things slowly."

"I get that." I looked over at the building and wondered if Avery had any idea his sister was dating Garrett. I smirked at the thought. Now, that would have killed him.

"She's a good person, with a big heart. She was a little rough around the edges for my liking, but given her past, it all kind of makes sense."

"Yeah," I sighed, still not able to process that shit. "We're good, Garrett, seriously."

"Yeah, all right." He nodded, started the car and we continued with our shift.

***

297

THREE WEEKS LATER

Emily

"Step away from the barbecue, MacPhee." Garrett pointed a water gun at me. "So help me God I have the best shot on the force, so don't tempt me."

I laughed and handed the tongs to him. "Believe it or not, I do know how to Q, Garrett."

"Did Erin get off okay?"

"Yeah, she's incredibly excited. A month backpacking through Southeast Asia sounds pretty fun. I think Alex hit a homerun with that present."

"I'd say so." Garrett grunted and pulled his secret sauce out of his pocket. A quick glance at the door, and I braced myself and hoped for a different answer to the question I was about to ask.

"You ever gonna tell us how you met Alyssa?"

Garrett gave a sad shrug as he answered. "We dated a little. She seemed nice enough, but now there's just no way."

I didn't bring up the fact that he avoided whenever I asked *how* or *where* he met her. I sighed inwardly. "So, how is he really doing?"

He glanced at me sideways. "Seth is okay. I know he's relieved that his family didn't press charges. Alyssa really is a lost soul."

I watched Garrett as he carefully turned the steaks. I kept my voice low. "I know he set her up with money and a job in Florida, even sent that damn dog with her." I shivered at that comment. "I don't blame her for wanting to start fresh. I don't think I would ever feel part of the family after all that's happened." I handed Garrett the salt. "I'm proud of Martha for leaving Jack. She plans to rebuild on her land. She needs a fresh start too."

Garrett gave me a smile. "Crazy how things turned out, but at least we are finally free of that crazy bunch." He nodded over my shoulder. "Someone is here to see you."

"Oh, hey, Travis." I walked over as he held up a brown piece of rope with a key attached to the end. "What's this?"

He pulled my arm and tugged me out of earshot of Garrett.

"I haven't been completely honest with you, Emily. I know you've been through so much, and I feel it's time to come clean." My stomach sank. I couldn't handle any more crazy. I looked back at Garrett, who was watching us carefully. "Em, the woman in the photographs in my house, she wasn't my best friend who died of cancer. She's actually my ex-wife." *What?*

"Okaaay," I whispered.

"We had a nasty divorce, and I went a little weird. I, ah, roughed up her boyfriend and broke into her house a few times. I really wasn't myself. That's really not me. Anyway, I wanted you to know I'm due in court next week, and I have a feeling I won't be back for a bit. I was wondering if you could keep an eye on my place."

I looked down at the key as I thought about what he had shared. I didn't like having it. It felt like it meant more than just watching his house. It was time to cut ties with my neighbor.

"You know what, Travis? I'm not sure I'm the right person for that." I handed him back the key. "Good luck, I hope things get better for you."

He closed his eyes and gave me a little nod. "You really do love him, don't you?"

"More than I thought possible."

"He's a lucky man."

"No, honestly, I am the lucky one."

I watched him wave to Garrett and jog off toward the tree line. I turned and jumped when I saw Seth in the doorway, and he gave me a sexy side smile. He started to say something, but laughed when a familiar voice found us.

"Everyone can relax," Pete announced as he slapped Seth's ass and kissed my cheek. "I am here."

"Aren't we lucky?" I laughed and thought how great it was to have my life back. My mother was gone, I had my house, and I had my family.

***

EARLY THE NEXT MORNING

The sea lapped against the shore, and the morning breeze kissed my face, leaving a salty reminder that this was my favorite place to be. Two years of hell, and I finally felt at peace. I was stronger than ever now that my nightmare was over. Though I knew it would be a long time before I would be able trust people again, it was nothing compared to what I could have lost. The worst was over. Now it was time for me to move forward and not dwell. I'd cut all ties with my mother and couldn't be happier with the decision. Shawna and David had started to visit more, and I promised I would visit them more too.

My toes dug into the cool sand, and I closed my eyes and waited for my old friend to arrive.

A pair of warm arms wrapped around me while his legs pressed against mine.

"Good morning." His raspy voice made me sink further into his hold. There was no way to describe how much I loved this man. He completed me. I needed him in my life as much as the sea air, and I could honestly say I would go through all of that hell again if it meant I could have him. I leaned up and kissed his lips with a happy grin.

"You made it."

"Of course."

"Thank you."

He nuzzled his cold nose into my neck and gave me a little nip.

"I'd meet the sunrise with you any day, McPhee."

And we did. Every weekend we'd sit in that spot and watch the sun come up over our beach and remember that we made it out the other side together.

THE END

ACKNOWLEDGMENTS

A huge thank you to:
Ana Armstrong
Sergeant Che Chonnolly Heron
XL and Lauren Schöenherr
Adam Treat

ABOUT THE AUTHOR

J. L. Drake was born and raised in Nova Scotia, Canada, later moving to Southern California where she now lives with her husband and two children.

When she is not writing she loves to spend time with her family, travelling or just enjoying a night at home. One thing you might notice in her books is her love of the four seasons. Growing up on the east coast of Canada the change in the seasons is in her blood and is often mentioned in her writing.

An avid reader of James Patterson, J.L. Drake has often found herself inspired by his many stories of mystery and intrigue. She hopes you will enjoy her books as much as she has enjoyed writing them.

Facebook:
https://www.facebook.com/JLDrakeauthor

Twitter:
https://twitter.com/jodildrake_j

Website:
http://www.authorjldrake.com/

Goodreads:
http://www.goodreads.com/author/show/8300313.J
_L_Drake

Made in the USA
Columbia, SC
12 June 2018